Praise fo
Legend of t

⋆*RT Boo*

⋆*Barnes & Noble Re* ⋆⋆ *2013*
⋆*Library Journal* Starred Review
⋆*Booklist* Starred Review

"The mix of hardheaded realism and fantasy in this novel is enchanting... Victorian mores and melodrama are cast in sharp relief when dragons and fantastical quests are thrown into the plot."

—*Barnes & Noble Reviews*,
a B&N Best Romance of 2013

"An outstanding read! A fast-paced, smartly written plot—fraught with danger and brimming with surprises—makes it impossible to put down."

—*RT Book Reviews* Top Pick, 4.5 Stars

"Mesmerizing, ingenious, slyly humorous, and wonderfully romantic, this unusual charmer is a winner for fans of paranormals. A Highland dragon? How can it miss?"

—*Library Journal* Starred Review

"A light romance with strong character development and a plot rich with supernatural themes... Comical and genuine."

—*Booklist* Starred Review

Also by Isabel Cooper

No Proper Lady

Lessons After Dark

Legend of the Highland Dragon

The Highland Dragon's Lady

NIGHT *of the* HIGHLAND DRAGON

ISABEL COOPER

sourcebooks
casablanca

Published by Sourcebooks Casablanca, an imprint of Sourcebooks,
Inc.
P.O. Box 4410, Naperville, Illinois 60567-4410
(630) 961-3900
Fax: (630) 961-2168
www.sourcebooks.com

Printed and bound in the United States of America.
RRD 10 9 8 7 6 5 4 3

To Serin Hale, for friendship, patience, and advice.

One

September 1898

"LOCH ARACH?" THE GIRL SHRUGGED, FLIPPING A straw-colored braid over her shoulder. "Aye. They're all queer up that way." Her accent was almost too thick to follow, but William easily recognized the just-for-your-information tone at which girls of twelve seemed to excel in every place and generation.

Her brother elbowed her in the side. "No such thing," he said to William. "It's only that 'tis a very small village, ye ken."

"And backward," said the girl, refusing to be squelched. "Havena' even got the telegraph in."

"Have you gone there?" William asked.

The boy shook his head. "The farmers come in for the market day, some of them. We're there with the wool, so we've a chance to talk at times."

"Mostly with their daughters," said the girl, and she received another elbow for the information—sharper, if her indignant squeal was any sign.

William smiled and reminded himself to be patient.

Youth was youth in all corners of the world; shouting or snapping wouldn't get him the answers he wanted. He would have found the bickering funny another time, if he hadn't been thinking about murder.

Neither of the youngsters knew his thoughts, any more than they knew about the body in the woods. William wanted to keep it that way as long as possible. With luck, he'd be long gone before they heard rumors about the dead boy. With more luck, nobody in Belholm would connect him or his questions with those rumors—at least, not where his quarry could hear.

He focused on the siblings again. Elsie and Tom Waddell lived at the edge of the forest, like all the poor-but-honest woodcutters in fairy tales. By local standards, they weren't poor—their father owned a healthy flock of sheep as well as his house and farm— but William hoped they were honest and that they knew the land well enough.

Under his gaze, they left off their argument. Tom, a few years older, had the grace to look embarrassed. "Sorry, sir. We're not very much acquainted with them up at the Loch, to tell the truth. I wouldna say anyone is. But they're fine folk, I'm sure of it," he added with a glance at his sister. "Will you be wanting to go up that way?"

"Perhaps," said William, and he took a measuring look northwestward, where the mountains rose to meet the bright autumn sky. In theory, there was a lake somewhere beyond that line of hills, and a village nearby where "backward" people lived, "queer" individuals who were nonetheless "fine folk"—except that one of them might be a killer.

One of them might be a victim too. The dead boy might not have been local. By English standards, or at least by William's, Belholm was a small village, but it was big enough for the train to stop there twice a day, and there were plenty of farms on the outskirts where people kept to themselves. Nobody had reported a missing man, whether son, husband, brother, or farmhand, and William wasn't in a position to go making that sort of inquiry.

Even if he had been, he wouldn't have been able to give much information. The body he'd found had been almost unrecognizable. He'd made out sex, species, and rough age, but that had been all. Animals had done some of the damage—by the time William had arrived, the poor chap had been lying out for three days in a forest full of scavengers—but the worst of it had come from human hands. The killer, whoever he or she was, had pulled the boy apart in a manner that called to mind the killings in Whitechapel a decade back or the dissecting table—

—or a sacrifice.

Save when a mission called for it, William wasn't a gambling man, but he knew where he'd have put his money if he had been.

"Does the road lead anywhere else?" he asked and gestured toward the mountains. "Going that way, I mean."

Elsie shook her head. "Who else would want to live up *there*?" she asked, wrinkling her freckled nose. "Bad enough to be this far away from everything, isn't it? At least here there are the train and the telegraph, and we're getting the papers from Aberdeen every day now. Up that way's just Loch Arach and the devil of a lot of forest."

"She's right," said Tom, albeit reluctantly. "If anyone else lives that way, they keep to themselves even better than the folk of Arach. I suppose you'd get over the mountains eventually, but there are plenty of easier ways to do that."

"And the people there are…strange? Backward?" William kept his voice light, sounding simply curious—if a shade tasteless—rather than as if he was fishing for information. So he hoped, at least. It had been a long few months.

"Ah, well," said Tom with a more stoic shrug than his sister's, "they are a bit closed-mouthed, is the truth of it. And there are stories, of course, but that's just fancy," he added in a skeptical-man-of-the-world voice.

"Stories?"

"They *say*," said Elsie, eager to contribute where her brother was too embarrassed, "that people disappear up there."

Tom snorted.

Ignoring him, Elsie dropped her voice. "And I heard that the lady doesna' ever grow any older."

"The lady?" William asked.

"Lady MacAlasdair. She lives in the castle, and she's been there years, but she stays young and beautiful forever. And how would ye do that?"

"Hair dye," said Tom, "and rouge. And having silly little girls tell romantic stories about people they've not seen once."

Ignoring Elsie's violent outburst at *silly little girls*,

William chuckled. "I see," he said. "Have you met this young and beautiful lady?"

"Nay. She doesna' come out of Loch Arach much, 'tis true," said Tom, once he'd successfully dodged his sister's foot. "But the gi—the *people* I've talked to say she's in the village often enough. And they do say she's comely."

"And—people disappearing?"

"Stories," said Tom firmly. "Stories, and maybe old men who went hunting in their cups and broke their necks, or a man's wife running off with a peddler. There's no one bathin' in maiden's blood up at the Loch, sir—and none who should believe it, Elsie."

"Jolly good," said William and laughed again, as if he were just as skeptical as Tom. It was a bit hard on Elsie, of course, but there was more at stake here than the feelings of one youthful maybe-Cassandra. "People *do* go there and come back again, I assume."

"Oh, aye, of course. Not a terribly great many of 'em—"

"Who'd *want* to?" Elsie put in, sullen now.

"—but there was a painter came through the summer before last. He stopped here on the way back and gave me sixpence for carrying his wee painting kit," Tom added in what might have been a hint.

"I think I can do a bit better," said William and dug two half-crowns out of his pocket.

Elsie squealed again, this time with delight. Tom just grinned and bobbed his head. "Thank you, sir. Very much obliged."

"Think nothing of it," William said, wishing he had the power to turn the polite saying into a command. "I won't trouble you any further."

He could ask nothing else. Oh, he could *think* of things to ask, but the children probably wouldn't know the answers, and they might start wondering why he wanted to know.

A day or two from now, someone else—hunter, peddler, painter, or possibly but hopefully not another child out playing—would stumble over the body in the woods. Then the hue and cry would go up. Men would go around to the houses to ask and find out whether the poor soul had belonged to Belholm. They might even find out who he'd been. They *would* be Scots, those men, and they would have no connections to D Branch, nor prior encounters with the Consuasori, the Brotherhood of the Grey Duke, or any other of the mad and maddening cults that grew these days like mold after rain.

Nobody would be surprised at such an investigation, and the guilty party would take no particular alarm from it.

William couldn't afford to seem interested.

The children left, keeping to a polite walk as long as he was watching, but he knew they'd break into a run afterward, eager to get home or down to the shops with their windfall. As he followed their progress, he went over the facts he knew.

Item the first: the dead boy's ghost had managed to get itself to Miss Harbert in Edinburgh before going on to whatever lay ahead. By the time the medium was in position to receive, the boy's spirit had been fading, but he remembered the essentials: the chloroform, the Latin, the sense of what Harbert and William knew was magical force, and perhaps most importantly, the location. From what Harbert had said and William himself had encountered, remaining so long and so coherent when away from his body had taken both considerable strength from the ghost and some relaxation of certain boundaries from the other side.

Neither of those was a good sign.

Item the second: the killing itself. Chloroform argued that pain hadn't been a necessary component, but the killer had bled the boy thoroughly, then removed eyes, tongue, and hands. Symbolically, that probably meant sight, communication, and action—but William didn't know whether the killer had been enhancing his or her own faculties or restricting someone else's.

Item the third: tracks. There hadn't been many in the physical world. Even in good weather, a footprint wouldn't last for three days in the forest. But William had a few resources most men didn't, especially when he was certain he wouldn't be seen. The equipment that let him look into the past—two silver chains etched with runes and tipped at either end with onyx—was clunky and obvious, and the procedure not always reliable, but it had proved a godsend more than once in the last five years.

This time, the results had been mixed. As always, he saw the past through a thick haze, as bad as the worst of the London pea-soupers. While a clearer view would have been more *useful*, the blurred sort was often better for his peace of mind, as in this case. He'd seen the killer's form stooping over the boy's unconscious body and witnessed the slow process of the death, but the fog had hidden all details.

The killer was human, or human-shaped. He or she was tall for a woman or middling height for a man, relatively thin, and moved like someone whose joints still obeyed without a hitch. Otherwise, the murderer had only been a dark shape, lost in more darkness soon after he or she had left the body.

Before the shape vanished, it had headed up the road. It had gone up toward the mountains, where the children said there wasn't much but a reclusive village with a strangely young-looking lady, and past a forest where men had been known to disappear.

Up the road then was William's destination too. If he left now, he might get there before sundown, but that didn't seem very likely.

He adjusted his bag—clothing, the silver chains, guns and ammunition, and a book for the train—on his shoulder, faced the road, and couldn't help but sigh.

He envied young Tom. He envied the boy's parents, who'd doubtless had some part in his hardheaded skepticism. He envied any man who could look down the road that faced him now and tell himself that this was practically the twentieth century, that he was in Scotland, not darkest Transylvania, and that really and truly nobody around here *was* bathing in maidens' blood or ever would.

Maidens' blood would be fairly mild—especially as one could only go through so many maidens, even in a wholesome rural community.

As bad as the legends were, the truth would probably be worse. William had found that it generally worked that way.

Two

THE RESTFUL THING ABOUT AGNES, JUDITH THOUGHT
as she watched the other woman pour tea, wasn't that
she didn't ask questions. She asked plenty. She was
asking another one right now, her long acquaintance
and current position as Judith's hostess making her
bolder than another villager might have been. "I canna
think it's at all safe, can you? All of those wires right
there in the house, and what if one of them breaks?"

That was the kind of question Agnes asked. That
was the kind with which Judith could live very well.

"Then you die," said Judith. She broke open a
muffin, still steaming hot, and reached for the butter.
Even looking human, she had certain advantages over
those with only mortal blood in their veins, including a certain imperviousness to heat. "Probably most
unpleasantly. You'll remember I wasn't very enthusiastic about Colin's ideas."

Besides, she could see perfectly well in the dark, and
she had no need to keep her servants up at all hours.

"You never are that," said Agnes.

"Not *never*. There's been an occasion or two. I like

his wife well enough. That has to count for something, doesn't it?"

"More than many sisters would admit." Agnes smiled. "Will they be coming back soon, do you think?"

"I don't know," said Judith.

She knew that Agnes wouldn't ask *why* she didn't know or how long Colin had been away before or how old he was. Most people in Loch Arach wouldn't. Agnes was one of the few with whom Judith didn't always hear the unasked question, one of the few who lived comfortably without the answers she would never hear, and therefore one of the few mortals Judith could come close to calling a friend.

That was why she told herself that the gray in the other woman's hair was only shadows, and that she saw no lines at the corner of Agnes's eyes. Judith was decent at lying to herself, though not as good as she once had been.

"Aye, well," said Agnes, "it's been a great year for visitors in any case. Your brothers and that friend of the doctor's, and now Elspeth MacDougal's son's come back. I dinna' know if you'd heard that."

Judith shook her head. Mrs. MacDougal had been a housekeeper at MacAlasdair Keep for forty years before old age had made her retire to a cottage with her daughter's family. She remembered the MacDougal boy vaguely as a towheaded youth running around the village. She thought he'd taken after the father, whom she barely remembered more of.

"Come back for good?" she asked Agnes.

"He didna' say. Not but what it would do them good to have another man about the house, with the third bairn on its way and the harvest coming in. But he's been living well down in London—"

Anywhere south of Aberdeen and west of Calais was *London* to Agnes. She knew the difference, Judith was sure. She just didn't care.

"—and few men want to give that up. His mother's that glad about it, though. I dinna' think she'd more than three letters while he was away."

"Maybe he went to sea," said Judith, "and couldn't write regularly."

"Maybe," said Agnes skeptically. "I'm just glad I've a daughter, that's all."

"Women go out into the world too, I hear." Judith smiled across the teacup. "More and more in this degenerate modern age."

"Aye, but still fewer than the men. And they've more feeling for what they leave behind. I'm sure of it."

"Maybe," said Judith, and it was her turn to be dubious.

"You're here, aren't you? And your brothers all away?"

"Yes," said Judith, and she didn't add "for now" or "after a hundred years or so" or any of the other replies that might have sprung to her lips.

She was trying to think of a less-revealing argument when the door opened a crack. "Mum?" Agnes's daughter, Claire, stuck her face through the opening. She was sixteen, all blithe, blond prettiness, and Judith still couldn't get used to it. In her mind, Claire was still a toddling girl with braids and a jam-covered face. "There's a man here looking for lodgings."

"You might be right," Judith said to Agnes. "Not about men and women—about this year."

"It's the railroads. I'm sure of it. Show him in, Claire," Agnes said. "We'll give him a cup of tea while we hear what he has to say. And," she added, lowering her voice as her daughter headed off, "you might as well get a look at the man. He's likely to be the most excitement we have around here for a fortnight, unless someone's barn catches fire."

At first glance, the guest didn't *look* particularly exciting.

Oh, he was handsome: tall but not lanky, with broad shoulders and muscular legs and neatly cut hair the color of the turning leaves outside, graying just enough at the temples to lend him a distinguished air. Looking at him was a pleasant diversion. But Judith, who'd diverted herself with handsome men a few times when she'd been younger and had more freedom, didn't think his presence was going to be the year's thrill for her.

Claire's sudden need to rearrange the parlor knick-knacks indicated that she felt otherwise, but that was sixteen.

Hat in hand, the visitor bowed smoothly. "I do hope I'm not disturbing you," he said in a voice thick with public school and university. His clothes were tweed, Judith noted, and practical but of good quality and—if she recalled her brothers' wardrobes correctly—in the latest London fashion.

As he spoke, he looked around the parlor, his blue eyes taking in the deep-red wallpaper and the stuffed horsehide chairs, the mahogany table and the damask cloth. In his face, Judith saw careful, if quick evaluation, then satisfied confirmation. All was in order; he'd found what he'd expected in a place like this.

"Och, no," said Agnes, giving him her warmest smile for prospective boarders. "Have yourself a seat and a wee bite. We've plenty to go around."

"I'm greatly obliged," said the man. "Do I have the privilege of addressing Mrs. Simon?"

Agnes smiled again. "Aye, you do. And this," she said with a gesture, "is Lady Judith MacAlasdair."

Already knowing what would happen, Judith saw the stranger's face freeze briefly in surprise. Where he was from, ladies didn't take tea with boardinghouse keepers. That had been true when Judith was young, and from everything she'd heard, the boundaries had only gotten firmer—Stephen's decision to marry a commoner from the East End notwithstanding. She smiled into the man's startled expression, as blandly polite as she could manage. "A pleasure, sir."

Soon enough, and quicker than Judith would have expected, she saw the man recover himself, no doubt thinking that a tiny Scottish village didn't operate by the same standards as civilized society. "The pleasure is mine, I assure you," he said. "I'm William Arundell."

Judith would have bet the castle and half a month's rent that he had at least two middle names too, at least one of them along the lines of *Percival* or *Chauncey*.

In the back of her head, a voice very much like her brother Colin's said that it was deuced odd for the lady with the title and castle to be bristling about snobs. Judith told that voice to hush. Arundell wasn't just rich and educated. He was an outsider, for one thing, and for another—she didn't like the way he'd looked at the room or at Agnes.

She certainly didn't like the way he was looking at her. It wasn't lust. She'd spent enough decades around soldiers and sailors that she wouldn't have batted an eye at mere lechery. No, Arundell's expression was gentlemanly enough, but underneath it she sensed the same evaluation he'd turned on the parlor, but without the satisfaction, she was glad to see.

What reason—never mind, what *right*—did he have for sizing her and her friend and her village up like so many horses at auction or so many freaks in a sideshow?

"What brings you up here?" she asked. "You don't have family in the village?"

Only politeness kept it a question rather than a statement. If Arundell had been anyone's relation, Judith would have known—unless he was a bastard who'd done incredibly well for himself. She was considering that possibility when Arundell shook his head.

"No, nothing of the sort," he said. "My physician recommended it. Not here specifically, of course, but getting away from city life, from crowds and smoke and so on. I've been touring the countryside. One of the villagers in Belholm mentioned Loch Arach. It sounded like an excellent—well, retreat, if you will."

"I suppose we are that," said Agnes, laughing. "And you'll be wanting rooms, then?"

"For an indefinite time, if it could be managed."

"And gladly." Agnes got to her feet—still easily, Judith noticed, while wishing she could stop noticing such things—and put her cup down on the table.

"Lady Judith, if you'll excuse us for a moment, we'll just be stepping into my office to settle the details."

Judith was glad to let them go.

Once again, the voice of self-reproach spoke up, wondering whether she was truly going to dislike the man because of the strangeness in the way he'd looked at her. Once again, she told the voice to be silent. If two centuries of life had taught her anything, it was to trust her instincts. At the moment, she couldn't act on this one—the man had done nothing overtly wrong—but she tucked the impression away to turn over and look at later from more angles and with better tools.

When Claire came over to nab a muffin, Judith thought she might have an idea where her distrust came from. A man who viewed Loch Arach as an interesting diversion might well look at its people the same way. Arundell wouldn't be the first man to decide that fresh things other than *air* would give him a new outlook on life. He was in his forties, if Judith was any judge, and Claire was sixteen. Agnes had probably told her daughter a few home truths by now—Agnes hadn't had much time for men even before her husband had died—but that could hurt as much as help at Claire's age.

"Did you talk to Mr. Arundell much outside?" Judith asked as casually as she could manage.

"Well, no," said Claire, sighing, "not really. He said good afternoon, and I said aye, it was bidding fair to be grand, and could I be helping him with anything, and he asked was I the proprietor of this establishment, only in a joking sort of a way, ye ken—and he has a bonny smile, Lady Judith, you should see it—"

"I'm sure he does."

"And I laughed and said no," Claire went on. If she'd noticed the interruption, she gave no sign of it. Sixteen, Judith thought, was in certain ways the youngest age. Her own time in the valley of that particular shadow was a dim memory now, which went a good way toward arguing for the merciful nature of the universe. "And I asked did he want Mum, and did he want lodgings for a time, and he said he couldna' imagine leaving soon now that he'd seen how lovely the place was."

Judith made a neutral sound. It didn't sound, in fairness, as if Arundell had said anything outside the bounds of polite flattery. Not yet, at least.

"And then I showed him into the parlor. Do you think he'll stay for a while? Do you think he'll be at the fair?" Claire caught her breath at this evidently new idea. "I'll be having a new dress. Of course," she added, suddenly downcast, "it's bound to be out of style by now, and I'm sure he's used to very fashionable ladies."

"I'm sure he's used to *older* ones," said Judith. "And if he isn't, he should be, no matter how pretty you are. You're old enough to know what I'm saying, aren't you?"

She hoped so. Pure human girls were so damnably *fertile*, and the world wasn't kind to an unmarried woman with a baby. Loch Arach was small enough that everyone would talk, no matter what Judith did; bigger places had their own dangers.

Claire was nodding now, chewing on her lip and looking about to go into a fit of sulks.

"Besides, isn't the Stewart lad chasing after you these days? And haven't you been doing a good bit of chasing back?"

"Oh, aye," said Claire again. If she wasn't completely mollified, the mention of her beau did seem to keep her from sinking completely into the doldrums. "But he's been all nervy lately. It's *tiring* for a girl," she added as the door to her mother's private office opened and Arundell followed Agnes into the parlor. "Just because a beast killed one of his old cows."

And at *that*, of all things, Judith saw Arundell's gaze sharpen.

Three

DAMN. DAMN, DAMN, DAMN.

Either the dead cow was completely irrelevant—
which was likely enough insofar as cows were reasonably common in the country and did get killed for
reasons other than their owners' desire for a roast—or
it was exactly the sort of thing William should hear
more about—which was *also* likely, since animal sacrifice was a decent way to summon and bribe demons
and thus relatively common among the smarter sort of
cultists, the ones who'd worked out that people did
eventually miss even street urchins in this modern day
and age.

He badly wanted to ask questions. He probably
could have gotten answers if he'd just been talking to
Claire, or to Claire and her mother. The girl clearly
found him charming—the day William couldn't
charm a pastoral adolescent, he'd retire to a Spanish
villa and fish for the rest of his life—and her mother
was inclined to indulge paying customers, particularly
strangers with potentially interesting stories. He could
easily have gotten off a series of "Sounds dreadful.

Do tell me more" questions without them thinking anything of it, and any suspicions they did develop would have been gone by morning.

Lady MacAlasdair was a different kettle of fish—and not fat, harmless goldfish either. Swordfish, maybe. Or sharks.

Meeting her, he'd understood the rumors. The lady's eyes, her speech, and the way she carried herself belonged to a woman of at least his age, but everything else about her suggested that she might possibly have reached twenty-five at the most. Her hair, pinned in a simple coil at the base of her long neck, was glossy black shot through with strands of bronze. William couldn't see a trace of gray there, nor any wrinkles at the corners of her wide mouth or her green-gold eyes. She wore a russet-colored walking dress with no frills or tight lacing to conceal her form, and the shape it revealed was straight and slim but, he noticed with a sinking heart, broad-shouldered.

In dim light and in the right clothing, she could have passed for a man, especially if she'd had her hair up. She could certainly have been the figure in the image William had seen.

Plenty of people could.

Plenty of people didn't inspire rumors about how they maintained their youth, nor were they heir to a small village and a castle in the back of beyond.

Nor did most people regard outsiders with the look of a magistrate hearing dubious testimony.

This was not a woman disposed to welcome him with open arms and questions about the latest London fashions. This *was* a woman well-positioned to make trouble for him if she had the inclination. William wasn't exactly up to speed on the law in remote parts of Scotland, but he had the impression that the local nobility still had a touch more power than the foxhunting-and-waltzing crowd he'd been used to.

Legal questions aside, she could probably command the loyalty—or at least the mercenary inclinations—of a few strapping local men. That could be enough of a problem for William. His training had carried him through a number of scraps, and he was still years from a walking stick or a chair in front of the fire, but he was one man, and mortal.

Being a man with sound tactical sense, he did not press his luck but simply listened.

"Now, Claire," said Mrs. Simon, "that's no' a fitting subject for the lady, nor for our guest to be overhearing."

Luck was with him—luck and the moodiness of adolescents. Claire pouted. "I dinna' see why not. If there's a wolf about, or a bear or a great cat, and it starts eating us all, it'll be her business, will it no'? And well for him to take care if he goes wandering about the place."

"There hasn't been a wolf here in a hundred years," said Lady MacAlasdair, quietly amused. "Nor bears for a century or five, and no cat larger than the tabbies in my stables for much longer than that. Graham's not talked to me," she added dryly, "nor yet has his father, but I'd imagine the poor beast broke its neck."

"It didna' look that way, from what Graham said. Of course," Claire added, "he'd not tell me much. But he did say as its eyes were gone, and its throat."

"That sounds more like crows and rats than wolves and bears," the lady responded without a trace of alarm or disgust. "Nothing dire there, unless you're the cow."

"Or the boy, I should think," said William, "if it was one of his father's beasts."

"She was that," said Claire, "and one of the best milkers, and Graham's da's fair taken him ower the coals for it. The which is noways fair." William guessed that was a comment on the injustice of the situation. Certainly Claire's blue eyes flashed in a way that suggested where her loyalty lay, no matter how attractive she might temporarily find a stranger. "He swears he latched the gate afore he came away, and he's never a dishonest lad," the girl added.

"If lying meant you could take your dinner sitting down for the next week," said Lady MacAlasdair, "nobody but a saint would tell the truth. Was the gate latched the next day?"

"Well, no," said Claire, flushing.

"It'd have to be a very talented wolf, then," William said gently.

As he spoke, he thought he heard Lady MacAlasdair's voice as well, too faintly for him to hear what she'd said. It almost sounded like Latin: a curse? He wouldn't have expected a woman of her rank and age to know Latin, much less swear in it.

He wouldn't have expected a woman of her rank and age to be sitting in a boardinghouse parlor and talking about dead cows.

When William turned toward Lady MacAlasdair, he caught a glimpse of narrowed eyes and thin lips.

She quickly made her face relax into a rueful smile, but he hadn't missed that moment of scrutiny, and he thought she knew it. She set down her teacup.

"I'd best be on my way. Graham and his father both have my sympathy, of course—and if anything similar *does* happen again, they'll know to come have a word with me." She turned her smile on William, showing more teeth than was entirely friendly. "I take care of problems around here, Mr. Arundell. I flatter myself that I'm good at it."

"I have no doubt," he said and bowed to her. "None whatsoever."

❧

Over supper and then breakfast the next morning, William solidified his cover. In answer to Mrs. Simon's questions and her daughter's, he said that he'd been born in Sussex and was an only child (both true), that his parents were both dead (also true, as of five years ago), and that he had no real profession, which might have been true from a certain angle. Membership in D Branch didn't come with a regular check—just the ability to draw on various funds and the vague promise of a sinecure when he grew too old for his regular duties.

It was rather like being a kept woman, without the jewelry.

Of course, he didn't say any of that to his outwardly respectable hostess and her young offspring. He just said that he was "rather aimless most of the time." They assumed he was a gentleman with funds in the Exchange—another truth, though that inheritance wouldn't have covered half of his expenses on missions—and William distracted them with tales of the Diamond Jubilee.

Mrs. Simon looked intrigued at that, and Claire starry-eyed and wistful. "Och, but it must ha' been something to see. There were the pictures in the *Times*, of course, but they were wee an' with no colors an' a whole week behind. I wish I'd ha' been there."

"Aye, well," said Mrs. Simon, "when I was a girl, we'd not have even had the pictures, only the engravings. And we didna' get the *Times* at all save when someone went to Aberdeen. We have it every week here down at the store," she added to William, by way of being a helpful landlady, "only it's often behind. Young Hamish Connoh rides down to Belholm for the post every twa' days, you see—or he's supposed to, but he was in bed with a sore throat that week, I recall. You'll not be needing anything urgent? We've no telegraph, though it's no' very far to Belholm when the weather's fine."

"No," said William. "No, I don't believe anything of that nature should arise."

It was rather his job to see that nothing of that nature *did*. He knew that job, had done it for years, had accepted its nature when he was a much younger man—and yet, after he answered Mrs. Simon, he looked out the window to where the mountains rose dark and unyielding behind the much-smaller roofs of the town. Up here, he would be very much on his own.

He felt that isolation again after breakfast when he went out to explore and investigate.

If Belholm was small by his standards, Loch Arach was tiny—and old. Most of the houses were still stone, one-story cottages with thatched roofs and borders marked out with more stone walls. Sheep grazed inside some of those walls; an occasional pig rooted under trees; dogs, poultry, and children abounded. William spotted three larger farmsteads with wooden buildings bright white and red against the dark pines and vivid leaves, and sturdy fences to contain the herd or flock. One of those farms, he assumed, was the property of the unfortunate Graham's father.

The farms spread out around the lake that had given the village its name. Small in circumference, it glimmered cold and blue in the sunshine. One of the old men who fished by it told William that it was very deep and fell off quickly—no place for wading and a constant source of wariness where children were concerned.

The village proper was one short street where a few more of the newer buildings stood side by side, though with considerable room between. Mrs. Simon's house bordered a smaller but comfortable building where—according to the lady—Dr. McKendry lived, now with a friend come up from Aberdeen. On the other side, a pub announced itself as the Old Dragon with an appropriately lurid red sign. Opposite was a store, presumably the domain of young Hamish and his relations, and set some way apart from it, a blacksmith's forge with a stable in the back. A small stone church capped one end of the street, and at its back was a graveyard, the stones rough-carved and, in many cases, very old.

That was all—except for the castle.

Rather than being at the top of a cliff or built against the mountains themselves, both of which would have been quite defensible back when the broadsword and the longbow were the latest innovations in warfare, the castle sat on a small hill a mile or so from the village. From his window on the second story of Mrs. Simon's house, William could make out blocky towers of dark stone rising above the surrounding trees. For someone standing in the village, the building itself would be harder to see. A veritable Birnam Wood surrounded the place, near-black evergreens mingling with the vivid reds and golds of autumn leaves.

"That's quite a forest back there," William said to the man behind the counter of the general store. By his salt-and-pepper hair, not to mention his luxuriant mustache, William guessed this was not young Hamish.

"Hmm?" The man had been ringing up William's purchases: the latest outdated *Times* and a packet of biscuits. He looked up without comprehending for a second, in the way of people hearing curiosity about a constant feature of their lives. "Oh, the woods? Aye, 'tis large enough."

"Good hunting, I'd think."

The man frowned. His eyes were very dark, William noticed now, and their shape was almost Indian or Chinese. "I'd not venture verra far in," the shopkeeper said, "nor yet out by the castle, not without her ladyship's permission."

"Worried about poachers, is she?" William asked. "I wouldn't have thought it would be a problem in a place like this. There must be plenty of game to go around, and you couldn't ride to hounds out here."

"No," said the storekeeper, "no, nobody'd think of it. Galloping the horses on that ground?" He barked laughter. "It's bad enough riding down the road to get the post."

"Then—"

"She doesna' want people running about back there without her knowing it," said the man. "None of the family ever has. And it's not my place to be askin' why, lad, nor yours. Now, if I canna' be showing you anything else this day…"

Four

THE LAST TIME THAT JUDITH HAD GONE TO LONDON, ladies had made their round of calls in carriages, attended by maids. She didn't have the impression there'd been much change in that regard, which was another reason she was glad to be away from the city. She'd neither the patience nor the fleet of servants needed to have another body tagging along with her the whole time, and she would have liked to see the fine carriage that could handle the road out by the Gordons' house.

Instead, she rode astride on a stout dun pony from her own stables, bred over the centuries for hardiness, tractability, and a near insensibility to the smell of large predators. Most animals knew what the MacAlasdairs really were, even in human shape. The elegant horses that the London crowd rode would have shied and bolted if Judith had even put a foot in one of their stirrups.

That reaction had made for a few awkward moments in her youth. More than one officer had seen a vacant spot in his cavalry or the need of a mounted messenger, and thought that "the MacAlasdair boy" had the build and the bearing to fill it. She'd learned to shrug and look down and say that horses never had taken to her, sir. How fast the rumors spread after that had been a matter of chance, though better toward the end of her career when men were less superstitious.

The navy had been easier all around. Other superstitions aside, ships didn't care who sailed on them, or at least they didn't seem to mind the MacAlasdairs.

Hitching Dawn to a convenient oak, Judith remembered the sea for a moment—the smell of salt and brine, the almost unreal pink of sunrise near the Indies—and smiled. Then she straightened her skirt and her hat, secured a package under one arm, and walked up to the cottage's front door.

Her tap brought first small Ronnie—an eight-year-old with his father's black hair and eyes—and then after the child's quick and loud exclamation, his mother. Encumbered as she was by the sixth month of pregnancy and a baby in one arm, Gillian Gordon bobbed respectfully nonetheless and smiled, though wearily. "Good day, your ladyship. You'll be here to see Ross?"

"And the rest of you, aye," said Judith. "I hope I'm not troubling you."

"Nay, not a bit of it," said Gillian. "Come in and sit yourself down."

The cottage was a large one, with a curtain-covered doorway on each side of the main room and a loft over the fire. Inside, it smelled of peat and baking bread, odors that relaxed Judith as quickly as her own scent would frighten a horse. A smooth wooden table and chairs were tucked against one wall; a rocking chair and a long bench sat by the fire. Elspeth MacDougal occupied the chair, knitting a small garment.

On the bench sat a man, young but not too young, who looked almost as out of place in the cottage as Arundell would have. With the years, Ross MacDougal's unruly blond curls had become light brown and fashionably clipped, and he'd grown a small, neat mustache. When he saw her, he got to his feet smoothly, showing a well-tailored tweed suit, and smiled. "Lady MacAlasdair." There was little of Loch Arach in his voice, little of Scotland in general. "You've not aged a day."

Long since, Judith had learned not to flinch at such comments, nor to suspect that they had any ring of actual suspicion in them. This time she hesitated, though she didn't know why. She felt off balance for a second, as if she'd caught her heel on a bump, but the carefully sanded floor had no irregularities.

"Eighteen's a grand charitable age to remember, I see," she said, recovering herself with a laugh, "or you've learned courtly manners in your time away. It's good to see you back, Ross." She turned to Mrs. MacDougal, holding out the package. "Mrs. Lennox says she's sure her jam isn't anything to what you used to make, but she'd be obliged if you'd try it. I'll not venture an opinion one way or the other, before you ask."

"Ha," said Mrs. MacDougal, her tone familiar in both senses of the word.

She had the right if anyone did. Alone among mortals now, she had been there during the first awkward years after Judith had come home permanently. Judith's mother had been dead, her father increasingly in seclusion, Colin off in France, and Stephen preoccupied with the curse he'd brought upon himself in his own travels. Mrs. MacDougal's advice had been invaluable then, her sympathy even more so.

Had Judith's father revealed the MacAlasdairs' true nature to his housekeeper? Had it been her mother before she'd died? Stephen? It didn't matter. In the end, the senior servants took oaths more powerful than mere words, and if Mrs. MacDougal had ever tried to get around them, the results had never troubled Judith's ears.

"Fiona always did worry about filling your shoes," said Gillian, who'd grown up with Mrs. Lennox. The two had been maids at the castle together—ten years ago that was, before marriage for both and widowhood for one. Judith had almost gotten used to Mrs. Lennox as a housekeeper. Gillian as a housewife was still odd, and odder still when she referred to the past as if it was so far away.

"Fiona was always a likely girl," said Mrs. MacDougal diplomatically. "'Twas a shame about her husband, but she's managed fine. Got a chill twa' or three year after ye left," she added to her son, "and it settled in his lungs. Dr. McKendry still feels it, aye, though he did all a man could."

"It must be difficult for him up here," said Ross. "For any doctor. And he was middle-aged ten years ago."

"He's got life in him yet," said Mrs. MacDougal. "More of it now with that Mr. Hamilton up to bide wi' him. A nice, homely sort of man that, even if he is used to city ways. But then, we've no shortage of those round here now, do we?"

Judith laughed. "Certainly not."

"Are your brothers about, then?" Ross asked. "I don't think that I caught more than a glimpse of either when I was a boy."

"You've just missed them, I'm afraid. *And* their wives." She had to laugh again at Ross's startled look. "Aye, it was a shock to me too, though a pleasant one. I don't *think* they met and decided it was time, but I could almost believe it."

He smiled. "It'll be you next then."

"I shouldn't think so," said Judith cheerfully. "Everyone's better off with me being an old maid. I doubt I could manage the castle *and* a husband."

It was the sort of polite deferral that she always used when people asked certain questions. Usually her response got a smile, varying from sympathetic to indulgent depending on the audience. Ross's was definitely on the indulgent end, but before it appeared, Judith thought she saw another look on his face: weary and disappointed.

Well, that made two of them.

"I'd think the right husband would take that burden from your shoulders," said Ross.

Judith held her smile and searched for a suitable reply.

Luckily, Gillian stepped in, shaking her head at her brother. "Och, leave off, or her ladyship will think you've a man in mind for her."

"I'd hardly presume that far," said Ross, his smile

more ingratiating now. "I'm sure I don't know anyone suitable."

"I'll no' believe that," Mrs. MacDougal said. "Not wi' the letters you've been sending, nor the stories you've been telling us now you're here. He's a great man in London," she said to Judith. "Dines with lords and bishops and captains of industry."

"Oh, Mother, don't exaggerate." Ross looked down and waved a hand, the picture of self-deprecation. "It isn't as though it happens every night, and most of the time there are dozens of other people about. Besides, it was only chance that I struck up an acquaintance with Southbrook. I was as surprised by it as anyone."

"And the bishops and merchant princes?" Judith asked, biting the inside of her cheek to keep from laughing.

"Oh, them," Ross replied with studied casualness. "Well, that's largely been on parish business. Or on other business. I work on the Exchange, you see, though I won't go into detail about it. I'm sure it would put all three of you to sleep."

This time, Judith did let herself chuckle, though only partly at the actual joke. Young men writing to their mothers—it was hard to top them for cheek. She wouldn't have been surprised, for that matter, if half of her early letters home had given the impression that she was in the confidence of Admiral Lord Anson himself.

"Stephen does handle all of that, thank God," she said. "I've a decent head for figures on a small scale, but I've never been much good with the funds."

"He's gone down to London again, my mother tells me," said Ross.

"Aye," said Judith. "And I'll not ask if you've seen him there—country cousin I may be, but I know well enough that London is a bit larger than Loch Arach."

Ross's face tightened again, just for a moment. "Large," he said, "and getting larger all the time. Not always in the right ways or with the right…elements. I think you're wise to stay up here, Lady MacAlasdair, since you can manage it."

He could have managed it too, Judith thought—he hadn't *had* to go chase after being a fine businessman. But the thought passed unsaid as quickly as it had come. She'd been about Ross's age when she'd left Loch Arach, and she'd not *had* to leave either.

"Wise or lazy," she said. "But Colin's fond of the city, I believe, and even Stephen says it has its advantages."

Privately, she wondered what had happened to Ross down in London. Men had come back like him before, with bitterness coating every shilling of their new wealth. Girls were behind it usually, or business gone bad. Occasionally the causes were more violent. Judith looked surreptitiously back and forth between Mrs. MacDougal and Gillian, and got blank expressions from them both. If they knew more than she did, they didn't consider it a public matter.

That was fair enough. Mortals didn't have her reasons not to want people prying, but they did have reasons.

"Will you be staying with us for a while then?" she asked.

"At least until the winter, I should think. After that"—he spread his hands—"we'll see."

"We're hoping to persuade him to stay a year," Gillian said, "though of course his business may need him back well before then. The telegraph can only do so much, aye?"

"Even once it arrives," said Mrs. MacDougal.

"But he'll stay at least through the harvest and the fair," said Gillian, and rumpled her brother's hair. "I've his word on that."

"I couldn't miss that," said Ross. "Not now that I'm back. I've too many fond memories."

"I'd imagine," said Judith.

As its neighbors did, Loch Arach always celebrated once the harvest was in. In Judith's girlhood, that had meant a meal at the castle with all the tenants. Over the years, it had come to include pony rides and boiled sweets for the children, a few contests of a largely physical and messy nature, and dancing in the evening for as long as the band's fingers and the dancers' feet held out.

"Well, I warn you," she added, "you're likely to get a fair few questions while you're here. Your family's not the only ones who'll want to hear stories—and as for the fair, lad, I hope you came prepared to dance. New faces are rare around here, as I think you recall, and handsome ones who've lived in London rarer than that. If every girl in the village isn't making eyes at you before the week's out, I'll be very surprised."

"Aye," teased Gillian, "but he'll not be the only one, from what I hear."

"The doctor's friend? Nay, too old by half," said

Mrs. MacDougal. "Or d'ye mean that Englishman who's stopped wi' Mrs. Simon?"

"That's the one," said Gillian. "Have you seen him, your ladyship?"

"Aye," said Judith, not changing her expression or the tone of her voice. She'd known since Arundell arrived that he'd make a stir in the village; there was no point in pouting about that. "He's well-looking, I'll say that for him."

"I've not heard very much," said Ross. "What can you tell me about my competition?"

"Not much. Mrs. Simon and her daughter could say more by now, I'm certain. He's a bit older than you, and a gentleman by his dress and his manners. He says his doctor's sent him away from the city for his health." Judith shrugged. "Arundell's his name. I can't say that I know anything else."

"Arundell?" Another moment of unknown emotion flickered across Ross's face.

"Do you know him?"

Ross frowned and finally shook his head. "I don't know that I can place the name. Perhaps I will when I meet him—but the odds, as you've already observed, are against it."

"Aye," said Judith, though she hoped otherwise. Most likely Mr. Arundell was only what he seemed, and she was too inclined to jump at shadows—but she would have felt much better with confirmation.

Five

REMEMBERING HIS OWN ADOLESCENCE, PARTICULARLY the part connected to Miss Susan Levett and an unfortunate fire in a wastebasket, William steadfastly ignored Claire's tendency to blush and walk into walls when he was around, just as he did with a few other girls her age. A few of the young men had shown tendencies to sulk, which William also pretended not to see. None of it was really about him, after all. He was a new face in a village that didn't see many.

Other young men, and one or two young women, asked questions instead, wanting his opinion on the wider world. They wanted to know what it was like to live in the cities, how long train journeys took and how often the trains broke down, and how hard it was to earn a living. Their younger brothers and sisters just wanted stories of steamships and royalty and battles; while their grandparents asked after politics and war, and told their own stories, as glad of a new audience as of information.

William answered everything as best he could, cultivated who he might without hurting any feelings or incurring the wrath of fathers or brothers, and found some information in his own turn, although not nearly as much as he'd have liked.

Neither Graham Stewart nor his father were among the men who talked with William, and their cow, whatever might have happened to her, was not a great subject of discussion for anyone, even Claire, after the first day or two. Without any plausible way to broach the topic, William let it lie and concentrated on other angles, though those didn't prove much more fruitful.

Lady Judith was at least forty and had come home "about twenty" years ago after her mother died. Popular consensus had her in England or maybe Ireland before then, living with an aunt or maybe her grandmother on her mother's side, or maybe going to school and then taking rooms with a friend, as young women would do these days instead of getting married like sensible creatures, according to one of the old men at the pub.

She had two brothers, and William had just missed seeing them. They were both married and living elsewhere now. On that last, public sentiment was mixed. The young regarded such defection as only natural, while the old said that it was a pity—but that it had always been the MacAlasdairs' way to wander about. Either way, general agreement had them being fine, handsome young men, with a minority (a spotty youth being most vocal among them) voting for "think they're too good for the likes of us, of course" or just taciturn shrugging when the subject came up.

Nobody could recall or had even heard of a time when the MacAlasdairs hadn't been in the castle.

Nobody had heard of any mysterious deaths recently either. Every few years, a man might break his neck hunting, but that was generally due to bad luck or drink. Disappearances were more common, but mostly young people running away to try their luck down the mountain, getting shed of their parents or the girl who'd turned them down, or in at least one winked-at case, the boy who hadn't been turned down and the unfortunate results.

Nobody could say for sure how old Lady Judith's brothers were or how old her parents had been when they'd died. They had to have been close on ninety, William's informants had said, though neither of them had much looked it, and Lord MacAlasdair in particular could have passed for a man of sixty. "Well-preserved" was the term. It made William think of jam and reflect that, generally speaking, preserving was an intentional process.

Nobody knew exactly why the MacAlasdairs didn't want anyone in the forest.

People did keep to themselves, particularly up here. Particularly when the other party was nobility. William tried to remember that and not jump to conclusions.

Then he met Ellen Ruddle. One of Claire's friends, she was short and cheerful, as ready to giggle as any of the other girls. She had a touch more composure though, a sense about her that she wasn't going to lose her head easily. That might have come from being a couple years older than the rest, but William was more interested in the other potential reason: her work at the castle.

"She's got a half holiday today," said Claire by way

of introduction. William had come outside to find the two of them leaning on a fence and talking, a dust rag tucked absently into the waist of Claire's skirt. "Ellen's a housemaid up at the castle. An' not the most junior either."

"Aye, I'm an old hen," said Ellen, elbowing the younger girl in the ribs.

William produced a greeting just on the charming side of polite and, after providing the requisite few sentences about himself, added, "I've only seen the castle from a distance. Vast place, from the look of it. And you're in charge of the whole thing?"

"Get out of it, you fooler," said Ellen, waving a hand at him as if to shoo a fly. "There's a head housemaid and Mrs. Lennox over me, as I've no doubt you know. But Mrs. Lennox did say as how she couldna' do without me," she added, shaking back her dark curls.

"I've no doubt. It looks like quite a job, even for a whole army of housemaids—or are some of the rooms shut up? I've heard that about some of these old castles."

"There's the north wing," Ellen began, "but—"

She stopped, frowned, and shook her head.

"But?" William asked, not sounding eager despite all temptation.

A curious look came over the girl's face then, a mixture of surprise and annoyed resignation. If an expression had words, this one would have said, *Oh, fine* then. *Have it your way!*

She shook her head again. "Oh, nothing important. 'Tis shut up, is what I meant to say, and we're not to

go into it, but I canna' imagine it's as bad as all that."
She stopped for a second. "They're not the sort to be
letting a place fall down, aye? Even if they dinna' use a
part of the castle, they'll be keeping it in repair."

"How industrious," said William. "And less for you
to do, which must be convenient."

"Oh, aye. I'm glad enough of it," she said. "Especially
these last few months with the whole family up. I
thought for a bit that we'd have to take on extra hands."

"But you didn't?"

"Too hard to find folk we can count on," she said
and then changed the subject.

Looking back, William could only think of that one
moment, that brief look that had been anything out of
the ordinary. If it hadn't fit the pattern he was starting
to perceive, if not understand, he wouldn't even have
noticed. Small towns were odd. Everyone knew that.

William knew that. He also knew just how dangerous "odd" could be. He'd tried to find the missing
children of an "odd little town" in Ireland and had
only succeeded in killing the gnarled man-thing that
had sent them *elsewhere*—not the last of its kind, he
was sure. He'd infiltrated an "eccentric gentleman's
club" in London and discovered the Things to whom
its members dedicated themselves and the methods by
which their allegiance was bought.

At times, perhaps usually, odd was just odd. But his
duty to Queen and Country meant he could never
assume that.

When the note arrived from Dr. McKendry, offering dinner and cards "if we can dig up a fourth," he
was glad to go—not just to have mature masculine

company for a whole evening, but because McKendry was likely to at least have been educated in a city, and his friend Hamilton came from Aberdeen. William's perspective was skewed one way, while the locals' perspective, and perhaps their loyalties, leaned in the other direction entirely. He wanted to hear a voice from the ground in between.

He was almost on the doctor's doorstep when he heard trotting hooves and looked up to see Lady MacAlasdair.

As he might have expected, she rode astride. When she passed William, he could see the outline of her leg pressed clearly against the yellow flowered cotton of her dress. It was a rather shapely leg too, he noticed, being a man of some experience. Being also a gentleman, he quickly lifted his gaze.

She nodded at him but didn't speak until William went to help her down and she waved him off. "Oh, Lord, no. Thank you," she added a second later, and she swung down out of the stirrups, apparently not caring about any stray flash of petticoat that resulted. As if he had been one of the horses, she brushed past him, stepped briskly up to the door, and rapped several times.

"Tell Dr. McKendry that I need him up at the castle," she said when a maid answered. "Jack Shaw's fallen and broken his leg. It looks bad. I'll wait for him here."

Ave Caesar, William said mentally.

Imperious as Lady MacAlasdair sounded, neither her tone nor her posture was that of the typical lady making demands.

William hadn't served under many officers in his life, his position being very irregularly attached to the army, but he knew how they spoke. Make Lady MacAlasdair male and give her a few bars across her chest, and she would have passed nicely on any parade grounds.

As he smiled at the thought, the door closed, leaving the two of them alone together. Quickly, William banished any trace of mirth. "Sounds like a nasty fall, by Jove," he said, turning to face the lady. "Is there anything I can do?"

She regarded him from under the thick darkness of her braided hair. The excitement made her eyes almost glow, like fireflies on a summer's evening, but William wouldn't have envied the lad who tried to catch them. "Set any broken bones, have ye?"

"Afraid not," said William. In fact, he knew the theory. He knew a lot of theory, but so far he'd mercifully escaped the need to practice. "I could hold the chap steady though, or fetch water and bandages or whatnot."

"We're no' so short of servants as ye might think," said the lady. Her accent was thicker now than it had been in Mrs. Simon's parlor and different from what he'd heard from the locals, though William couldn't say why. Lady MacAlasdair let out a breath and then added, "But 'tis good of you to offer, all the same."

"Oh, one tries to be helpful. I hope everything turns out well. What happened?"

"He'd been mending the roof," she said after a moment, during which William could almost read her thoughts: *It'll be all over the village tomorrow. May as well tell him myself.* "The ladder broke. Not while he was at the top, God be thanked."

"Indeed," said William. "Not his first day on the job, was it?"

"No," said Lady MacAlasdair, her eyes narrowing. "They've been mending the walls for five years, Jack and his father, and there's no' been any broken bones before."

"First time for everything, I suppose," said William. He looked over the lady again as she stood waiting with her hand on the horse's neck. She was a fine-looking woman, even in a plain dress and with her hair in a hasty braid. Her body rose from the ground like an oak sapling, graceful and yet with the implicit promise of strength and power.

He wished he could have viewed that last as an unqualified positive. "Will you be able to hire other men from the village, or will you send to Belholm?"

"I hadn't thought about it yet," snapped Lady MacAlasdair, and her horse shied suddenly, though William hadn't seen any movement in the doctor's yard. She took a slow breath. "You'll forgive me, I'm sure."

"You're worried. It's commendable."

He wished that he hadn't been sincere when he spoke. Admiration would only make his job harder.

The lady's mouth twisted into a hard smile. "I'm glad you approve, sir." Before William could protest, she went on. "The repairs aren't as urgent as all that. I'll see if anyone from the village is willing and able. Then maybe Belholm."

"You don't go often, do you?"

"I wouldn't go this time," she said. "My steward's better at hiring, and Mr. Shaw knows best who'd be a good partner."

The doctor came out the door again, thick-bearded and short and grim, gripping a medical bag in one hand. William made a polite answer to his distracted apologies, got out of the way, and noted silently that Lady MacAlasdair had not actually answered his question.

Six

By the time Judith and Dr. McKendry reached the castle, Jack Shaw the Younger was unconscious. Shock might have done that, or lost blood—the lower part of his right leg looked badly broken, and the skin was punctured in several places—but Mrs. Lennox was holding a large brown bottle that also went a way toward explaining his condition. Judith was glad to see it. Setting a leg was no comfortable matter, even in these days when there was a fair chance it would succeed, and she disliked screaming. It brought back too many memories.

Healing magic had never worked for the MacAlasdairs. During one of his scholarly periods, Colin had rooted out a few spells that were supposed to work all right, even if one of them did involve unpleasantly close contact with a chicken liver. One of them, *not* the chicken-liver one, might possibly have helped a cut mend faster than it would have already and hurt less in the process, but there wasn't enough difference to be sure. The others, even the ones Colin had seen humans cast on each other with success, did nothing. Moreover, none of the spells worked when a MacAlasdair cast it on a human being. Colin had talked about "the law of similarity" and found it all rather fascinating.

For themselves, it didn't really matter. Their blood did more for them than any spell, particularly when they were in dragon form. Magic could do lasting damage, as could silver and a few kinds of wood. Wounds to the heart and the brain were generally fatal because they didn't give one any time to heal. The rest got better, generally at ten times or so the speed of human wounds.

But she could lend nothing of that to her tenants.

Judith kept out of the way, letting McKendry do his work with one of the two grooms to assist him. Having played her role, Mrs. Lennox was shooing the three maids back into the castle, saying firm things about the lateness of the day and the amount of work still to be done. In all likelihood, Mrs. Frasier and Mr. Janssen were still inside, neither cook nor butler being terribly burdened with curiosity.

Most of the servants weren't, when one came right down to it. Judith looked for that quality, as her father had done before her.

Standing in the shadow of the castle, she felt the hairs on the back of her neck rise. She turned quickly but saw nobody—and who was there to be seen?

Clearly, the last few days had not been good for her nerves. She'd have to go hunting soon and work off the tension. The body, she'd learned before she'd become a woman, responded very much to the mind. With her family, that could end badly.

She cleared her throat, stepped forward, and did her duty, addressing herself to Jack Shaw the Elder. He'd been watching the doctor's progress with his son's leg, his face beneath its gingery beard distinctly grayish, and it was probably time for him to turn his attention elsewhere.

"I'm sure he'll be all right," Judith said. She was telling the truth by the standards she'd grown up with. The boy might walk with a limp, but he'd probably keep the leg, and now that doctors used alcohol and carbolic acid and whatever else was in McKendry's bag, there wasn't much chance of blood poisoning.

She hoped she was telling the truth by Shaw's light as well.

Regardless, he turned to her and managed a nod. "Thank you, m'lady." He glanced over his shoulder to where the broken remains of the ladder lay at the foot of the castle wall. "Devilish thing. I—I would swear it was whole enough this morning. Would ha' sworn so," he added, looking back at the still figure on the ground.

"I'm sure of it," Judith said. "I've never known you to be a careless man. I expect," she said, letting the words come to her as they might and bring what comfort or reassurance anyone in her position could give, "I expect that wood goes bad from the inside at times, and anybody might miss that. Certainly when a thing has so many parts."

Shaw nodded again. He still stood stiff, his hands clasped in front of him and his face set like one of the stones he worked with. There was no knowing if what she'd said had been helpful; there so rarely was. "It wasna' new, like, but no more than two years old. I recall Keir makin' it that spring when the river near flooded."

"Keir's a good hand with woodworking," Judith said. The man who served as groundskeeper and herdsman and general jack-of-all-trades was off keeping a watchful—she hoped—eye on the sheep.

"Aye," said Shaw, "and it never went at all bad afore this. Not wi' all the climbing we've been doing, an' all the stones an' mortar. So I'm no' saying 'tis any fault of his."

"No, of course not," said Judith.

She would have wagered half her fortune and all her lands that Shaw didn't know *what* he was saying, or at least that he wouldn't remember it by evening. Men rambled at times like these. If you had to talk about things you couldn't fix, you at least picked the ones that didn't cut so close.

"Bad luck," she said. "Rotten bad luck, and I'm sorry for it. You know he'll have a place here whatever comes, d'you no'? A likely lad like him can always be useful."

She would also pay McKendry's bill, but quietly. One didn't say certain things aloud.

"Aye," said Shaw, and he did relax a bit at that, if only a hair. "Thank you, m'lady."

They stood there for a while. There were no more words to distract either of them, no words at least that could pass between a stonemason and even the eccentric lady of a small village, perhaps no words in any case. Behind them, the cracks and squelches came at irregular intervals, without even a rhythm one could eventually tune out. Sounds like that drowned out all words over time, even all thought.

The castle's shadow stretched long and cold around them. Judith generally wasn't fool enough to envy her servants—she treated them well but knew her own good fortune—but just then, she would have liked to have been a housemaid, whose duty lay inside.

For all Ross MacDougal's comments, Dr. McKendry moved swiftly, and his hands were steady on the wood and leather of the splint he was constructing. Judith seized on that as one good sign in the day. All sentiment aside, she didn't want to have to bring a new doctor up to Loch Arach any time soon. Nobody in the village showed signs of going into the profession, and introducing men from outside was always tricky, particularly in these days of telegraph and photograph.

Arundell hadn't shown any inclination to tromp about with a camera, at least. Not that there was anything for him to see—not unless he really managed to go where he'd no business being—but men with cameras tended to pry more than those without, in Judith's experience. Arundell asked too many questions already.

She wondered if that was the way of city men now. The painter hadn't pried, but he'd been artistic. Mrs. Simon had told stories of him coming downstairs with one boot unlaced, or of not showing up for meals at all because some view had distracted him. Although city-born, Mr. Hamilton was McKendry's friend and so far seemed willing to imitate his host in discretion.

She would have preferred to think that impertinent questions and searching looks just came naturally to city men. The alternative meant trouble. She doubted Arundell, or whatever object he might have, was magical. The brief glimpse she'd gotten of his aura, in Agnes's parlor, had shown it to be an unremarkable and irksomely pleasant shade of silver-gray.

He could be after money in one way or another. Judith had turned down two offers from mining companies since she'd returned to Loch Arach. Arundell could be working for either or a third, and trying to find anything they could use. He could be a newspaperman who'd run into one of her brothers and was looking for scandal—or who thought a "quaint, old-fashioned village" in the Highlands was just the sort of place his readers might want to visit, which would actually be worse.

He could have heard rumors or legends. Judith knew they existed, but she didn't know how far the stories went, or what shape they took outside Loch Arach itself. As her mother had told her, there was only so much you could do to keep people from talking, and then the key was to make sure nobody really knew what they were talking about.

There was a great deal she didn't know. There was a great deal she'd chosen *not* to know in the last twenty years. Now, recognizing that lack, she had the urge to arch her neck and bare her teeth.

Of course she didn't. Only so much eccentricity would pass without comment, even in Lady MacAlasdair. "There, poor lad," said Dr. McKendry, tying a last knot and stepping back. "I've plaster with me, but I'll want to be making the cast properly once he's in his own bed. If you'll help me get him to his home," he said to Shaw Senior and to Peters, the groom, "I'd count it a kindness."

"He'll stay here," Judith said and then looked at Mr. Shaw. "If you'd like, of course. It being closer to hand and all."

The castle would also have more room for the doctor to work, and it'd be far less hardship for one of the maids to bring young Jack his meals than it would be for his mother or one of his sisters. Such things were like McKendry's bill though. One didn't say them out loud.

"Aye, that'd be most kind," said Shaw.

"It's the least I can do," said Judith, since they both heard what she didn't say. "It was my roof he was mending, and my ladder that failed on him."

They passed through the great doors, heavy oak-and-brass monstrosities that Judith only had closed at night, and entered the castle proper. Walking was more of a relief than Judith had anticipated. As she went inside, a restlessness, almost an itch, lifted from her. Standing around never had been good for her peace of mind, particularly when others were working.

They trooped across the courtyard like the soberest parade in the world, and then, thank God, Judith was able to step aside and let the others go up the servants' stair. "I'll only be in the way up there, I'm afraid," she said. "You'll let me know what happens, Doctor."

"Aye, I will that," he said, distracted as a man in his position ought to be.

Judith turned to her office and her own distractions—factoring McKendry's bill and the cost of boarding Shaw into the month's accounts and going through the list of able-bodied men in Loch Arach. Most of them would be busy with the harvest now. Winter would see them with more time on their hands, but winter was not when one wanted a hole in the roof, even above a seldom-used attic. She'd likely have to send to Belholm.

Perhaps she'd even go this time. A change of scene might do her spirits good—and it would show Arundell that she got out more often than he might think.

Seven

"MR. ARUNDELL," WILLIAM SAID, HANDING HIS CARD to the surprisingly young man in a butler's uniform who'd answered the door. "Calling on Lady MacAlasdair."

More open as well as younger than his counterparts in the city, the butler stared for a second, either genuinely surprised or trying to remember rules of etiquette he'd likely thought he'd never have to use. "I'll see if she's at home, sir."

William fully expected to be shown into a drawing room, to wait there for a few minutes, and then to hear that Lady MacAlasdair was most definitely *not* at home. His gamble would at least have gotten him entrance to the castle and a bit of time in which to look about.

He hadn't expected the lady herself to come through one of the doors at the end of the hallway, striding across the thick rugs with a list in one hand. "Janssen, have you seen—oh." She smiled thinly, obviously wanting to curse. "Mr. Arundell. This is an unexpected pleasure."

"He'd come to call on you, m'lady," said the young man who presumably was Janssen. "I'd been about to show him into the drawing room, not knowing if you were at home."

"Of course," said Lady MacAlasdair. She was good, but William was better, and he saw her face change as she thought out her options. She clearly *was* at home, turning him out in front of the servants would cause talk, and if she pled business, he might ask more questions. She was trapped and she knew it.

William knew it too, which made him feel rather like a cad. Had the lady not been a possible murderess, he would have felt worse.

"We'll be in the east drawing room, Janssen," she said with another patently false smile. She handed the list to the butler. "Ask Dunbar to go over these figures, and tell him I'll meet him in half an hour in my office."

"I hope I'm not inconveniencing you," said William as Lady MacAlasdair led him through a door.

"No, not at all," she said, giving him the polite lie.

Like the front hall, the east drawing room was stone-walled and stone-floored, smaller and darker than any such room in London would have been. Two high windows let in some afternoon light, but the oil lamps were lit even this early. The furniture was dark and old, polished wood and thick plush, and a stag's head mounted over the mantel gave William a resentful stare as he walked in.

"Alas, Actaeon," he murmured.

Lady MacAlasdair flicked a glance at him as she took a seat on an overstuffed sofa. "You're well-schooled."

"One can learn a great deal from myths."

If the smile she gave him was more genuine than any she'd produced in the front hall, it was also far more predatory. William fancied for a second that he saw fangs. "Such as the dangers of trying to see what you shouldn't, aye?"

He took a seat opposite from her. The wooden chair was less comfortable, but the couch didn't quite seem safe.

"Or the need to know you can trust your companions," he said.

"You can trust dogs to be dogs. Just don't be fool enough to hope for more." Lady MacAlasdair sat with her hands clasped in her lap. What would have been prim and correct in any other woman merely highlighted the restless way her fingers brushed against each other as she talked. "What brings you here? Or is this a social call? You'll have to excuse me—it's been some time since I was in society."

She threw the last words out at him like a challenge: *See? I've said it, and now you can't imply it.* Then she smiled again. Her lips were slim, William noticed, and darker than he would have expected from a woman of her complexion.

"Primarily social," he responded a second later than he should have. "I wanted to ask after that poor chap who'd broken his leg the other day. Dr. McKendry says he's recuperating here."

"Kind of you," she said. "Mr. Shaw's doing as well as anyone can in his condition. The break was bad, I hear, but healing well. Or so I understand."

"I'm glad to hear it," William said. "And it's kind

of you to put him up. I hope he appreciates his good fortune in employers."

Lady MacAlasdair's eyes narrowed, blazing green between long, dark lashes. "He's been a good tenant and a good worker. I owe him this much at least."

"Yes, you seem very much alive to your responsibilities," William said. "It's refreshing in this day and age."

She shifted her weight, leaning forward on the couch, and swept her gaze over him from head to foot, stopping finally on his face. "What are you after, Mr. Arundell?"

"I beg your pardon?"

Beautiful as Lady MacAlasdair's eyes were, he'd seen the expression in them from men with their hands on knives or their fingers on triggers.

"What do you want here?" she asked, pronouncing every syllable carefully and clearly. "What do you want with Loch Arach? You'd not be asking so many questions if you were only after a change of scene, and you'd not be going to any length to charm me—which you're not managing, by the way. So what is it you're here for?"

Responding wasn't a matter of making up an answer, but of choosing the option he wished to use, like picking a waistcoat or a rifle sight. As always, William thought of plausibility, effectiveness, and closeness to the truth.

Then he sighed and gave in—just not all the way. "An acquaintance of mine met a nasty end in these parts recently," he said. "I thought perhaps if I spent some time near where he died and learned a few things about the place, I might gain a better perspective."

Lady MacAlasdair's eyes didn't change. "Nobody's died in Loch Arach this year, nor last," she said without even hesitating to think about it.

"He wasn't from here," said William. "He was traveling. They found his body in the forest near Belholm," he went on, heading off her next objection. If the stakes hadn't been so high, he would have enjoyed the challenge of anticipation and response. Part of him did anyhow, which probably spoke volumes about his moral character, none of them good. "But he hadn't been there very long either, and I thought he might have come here, or meant to. Places like this appealed to him."

"Places like this? Hah." Lady MacAlasdair breathed the syllable out on a laugh. "I'm sorry for your loss, I'm sure, but what do you know about places like this?"

"Not very much. That's why I'm trying to find out."

She tilted her head to the side and watched him. Gradually, a little of the tension left her. It wasn't much, but she'd shifted her weight back, metaphorically speaking. The defense was still very strong, but she'd dropped the offense for the moment. "What was he like, this friend of yours?"

"Younger," said William. "Black hair, brown eyes. Tall, for his age. Girls might have thought him handsome." He called to mind all the description that Miss Harbert had given him. "Not very well off. He might have been selling things, trying to pay his way along."

"He doesn't sound like your sort of company," said Lady MacAlasdair. She cast a significant glance at his well-tailored suit, paused, and frowned again. "From the sound of it, you didn't know him well at all."

"I'm here on behalf of someone who did."

"Hmm," she said, and William could see her going through the possibilities. He knew what she was thinking when her lips twitched. If the woman had a poker face, she didn't bother with it now. Her fingers brushed over the fabric of the sofa's arm, fingertips going back and forth in a steady line. Her fingers were very long, the nails smoothly tapered. On her left hand, a large square-cut emerald flashed in the lamplight.

She hadn't been wearing a ring when they met the first time. And her clothing now was plain: a dark skirt and a high-necked, long-sleeved shirtwaist in a blue-and-green swirling pattern. It was pretty, but it wasn't the sort of fancy that would justify extra jewelry.

"Are felicitations in order?" he asked, though the finger was wrong.

"What?" She followed his gaze to the ring. "No. It's been in the family for a while. I dig it out and wear it on occasion, usually when things go a little mad. It'd be a waste otherwise."

William smiled. "A good-luck charm? Better than a rabbit's foot. I'd a friend at school who carried one around, though if it helped him with exams, I never noticed."

Lady MacAlasdair laughed again, more willingly this time. "Both less messy than pouring wine on the deck, as they do for long voyages," she said. "Though I'd never thought of it as a charm. It"—she touched the ring absently—"keeps my feet on the ground, maybe. Reminds me of where I come from and where I am now. I never thought of luck."

"Not superstitious?"

"No," she said. "Either you can change a thing straight out, if you know the way of it, or you can't change it at all. No point asking favors." She cleared her throat. "How did this man die?"

"Badly."

She nodded. Then, as calmly as she'd asked about his friend: "Are you a policeman?"

He felt the wind from that shot. "No," William said. "Nor do I work for them. I'm not here to see anyone arrested. I'll give you my word on that."

"Your word as a gentleman?" In her mouth, the common phrase took on an exotic flavor, or perhaps an antique one.

"If you'll take it."

"I never doubted you were a gentleman," she said. "I'll believe you."

The way she said it, William knew it was a choice. He hadn't convinced her, this sleek, dark woman who he'd never yet seen looking less than watchful. She wouldn't take anything on faith. She had consciously decided to accept what he said—for as long as it made sense to do so. He didn't think she gave a damn about his word.

"I hope I've set your mind at ease," he said nonetheless, because one said certain things.

"I wouldn't hang well," she replied with a grim little smile, and then went briskly on. "I don't recall this man you talk about. We do have peddlers once in a while. Once in a great while. It's possible."

"Possibilities are all I have to go on just now. It's my duty to look into them."

"Ah," she said. "Speaking of duty, I should be getting back to mine."

The lady got to her feet. Naturally, he did too, and the size and excessive furniture in the room meant they stood facing each other for a moment, only a step or two from touching. Close at hand, Lady MacAlasdair smelled of autumn leaves and woodsmoke. William felt his pulse quicken.

Being a gentleman, he kept his eyes on her face. He did not let himself regard the way her breasts swelled beneath her blouse. He did, however, see the movement of her throat as she swallowed before speaking.

"I still don't know what you're hoping to find here, Mr. Arundell," she said. "Dead is dead. Bad, good— once it's over, it's over, and most of the time it's better that way. No answer you'll get here will change that, not from me nor from any of my folk."

Eight

JUDITH DIDN'T SLEEP EASILY THAT NIGHT.

She couldn't blame all of that on Mr. Arundell. Sleep wasn't as chancy for her now as it had been when she'd first come back from the outside world, but she still had bad nights caused by a scrap of conversation troubling her dreams, or a face looking too much like one she'd seen in pain, or seemingly nothing at all. Changes in weather, phases of the moon—the mind turned on itself once in a while, and it did little good to ask why.

Why was never a good question. She'd tried to tell Arundell that. She doubted he'd take it to heart. People always wanted reasons—and he wasn't the one to convince, if he'd been telling the truth.

Judith thought he'd come closer to honesty than on the day he'd met her. The thought brought her no triumph, nor any real sense of relief. It was almost more disturbing to know that she could get a straight answer out of him if she pressed hard enough. It made her feel almost obligated to try.

Almost compelled to.

She paced the room in the moonlight, feeling the floor beneath her feet—reassuringly solid and cold, motionless and dry. She had learned that pacing helped. Flying didn't, not unless she gave herself so fully to the flight and the hunt that she risked discovery. She had lived too long among humans to find comfort in inhuman things.

Men had made the floor and the walls. She could not break them, not in this form and not without difficulty in the other. The rugs were braided wool, the dresser carved oak, the lamps on the wall brass and oil that she'd seen put in herself. These were normal things, everyday things. Judith caught them with her mind and steadied herself, turned away from the fields of blood and the sound of cannon.

Once it's over, it's over, she heard herself say.

She laughed into the empty room.

Well, it *was* over, but nobody got through life unscarred, and a sleepless night had never killed her yet. She did hope Arundell was having as restless a time. She wouldn't wish her dreams on him, but maybe a screech owl could take up residence outside his window. He hadn't given her the dreams, but he'd certainly stirred them up this time, he and his need for perspective.

He'd stirred up a few other things too. She'd meant to be disparaging with that glance at his clothing, to show that she was no country fool and to question why a man who could afford Savile Row suits would know a boy who had to go peddling to make his living. She'd ended up taking in the breadth of his shoulders and the strong line of his jaw, and she'd sworn inwardly at the tightening sensation low in her body.

Then, in those moments when they'd stood facing each other, she'd been damnably aware of his presence, his size, his masculinity. She'd felt it in her blood like wine. She'd wanted to pull him toward her, to taste his mouth and feel the muscles in his back beneath her gripping fingers, to hear the catch of his breath as she took him to the floor.

When she'd been younger, she might have done it. Even knowing as little as she did about him, even with as much as he shouldn't know about her, she might have—probably would have—either leaped on the man or at least made him a proposition in no uncertain terms. Back then, pleasure had always been worth the risk.

Youth was very stupid. Age—she didn't know what age was except tired and unsettled and beholden to too many talkative people.

She'd taken care of her body's immediate urges easily enough. Now, as she stood and leaned her head against the windowpane, she pictured Arundell's face and felt her excitement return, not as strong as it had been that afternoon, but strong enough.

A trip to the city wouldn't help, then. It was like having a bad song in her head. The only way to get it out was to wait or find a worse one.

Damn.

At least lusting after Arundell kept her mind off the dreams, now that she was awake.

It wasn't the end of the world. She'd desired men before, some of whom it would have been impossible or unwise to bed. Waiting did work. If nothing else, Mr. Arundell was temporary. He'd stay as long as he felt he needed to, or as long as he'd promised his friend he would. Then he'd go back to London: out of sight, out of mind.

If nothing else, they were *all* temporary.

The chill of the floor was no longer comforting, only cold. The half-shaped figures from her dreams had retreated. It generally took them a few months to regroup. Judith crawled back into bed and stretched out, staring up at the canopy overhead.

The dreams didn't return. But she still took a long time to get back to sleep.

❧

Morning was easier. It always was. Judith knew the night well and loved it most of the time, but daytime was like the stone walls and the emerald ring—an anchor to solid things, to the present, to the world of men. Human hands hadn't created the daytime, but human movement and voice shaped it, at least for Judith. As long as she was in the castle, she could almost always hear the sounds of working or talking a short distance away—reminders that life went on and the living were all around her.

By the time she got through with her morning's tasks, she didn't need much more reminding.

Rain fell outside with a raw edge to it that reminded Judith how close winter really was. She'd have to check that afternoon and see how soon the cold was likely to set in. But that meant two hours in the north wing, which was almost always chilly, and even such a limited vision of the future as the weather left her wrung out. She'd do it in the afternoon, she decided. Meanwhile, she'd put her mind at rest by checking the castle's stores of food when she gave Mrs. Frasier the day's menus.

One of the reasons Judith never felt truly alone during the day was that she could hear voices through fairly thick wood and across a considerable distance. Even before she opened the kitchen door, she knew there was a man in the kitchen, and that while his voice was not entirely English, it was too close to be that of any of the castle staff or most of the villagers. She pushed the door open and, without surprise, saw Ross MacDougal sitting at the kitchen table having tea with Mrs. Lennox.

"I hope you'll forgive the intrusion," he said after Judith had waved them all back to their seats. "I have so many memories, and I felt myself rather in the way at home. I hope I'll not be any such thing here. I told Mrs. Frasier to box my ears and pack me off if I was," he added with a smile toward the cook.

Mrs. Frasier, kneading bread dough, looked over her shoulder and chuckled obligingly. "You're a bit big for it now, lad."

"If they don't mind having you here, I can't imagine I would," said Judith. "Nothing unusual today, Mrs. Frasier," she added, leaving the menu near the cook, though out of the way of stray flour. "I hope everything's well at your house."

"Oh yes, quite," said Ross. "Mother and Gillian send their regards, of course. An extra body does get underfoot in a place like that when it rains. I never noticed it growing up."

"Aye, everything's smaller when you come back home," said Judith.

"I wouldn't have thought that in your case," Ross said.

She shrugged. "The castle's larger than most buildings, but Loch Arach's smaller than most towns. It rather balances out. Although," she said, changing the subject before anyone could ask questions about where she'd been, "it did seem a bit oversized just after my brothers left."

"Aye, and quiet," said Mrs. Lennox, shaking her head. "It was grand to hear a child's voice about the place. Though, if you dinna' mind me saying, m'lady, I'll not entirely miss Master Colin doing chemical experiments in the middle of the night."

"Colin's always been too enthusiastic about his hobbies for anyone's tastes," said Judith as Ross's eyes widened. "Except Regina's, I gather. But if you have the patience for motorcars, Colin might be tame and predictable by comparison."

"What kind of chemical experiments?" Ross asked.

"Och, who can tell? Goin's-on that went *bang* and had the whole downstairs hallway smelling of smoke. We're lucky the castle didna' fall in around our heads."

"Oh, I think this place has been through worse in its day," said Judith. The experiments in question hadn't dealt with chemistry as most people understood it, but neither Ross nor Mrs. Frasier had any reason to suspect otherwise. Every family these days had an amateur scientist or two in it, she'd heard. "And you have to be fair. To Colin, ten o'clock is hardly the middle of the night."

"Hmm!" said Mrs. Lennox, unimpressed. "City hours. Meaning no disrespect, of course."

"Of course," said Judith. "I promise, the castle still stands as it always did."

"I'd be grateful for a look," Ross said and coughed. "That is to say, I'm sure it's changed since I was growing up, and I know I didn't see everything, but while I'm here… You wouldn't have to give me a walking tour or anything—"

The words "walking tour" kept Judith from staring in shock. Down in England, she remembered, it was common enough for people to go and walk about great houses, particularly if they were large and old. It had happened in Jane Austen's books, hadn't it? If that was the standard Ross was used to, no wonder he'd asked.

"Not in much shape for visitors today, I think," she said. "I've still got to get the roof fixed, and there are a couple bad spots in some of the floors—I wouldn't want you breaking your leg. We have everyone into the great hall for the harvest fair though, remember? If you'd like to look about then, I'll even see if I can find you a guide who knows some of the more interesting stories."

"Thank you," he said. "I'll look forward to it. But—"

A knock interrupted him. Mrs. Lennox rose and opened the door on a young man, who Judith placed after a second: young Ken Finlay, whose family kept sheep on the edge of the village. His tanned face was drawn now, and his voice shook a little when he spoke.

"Morning, m'lady, ma'am, sir," he said and then addressed himself to Judith. "I'd not thought to find you here, m'lady, but as you are, I was hoping you could send Keir up to m'father's house."

"Keir?" Judith's gamekeeper, like Mrs. Frasier and Mrs. Lennox, had worked for the MacAlasdairs since before she had come back. From what she could tell, there was nothing Keir didn't know about the woods around Loch Arach—and only one or two things he didn't know about the family who employed him. "He'd be out back with the cattle, I think. I'll send him up—but what's the matter?"

"'Tis one of our ewes, m'lady. She's been killed last night. And"—he looked back and forth between Judith and the other two women—"and mangled, rather."

Judith remembered the Stewart cow and Claire's secondhand description. She'd dismissed that—but this was firsthand, and Kenneth Finlay wasn't looking to impress any girls nor to explain himself out of a hiding.

"Da says maybe a dog's gone bad, and we should find it before it bites someone," said Ken.

He sounded doubtful. There might be a hundred normal reasons for that. His father's explanation might be perfectly correct—but Judith knew that many creatures could go bad, not just dogs.

She sighed. "Mrs. Lennox? Send Keir up to Finlay's. Ken, I'll come back with you myself."

Nine

WHOEVER OR WHATEVER HAD KILLED THE FINLAYS' sheep had done the deed a long way off from its fellows, where trees had started to spike up at regular intervals through the sparse fall grass of the field. The great mass of the forest—and certainly the part the MacAlasdairs guarded—was still a good walk away, but the Finlays lived at the very boundary of civilization, such as it was in Loch Arach, and this was the edge of their land.

The earth soaked up blood well, but the grass still showed it, even after the farmer and his family had taken the ewe away. William stared at those few traces, tried to make something of them, and hoped they'd be enough.

He had heard of the killing late and thirdhand at best. One of Mrs. Finlay's neighbors, whose dog had been briefly under suspicion, had dropped in for her usual cup of tea and chat with Mrs. Simon. She hadn't given much detail, but she had mentioned that the beast's eyes had been gone.

Scavengers could have been responsible, as Lady

MacAlasdair had said about the first incident. But there had *been* a first incident. Once was chance, but twice might be more than coincidence. William alone knew there was at least the possibility of a third and what such a pattern might mean, if one existed.

"I used to be a bit of a naturalist in my younger days," he'd explained to Mr. Finlay, upon reaching the farm and finding the farmer in the midst of a small speculative crowd. "I'm not sure I *can* be of service, but I thought I might at least have a look."

"Keir's had a look at t'ewe already, and she's gone," Finlay had said and shrugged. "But you canna' hurt anything peerin' at the place where we found her, if ye like. 'Tis kind of you to offer. Amy," he'd said, calling over a girl of about ten with inky black pigtails, "show the man where we found Daisy. An' come straight back—your ma'll want help wi' the dinner."

He'd turned back to the conversation, where an older man was speaking. "Could be an eagle."

"For lambs, Da, aye," Finlay had said, "but she were a full-grown ewe."

Finlay Very Senior had snorted. "Ye're no' blind, lad, and I didna' used to be. The ones we've seen flying could take a ewe if they wanted—or a cow."

The conversation had faded behind William as he followed the child. "Have you ever seen an eagle?" he'd asked her.

She'd grinned up at him, two gaps in her mouth where new teeth would soon grow. "Flying, aye, plenty. Granda's right. They're *huge*."

"Ah," he'd said. "Should you be worried, coming out here?"

Amy had shaken her head, pigtails flying like wings. "They never come closer. Scared of people, Da says."

Then, William had thought, either her father was wrong or her grandfather was—or something had changed. There might be a natural explanation. Although wild creatures might start acting oddly for many reasons, and not all of those reasons had to do with the material world.

"This is it," Amy had said, pausing by the bloody patch of grass. "They wouldna' let me see her. But she's been cut up already. For the dogs," she'd added with a farm child's unflappability toward gore. "So they'll have a good dinner, aye?"

"Ill winds and so forth, yes," he'd said. "Get home safe now."

He'd watched her figure vanish into the distance.

The trees provided him some shelter, but using the chains required considerable privacy if he wasn't going to be run out of the village as a madman. Finlay had mentioned dinner, and it was about that time, which would give him a window, if only a small one.

William wasn't really sure that the process would work. Even when he'd first heard of the killing, he'd been doubtful. Human death, especially when there was magic involved, could linger on a landscape for days. Animal death lasted hours, if that. Magic might make the imprint last a little longer—he hoped so— but it was far from certain, and from what he'd heard, whatever killed the ewe had done it during the night.

He reached into his satchel. His hand had closed around the first link of the silver chain when he heard the footsteps behind him.

Spinning around to face the new arrival, he kept one hand still on the chain—silver was good against unnatural things, and links of heavy chain could give natural ones pause—and reached with the other for the revolver in his coat pocket.

Of course he found himself looking into Lady MacAlasdair's eyes.

This time, their color made him think not of emeralds but of deep water: dark, green, and deadly cold. Her body mirrored his, alert and tensed to spring at a moment's notice. Although her hands were empty, William thought that the results might be painful for him regardless.

She was the first one to break the silence. "Perspective." The word came slowly, the *r* rolled and every syllable laced with profound skepticism. "What perspective d'ye hope to be gaining out here? Now?"

"I thought I might be able to help," said William.

"Did you?" Aside from the necessary motions of her lips, her face was as still as the rest of her.

"I have no proof of my good intentions, of course," he said. "But this isn't the first body I've seen in the wilderness."

"So you decided to take an interest?"

"I thought there might be some connection to my friend," he said.

"Your friend was killed by a mad dog?"

"No," said William. "Nor an eagle. But I don't know that the ewe was either, and neither do you." He watched her face as he spoke and saw in its strong angles the slight hesitation, the moment of how-did-he-know uncertainty that gave him his answer. "For some men, animals will do when there aren't people to hand. Or when people are too risky."

He'd found that out twelve years ago in a small fishing village in Dover. It wasn't common knowledge, and it certainly wasn't the sort of subject one brought up in front of a lady. While he didn't expect vapors from Lady MacAlasdair, he had expected surprise and was himself shocked to see recognition instead.

"Why do you think I'd agree?" she asked.

"Because you're here. If you really thought it was wildlife, you'd have let your gamekeeper handle it." He looked around them at the dull grass and the trees. The farmhouse was a good quarter mile away. Nobody was nearer than that, and yet Lady MacAlasdair faced him warily but without fear.

What did she know that he didn't?

What did she *have* that she didn't think he did?

Reluctantly, he released his grip on the chain, but he kept the hand on his revolver. "Come to that, why are you here? Isn't there a constable?"

"In Belholm," she said. "We've generally no need here. And these are my folk. If there's trouble, I know of it."

This time, William kept his admiration to himself. Compliments, even sincere ones, would not help the situation just now. "You were here earlier then?"

She nodded.

"I didn't see the sheep. What happened to it?"

"There was a wound in her throat," Lady MacAlasdair said. "She would have bled to death. Her eyes were gone. Her chest and stomach were opened. Savagely. Whatever killed her ate her heart too."

"A dog wouldn't do that," said William, "and you know it."

"It could have killed her. The wound to her throat would have done it. And then it might have taken fright, and other beasts could have done the rest."

"Gone for the heart specifically? Do you know of anything that would?"

"No. But I don't know everything in the world, nor do you. We've no witnesses."

"True. Has anyone's dog run off? Been acting oddly?"

Slowly, she shook her head. "That's not the sort of business I'd hear about, though. Besides, the forest's large. I'd lay odds there are no wolves in it, but having a dog go mad in one of the other villages and run off here? Aye, that could happen."

"Could," William repeated.

"Could. Many things *could* happen."

"It's an unpleasant possibility. I understand that you don't want to consider it—"

"I am considering it," said Lady MacAlasdair. "And I don't think you do understand."

Of all the times that accusation had landed on William, this was the calmest. Oh, she was angry. He could see it in her tight jaw and hear it rippling under her voice. That voice was even, though. She was stating a fact. That the fact happened to displease her was secondary.

She folded her arms under her breasts and fixed him with a level, very knowing gaze. "Let's for the moment," she said, "assume we're both innocent here, aye? We can get back to checking each other's hands for blood afterwards. For now—something else killed this ewe and Stewart's cow. Something or someone."

"All right," said William.

"If I say it was a man," said Lady MacAlasdair, "it's likely someone will die within a fortnight. A month, at most."

"What? Why?"

He half expected the answer to be occult. Given his mission, given the rumors he'd heard about Loch Arach and the lady, William expected her to talk about a demon or a curse.

"Because stock is a man's living out here, and nobody has very much of it," she said instead. "That ewe could be half a year's profits for Finlay. If the killer was human, killing the sheep is a vicious thing to have done. And men are men, and there arena' very many of them nearby."

The wind swept past them, down from the mountains and across the lake, bringing the edge of winter with it. Under its touch, the grass around them rippled. Lady MacAlasdair's dress blew back, outlining her figure. She looked very strong and very alone.

"They'll look for someone," William said. "Someone to blame. That's what you mean."

"Oh, they'll find him. Whether it's the right man or not, they'll find him. Maybe it'll be a man who owes Finlay money or who's got a grudge against him from ten years back. Maybe it'll be Norris, who's got a bad temper when he's had a few drinks, or maybe it'll be old Alice MacRae, who keeps her own company and has three cats. Maybe even an outsider with no very solid past." She smiled thinly.

"It's been more than my lifetime since we tried witches by law, even in this part of the country, but they went hard at it when they did, and there are more ways than courts and ropes to break a man, if you've a mind to it."

His own memories made that impossible to deny. "But you'd take a hand, I'd imagine. To prevent that—to see real justice done."

"I'd do what I could. And I could do plenty," she added fiercely. "But I'm only one woman. It might be that what I could do would break me as well, in its way, and harm them almost as much. And I can't force kindness from anyone, nor stop poison where it spreads."

"That's happened before?"

"It's always happened before." Lady MacAlasdair sighed. "And I'll risk it if I must. If I'm certain that a man is responsible, I'll say as much, and I'll do what needs doing then. But I'll not plant that seed when I just think it's likely, and I'll not overlook any other possibility."

"I do understand now," William said. "But do you really think it could have been anything else?"

"Yes," she said in a tone that brooked no further discussion. "And now, if you've found everything here you think you're going to, perhaps I can show you back to the main road."

Ten

THE PROBLEM WAS THAT ARUNDELL WAS RIGHT.

At least, he would have been right according to the world most people knew. Judith had seen the ewe before it had gone for dogs' meat. The wound in the sheep's throat *might* have been the work of an animal, but it was much more likely to have been done by a human with a knife—either one who was trying to disguise his handiwork, who hadn't had much practice at killing anything, or both. As far as Judith could tell, the eyes and the organs had been taken at close to the same time.

If she'd been Arundell, knowing only what a mortal man knew of the world, she would have been certain the culprit was human.

The other problem was that Judith knew more. The hills around Loch Arach were old and had in their time contained stranger things than the MacAlasdairs. The world was wide, the places outside the world wider still, and the creatures in them did travel sometimes. Judith had grown up hearing stories. As an adult, she'd seen a few things for herself.

That angle would have needed a good hour or two of solitary explanation and then hard proof of the sort she didn't much fancy providing, certainly not to a stranger from London. Colin might have been able to manage it. But Judith knew what was outside her abilities, and persuading a man who already suspected her was well across that line.

Also, she didn't trust him.

When she'd walked out of the forest and seen Arundell staring at the bloody patches of grass, she'd felt the immediate urge to transform for her own safety. It was an easy enough instinct to push back— she'd spent enough time fighting in human form that her body no longer thought switching to dragon shape was the only way to handle a threat—but it had been there, lengthening her teeth and nails for a second.

Men who killed for pleasure did come back at times to reminisce. At the time, she'd thought of no other reason he could be out there. She'd seen Arundell reach for his own weapons: a gun in his pocket, Judith would have wagered, and whatever was in the satchel.

Why would a man come out armed?

Well, if he had thought there was a dangerous creature—man or beast—around, he wouldn't have wanted to be helpless if it came on him alone.

Why would he come out alone?

He might not have intended to. Finlay and his family were busy; if Arundell really had meant to help and had arrived late, he might not have had a choice where company was concerned.

That was the way her thoughts had circled through-out the day—not enough clear guilt to take action, not enough clear innocence to let her relax. As they'd walked in silence back to the main road, Judith kept watching Arundell, trying to see enough from his face or his voice to put her solidly in either camp.

She found nothing, and although she didn't mind silence as a general rule, this time it started niggling at her after a few minutes. She once again got the feeling of being watched and glanced twice back over her shoulder, only to find the road behind them empty.

"Expecting someone?" Arundell asked, damn him.

"A cavalry charge," she returned. "Any minute now."

"I didn't know I was so formidable."

"I just like to be thorough." He kept up with her well. He should—his legs were about a mile long. Judith looked sideways at him, watching the easy grace with which he walked. She could picture him on the floor of a ballroom—or the deck of a ship—without much effort. "Do you live in London?" she asked. "When you're not getting perspective on anything?"

"Part of the year. The city's too hot in the summer."

"So my brothers say."

He nodded. "Both just married, I hear. That must have been a change for you."

"Not really. They haven't lived at home for a long while. I'm glad for their happiness, of course."

Arundell smiled. "No 'of course' about it," he said, his voice teasing. "Many sisters aren't."

"Echoes of Mrs. Simon there."

"All my own ideas, I promise," he said, raising one hand as if to take an oath. "Great minds and all that."

"Which I can't dispute without insulting my friend.

I'll grant you the move. Clever," she said and realized to her dismay that she was smiling.

Tilting his head, Arundell surveyed her face. He still looked amused, but now he was clearly interested as well, and Judith felt her cheeks heat beneath his gaze. "You think I have an ulterior motive for everything?"

Quickly, trying to sound cool and composed, she shot back, "I'll make an exception for sleep and eating and so forth."

"Can I take that as a compliment?" Arundell asked, blue eyes glinting.

"Take it as you like. I won't fight the matter."

"You're a gracious hostess indeed." He might have meant that sarcastically, but he sounded playful instead. His voice, low and refined, took its time over each syllable and made the praise sound almost genuine—and certainly sensual.

They rounded a corner, their footsteps in a smooth rhythm. Sparring with him like this, Judith found it easy to forget what she had seen recently, what might be lurking in the forest or living like a normal man in Loch Arach, and just how wary she should be of the tall man beside her. She fell silent with the realization.

Arundell let her go without speaking for a minute or two, and then gestured to the hills beyond them. "What's over there?"

"The ocean, eventually," said Judith, seizing the opportunity to look away from him and ignoring the urge to look back. "Trees. Mountains. Some old roads, but they don't lead anywhere much. We used to go up when we were bored, look for arrowheads and old spears and that."

"Roman?"

"Some, likely. There'd have been the Picts living there too. Maybe even a few poor English who tried what they shouldn't," she added.

From Arundell's ready laugh, she could tell the barb hadn't struck deeply. "Nobody ever accused us of knowing our limits."

"Too late to learn now, I suppose."

"Oh," he said. Surrendering to impulse, Judith turned her head back toward him. The glance he shot down at her was warmth itself, and sent that warmth right through Judith's body. She realized that they'd slowed down. "Much too late."

"Even if you were inclined to take that instruction," she said.

"Why would I be?" Arundell asked. A breeze went past, not as cold as the wind had been previously. It ruffled his red hair, and he absently pushed a strand of it out of his eyes.

"Safety?" Judith suggested, not meaning it. She couldn't look away from his face or from the slow motion of his fingers through his hair.

Stopping, Arundell turned to face her. "Ah," he said, "but nothing's ever really safe. We're both old enough to know that."

Coming from a mortal, the phrase should have struck her as funny. It didn't. However old Arundell might be, the knowledge in his voice and eyes made him seem as if he'd seen as many years as she had—and there was a carnal aspect to that knowledge that made Judith catch her breath.

She could have kept on walking, she knew. She

could have shaken off Arundell's hand when he placed it on her shoulder, turning her toward him, or pulled back when he pulled her close. But her body found its own voice at his touch, as loud as an avalanche, and she went willingly, eagerly.

Judith hadn't kissed anyone for a long time. She'd clearly forgotten the intensity of it, the way it made the world fade into the background, the heady and terrifying joy of being lost in sensation. But she couldn't believe that she would forget anything like this.

Arundell's lips were firm when they met hers, his kiss demanding in a way that had nothing to do with roughness or urgency. He was thorough instead, determined, and very, very skilled. Before long, Judith was clinging to his shoulders, not out of any need for support—although her legs, strong as they usually were, suddenly were far less inclined to hold her up than usual—but out of the consuming desire to get closer.

From the way Arundell reacted, she was sure she wasn't alone in her feelings, and that this was no mere display of his skill. His arms were like steel around her. The hand that had been on her shoulder now cupped the back of her head. The other hand rested at the small of her back, fingers spread wide, and pulled Judith's body against his.

There she could feel his chest against her breasts, the friction increasing with each quick, unsteady breath either of them took. Her nipples, already hard, rubbed against the inside of her corset, the contact frustratingly pleasurable. She made an incoherent sound low in her throat and leaned up into the kiss, taking the lead back from him.

Some men, not many but some, objected at that point or at least hesitated for a moment. Arundell didn't. His lips parted for her as readily as hers had done for him, and he let out a gratified sigh when her tongue slipped past them. His hand slid lower, cupped the curve of her backside, and squeezed gently—appreciatively, Judith thought, and smiled against his mouth.

She had plenty to appreciate herself. The slight difference in their heights meant she couldn't quite reciprocate, but she could—and did—run her nails down the back of Arundell's neck and trace down his spine, making him suck in a breath. She could, and did, arch her hips forward, so that the two of them pressed together from neck to knee.

That sent another wave of desire through her, overwhelming with the sheer force of it. Part of it was being able to feel the substantial bulge of his erection pushing against her, just above her sex. Part of it was the delightful pressure of her breasts against his chest, and part was the way he kept very still for a second, when she knew he had to stop and really try to hold on to his self-control.

The effect of the whole was to make her entire body shiver, unable to hold still under the barrage of pleasure. Judith let her head fall back and felt Arundell's mouth hot on her throat, kissing and then nibbling.

That as much as anything else brought her back to her senses: the realization that she was literally baring her neck to this man who she didn't know or trust, who might be the worst kind of murderer, on a public road in the middle of the afternoon. The wind went coldly past again, and if Judith hadn't felt it before, she was conscious of it now.

She opened her eyes and pushed Arundell away.

"Nothing's really safe, maybe," she said, getting her breath, "but that doesn't mean we have to be complete fools. We're both old enough to know *that* too."

Too conscious of her flushed face, her swollen lips, and the damp heat between her legs, she turned and started walking again, quickly and utterly gracelessly at first. She was glad of the cold air. It might help her look presentable, and she'd need that before too long. The turn up ahead would take them back to the village proper.

Once again, Judith glanced over her shoulder, looking for eyes that she didn't see. This time she was sure she knew why.

"You should know," she said, "that the people here aren't likely to believe you if you tell them what just happened. And those who do won't care. I certainly won't. In case you were getting any ideas."

"What?" If Arundell wasn't actually shocked, he did a fine imitation of it, all open mouth and inward-slanting eyebrows. "My God, you don't think I'd—"

"I think plenty of things about plenty of people," said Judith, "and I don't know you from Adam. I will give you as much credit as to assume you'd no motive at the time but a carnal one, whatever may have crossed your mind afterwards."

"Nothing crossed my mind afterwards."

"Good. Don't bother to let it."

He studied her face, shaking his head slowly. "Is it

only me who excites this much suspicion? Or do you never believe that anything is what it seems to be?"

"Not *only* what it seems," said Judith, looking down the road toward the village. "There's nothing that's just what you see plainly in the moment—not fire nor water, man nor beast. Most of them don't seek to deceive. Most of the time. But that doesn't really matter."

"You must make life very complicated for yourself."

"No more than you do," she said, thinking of his questions and his probing looks. "Probably less. If I'd kissed *you*, I'd wager ten pounds you'd have wondered what I was after."

In half a minute, they came to the main street and to far too many people to continue the conversation. It had been enough time for a denial, but Arundell stayed silent.

"You see?" She smiled at him. "I wouldn't bother protesting now. It's been years since my heart was tender, and I've no time for much pretense."

That itself wasn't entirely truthful, of course, she thought as she headed off. She didn't have time for much *more*.

Eleven

RAIN SHEETED DOWN IN FRONT OF WILLIAM'S FACE, almost obscuring the path ahead of him. That wasn't difficult. The path in question was narrow and winding, leading around trees and over clumps of rocks, many of them covered in moss. Mrs. Simon had said that a couple of the village boys led sheep that way, but they were fifteen, not forty-five, and they'd probably been out in fair weather in the daytime. No man in his right mind would be scrambling over rocks on a night like this one.

On the other hand, few men in their right minds would be *out* on a night like this one, which was why William had chosen it. Odds were good that, after two days had passed, he'd lost his chance at seeing anything up at Finlay's, but he hadn't been trained to accept those odds when there was an opportunity to try. Besides, this way took him through the far edge of the forest, and it was past time to start exploring that. His job demanded no less.

His job, he thought, as he half slid down the side of another boulder, was rather a young man's game.

William had heard that before. In sunshine or in a warm train compartment considering his mission, he never believed it. Moments like this were different.

Yet he'd nearly jumped at the chance when the rain started that evening. He'd been half-wild with the ability to finally act, to have even half a chance of discovering a clue—to find more for his mind to dwell on than emerald eyes, dark lips, and a warm, strong body melting against his.

If he was getting too old to wander obscure pathways on rainy nights, he was assuredly too old to dwell on women who might as well have "Danger" painted on their foreheads, even when the women in question kissed like Judith MacAlasdair did. He didn't even have duty as an excuse for the latter foolishness. He'd been honest, and honestly offended, about his lack of ulterior motive in kissing her, and that had been puzzling too. He *had* used such tactics before and not turned a hair at that. When he'd signed up for D Branch, he'd put his body at their disposal in any number of ways.

This time had been different. For some reason, he'd wanted Judith to know that—and still did, even though she was the reason he was out getting soaked and scraping his knees on the local landscape, trying for a second chance at the rite she'd prevented.

Staying in the shadows, of which there were plenty, William rounded a clump of pine trees and came up to the place where he'd stood earlier. Off in the distance, he could see a few lights in the window of Finlay's farmhouse, but there was nothing closer, and he was sure he was too far out and the night was too dark for them to see him.

Finding where the sacrifice had been was a matter of guesswork and memory now. There were no signs to guide him, so he laid down the rune chains and hoped for the best. Not expecting anything, he spoke the words he'd learned by rote, words not quite Greek or Latin or anything of this world. "Enochian," his tutors had called the language. They'd spoken of the man who'd discovered it, D Branch's unofficial founder and namesake, but William had always been more interested in the practical application.

The words worked now. The world around William grew even foggier than the rain would have made it, and he stood torn between satisfaction and fear. He was glad to have the information—but the fact that it had lingered so long spoke of nothing good.

When he saw the shapes, he understood why the resonance had stayed. One of the shadows was still the human figure, without any more clues to indicate sex, age, or race than William had seen before; the scene was even blurrier than the previous one he'd viewed. That was the only human shape and the only one that looked remotely natural.

There were four others. All walked on two legs, with skinny, ratlike heads and tails. Each had six arms, ending in hands with sharp, dexterous-looking little claws. None of them was bigger than a house cat. Physically, as much as William could tell through the fog, they were anything but fearsome. But bits of them kept fading into the fog in a way that William had never seen anything do before, and that was only the problem he could put his finger on.

They looked *wrong*. Even secondhand, even after

two days, he could see that they were things that shouldn't be in the same world he walked in, and maybe things that shouldn't be in any world at all. Even the wrongness was hard to pin down. One second they twisted along at impossible angles; the next they seemed to eat at the world around them; and then they became too dark or maybe too bright to look at.

In the fog, the human figure gestured. The creatures leaped forward. The scene disintegrated around William, leaving him standing once again in a dark, rainy field, completely alone and never more relieved to be so.

Quickly, he grabbed the rune chains and stuffed them back into his satchel, then darted for the edge of the cleared land. Only when he was in the forest, with a solid clump of pine and oak and undergrowth between him and any onlookers on Finlay's land, did he let himself lean against one of the trees, catch his breath, and think.

He had been right. The killer was human, or at least human-shaped. He wouldn't have much luck convincing Judith of that, though. Even had the figure been alone, *I saw a magic vision* was not evidence she would readily accept. If he started talking about demons… There wasn't an asylum nearby, but that would be all William would have to his advantage.

"Demons" was likely the right word for the little things, he thought, while the forest around him rustled with the rain and the wind. Creatures that looked like that were almost certainly from the Outer Darkness. These no doubt had been summoned with blood sacrifice, probably the boy's in Belholm, and kept fed on a steady though reduced diet of livestock. William had encountered a few similar creatures over his years of service and had more often seen their powers channeled through human vessels, but the thought was still enough to make him shiver.

He didn't want to think more about demons in the middle of the night, not in a forest where all the shadows looked far deeper than normal. William made a vain attempt to wring out his hat, then stepped out from the shelter of the tree.

Instinct saved him. As in the past, he didn't know if he'd seen movement out of the corner of his eye, heard a sound his conscious mind didn't register, or even caught a whiff of a repulsive and alien scent. Without thinking, William turned and looked up.

Blackness plummeted toward him, screeching.

William leaped backward, but not quickly enough. Claws raked down the arm he threw up to protect his face, tearing effortlessly through the layers of coat, jacket, shirt, and skin. He felt no pain at first but knew that would change soon. He struck out and felt the claws vanish as a dark shape went flying toward a tree.

Unluckily for William, it didn't hit. It dropped to the ground and came up snarling, its teeth jagged and gleaming foully even in the darkness. The head of the creature was shaped vaguely like a cat's but gaunt, the cheeks sunken around the too-wide mouth and hollow yellow eyes. Its body was long and flexible, with many sets of legs and a whipping razor-edged tail.

The creature was bigger than the demons in his

vision. Much bigger. Its head came to William's thigh, and its body was at least two feet long. Collecting itself, it reared up on a foot or so of that length and screeched at him again. Even far away, William smelled a rankly sweet, burnt odor and felt the heat of the demon's breath go through his clothes.

The butt of his silver-loaded gun came easily to his hand, but the wet folds of his coat slowed him as he yanked the revolver free of its holster. His arm was starting to hurt now, sharp pain whose immediacy suggested that the demon's claws hadn't gone too deep, but which was an unwelcome distraction nonetheless. A burning sensation came with it, and when William inhaled, the smell was like the demon's breath, but more acrid.

Acid, he thought. Bloody *wonderful*.

He fired. The demon sprang. The first bullet whistled through the air behind it and buried itself in a tree trunk. The second struck the creature in the hind flank, and it screamed a third time, now in genuine pain. William fanned the revolver and kept firing, counting down each bullet. He had six before he had to reload; his other gun was full of plain lead, which only worked on minor demons, and then not always. He didn't know how minor this thing was, and alone in the silent, dark forest, he had no intention of taking chances before he needed to.

Bullet number three hit the demon in the side. Blood, a sickly glowing shade of green, ran from that wound and the first, but the creature kept coming. The force of the shots knocked it back so that it landed just short of William. It reared again and swiped at him with four sets of talons. He dodged sideways, and this time, though his coat ripped, the blow didn't carry through.

"Get *away*," he snarled back at the demon and kicked sideways, catching it in the face. Its teeth were formidable, but his boot leather was thick, and the blow caught the creature off guard. William heard crunching, saw the many-legged form scurry backward, and smiled, sickly satisfied with its pain.

Now he had room to aim again. A breath let him fix the demon's head in his sights. Another, and he pulled the trigger.

Bonelessly, the creature twisted itself out of the way, and the bullet hit the ground.

That was four. Two more bullets remained, and of course he'd had to block the demon's first attack with his good arm. But now he had an idea.

Before the demon could collect itself and come at him, William shot twice, aiming just a hair high the first time and low the second, fanning the revolver so that the two sounds were almost one. One missed, as he'd known it would, as the demon spun impossibly through space—right into the second bullet.

Silver flared behind its eyes for an instant before its head split open. The gout of green blood was vast. A few drops hit William, sizzling on his coat. The creature's body collapsed to the ground in the middle of a growing pool.

William watched it for a minute, reloading his gun as fast as he could. Even in death or apparent death, demons could be tricky. He found a suitably long stick and nudged the body, gun in his other hand. The stick hissed as it made contact with the creature's acidic blood, but the corpse didn't move.

Dead was dead in this case.

He might have felt a sense of triumph, except that the demon's master was probably still around. Such creatures did occasionally come through without being called, but those occasions were very rare, and with everything else happening in Loch Arach, an independent demon would be too great a coincidence.

Either the demon's master had sent it specifically after William, or it was here to guard the forest.

William didn't like the implications of either possibility. Also, his arm was bleeding, though not badly, and would probably hurt even more as his body stopped compensating for danger. His clothing was ruined in a damned conspicuous manner; he'd just shot six of his limited supply of silver bullets; and anyone wandering around the forest would have a very nasty surprise soon. Prudence suggested that he bury the demon and retrieve what bullets he could.

The rain didn't seem to be letting up at all, and he had nothing but his hands to dig with.

No, he didn't feel particularly triumphant.

Twelve

"Three mares in foal," said Judith, gesturing to the stables as she and Agnes walked past, "and coming along well. Campbell's beast did good work, though of course we've yet to see how they all turn out."

"Hoping for the color or the height?"

"Neither—I like the line as it is. But they need new blood if they're to stay healthy." Judith nodded to a few of the grooms out forking hay and using the sunny day to mend fences and turned onto the path that led to the gardens. "Come to think of it, a wee bit of height might not be so bad. Stephen and Colin have an inch or two on me, and the lasses they've chosen are both tallish. I'd not want my niece's feet dragging on the ground in a year or ten."

Agnes laughed. "Planning for her future already, are you?"

"Oh, aye. What else would a proud auntie do?"

"Teach her to ride, I'd think," said Agnes, "and the others who come along as well. Or will you let their fathers do it and save your brothers' pride?"

"That? Never," said Judith. She smiled and didn't let the grin fade when she added, "As for the rest, we'll see."

In a few years, wee Anna would be not-so-wee any longer and coming up on her first transformations, which were always hard to control or contain. Like MacAlasdairs had done in Judith's day, and as far back as family stories went, Stephen and Mina would come back to Loch Arach and settle there for a decade or two.

That was fine. Judith would be happy to see her family as always—for as long as she could. Stephen's return would be the first step in a transition, though. The wheel would turn, and her time to leave would come shortly after. When that had happened before, she'd never minded. This time, she was trying not to think about it.

"Just hope they get their mothers' temper," said Agnes, saving Judith from her own mind. "The foals, that is. I dinna' know if you've heard it, but Murray's horse kicked his wife badly the other day. Dr. McKendry had to see her, poor thing, and she's still abed from it. Cracked a rib or two, or so I hear."

"I hadn't heard," Judith said and made a note to stop by that house the next day. She had a vague mental picture of Murray's gelding: middle-aged, fat, and as placid as her own horses most of the time. "Odd."

"Aye, well, you never can tell with animals. It's a hard bit of luck for her. Claire says 'tis worse for her Mairi—the eldest, ye ken—but then, she would."

"A friend?"

Agnes nodded. "And 'tis an ill wind that blows no good, I suppose. They werena' speaking to each other until it happened. Had words, as lasses will do at that age. But Claire went over the moment she heard, and they've made it all up now."

"As lasses will do at that age," Judith echoed. The gardens wound out in front of them—almost all dark greens and browns now, dotted with red and pink where fuchsias and roses still bloomed. Her ancestors had never gotten very elaborate out here, but there were a few stone paths between hedges. When the weather was fair, it was a nice place to wander with guests—particularly when she didn't want to visit those guests at their homes because of who else she might encounter there.

On that note, she looked over at Agnes. "The fight wasn't about your lodger, was it?"

"Oh no," Agnes said, shaking her head so that the ostrich feathers on her best hat waved back and forth. "You'll have forgotten your girlhood, m'lady. They're all content with each other so long as none thinks she can have him for her own self, and he's given none of them any sign of that."

"Arundell's been a gentleman, then?"

"Aye," said Agnes, and then she hesitated. "Aye, he has."

"But?"

"It's nothing to do with the girls," said Agnes, and relief unknotted a muscle between Judith's shoulders. In addition to her earlier protective feelings, now that Arundell had kissed her, she would feel thoroughly ridiculous if he'd been trifling with girls Claire's age.

"And it could be that 'tis none of my business—each blade of grass keeps its own dew—"

"But he's your lodger, and it's your roof," said Judith.

"Aye," Agnes said again, but she drew it out more slowly this time and didn't say anything immediately afterward, until the muscles in Judith's back had begun to twist again.

Judith was a patient woman. She always had been, in her own way, even when she'd been traveling the world outside Loch Arach. Most of the time, she was content to stay still and silent, and to let the prey come to her or the enemy step into her sights. But just then, she wanted to shake Agnes.

Eventually, the other woman did talk.

"You'll recall a few nights past? When it rained so hard?"

"Yes," said Judith with a grimace. The hole in the castle roof, not quite fixed yet, had necessitated the hurried addition of a cooking pot to the furnishings of the room below. Luckily it was a spare bedroom without much that the water could damage, but it had been another reminder of how quickly time passed and how much there was to do before winter.

"Well, he didna' come in until late that evening. After dinner. I couldna' say the time exactly, but it might have been nine or ten."

"City hours run late, I hear," said Judith. "Later than that. Perhaps he was drinking with some of the lads."

"He does that at times," said Agnes. "But never

so late before, and never in the driving rain. I canna' think who he'd been out with."

Judith shrugged, forcing herself to show a casualness she didn't feel. "Women a bit older than Claire find him impressive, maybe," she said, although a liaison didn't seem the likeliest explanation either. Arundell had struck her as more discreet than to carry on at night that way, and fonder of his comforts than to come back through a downpour.

"And so I thought at the time," said Agnes. "But this morning, I saw the sleeve of his coat had been torn and mended. And then, when I did the washing, one of his jackets was mended in the same place, and I recall it being whole the last time. And there's no reason for a guest of mine to do his own mending, which I told him when he took the rooms."

"No obvious reason, no," Judith said. She gazed off over the gardens, not really seeing the plants or the forest beyond. "What did the tears look like?"

Thinking, Agnes closed her eyes. "There were seven of them," she said slowly, forehead wrinkled in concentration. "All on the forearm, just below the elbow. Long and thin, like. If there'd been fewer of them, or if they'd not been so orderly, I'd have said he'd fought a man with a knife."

"Don't tell Claire that," Judith responded automatically. "She'll think it's romantic. And we don't have many knife fights up here."

"Aye, none that anyone's talked about. Which they would. But—" Agnes's eyes, open now, were troubled.

It was a sense of trouble that Judith shared, particularly because her first impulse was to ask if Arundell was all right. If he hadn't been, Agnes would have been talking about *that* for the last three quarters of an hour, and the question was therefore stupid. Judith also didn't like the way her breath had caught in her throat when she'd thought of him being injured. He was an aggravating outsider, none of her concern beyond what trouble he caused in Loch Arach, and neither the lean strength of his body nor the sure heat of his kiss should change that.

Having thus remonstrated with herself, she forced her mind down analytical paths. "If he hasn't thrown out a shirt with a matching set of rips," Judith said, "I'll eat my hat. Or yours—it'd be less comfortable."

Agnes cast her eyes upward to the rim of her own creation of straw and ribbons and feathers, and then looked over at Judith's simple brown velvet with a smile. "One day, m'lady, you'll recollect which of us is supposed to be the staid and solemn widow," she said and then sobered. "But if he'd mended the coat and the jacket, why not the shirt as well?"

"Mending is one thing. Getting bloodstains out is another."

"Oh," said Agnes, round-eyed and round-mouthed. "And perhaps he has been favoring the arm a bit of late. I've not noticed, but I've not been looking. Do you think he met with whatever killed Finlay's ewe?"

"I hope not, for his sake," said Judith.

If the creature they were looking for was actually an animal rather than a man or a demon, odds were good that it was mad. She'd seen a man—more a boy, though he'd been old enough to enlist—die of hydrophobia once. War wasn't the only subject of her nightmares. She licked lips gone dry and asked, "Has he been in decent health since? No fever or headache?"

"Not that I've seen, no. But it wouldna' be so quick to set in," said Agnes, her own face grave. She rallied then and said, "But the tears looked too long to be bites, though I'm not so much of a judge. And even if they were, there's dogs as are mean without being mad, aye?"

"That there are." Judith shot her friend a grateful smile. If Arundell had gone poking around other people's property the way he had with Finlay's—especially if he hadn't bothered asking first—he could easily have run afoul of a dog doing its right and proper duty. "And even with what I told Claire, there are other creatures in these mountains that could damage a man. Wildcats, for instance. If he stumbled across a female with a set of late kittens, he'd be lucky to come back with all ten fingers and both eyes."

"We'd a barn cat like that," said Agnes, "when I was a wee girl. My brother's still got a scar on his wrist. Though I can't see why he'd keep the matter so quiet, whatever happened."

"Neither do I," said Judith. "And I don't know why Arundell would have been wandering around where any such creature could get to him in the first place, especially in the rain and the dark."

She took a quick mental tally of the village women who might have been both alluring and willing, and came up with around a dozen. Of those, at least half had fathers or husbands who would take Arundell's advances badly—and who would have been at home before nightfall, particularly in the rain. The others lived near the main village, not out anywhere wild. It was rare for lone human women to live much outside civilization. There was too much work that took physical strength, and there were too many predators, men included.

Drinking at the Dragon would have put Arundell well in sight of Agnes's house, not to mention a number of others. Most people kept their dogs fenced and tied on their own property. If a mad dog or a wildcat had been wandering the main street of Loch Arach, it would have damaged more than just Arundell, and more people than Agnes would have been discussing it.

Agnes was talking again. "That said, it's over now, and perhaps I shouldna' have mentioned it. It's not as though he's harmed anyone but himself, whatever he was doing."

"No," said Judith, and she thought, *not yet*.

That might have been unfair. Arundell wasn't just on holiday, but she didn't know that what he *was* doing would hurt anyone. That was the problem. She didn't know, and she couldn't afford ignorance.

"Can I ask a favor of you?"

Agnes nodded. "Of course, m'lady."

"If this happens again, or if Arundell does anything else that strikes you as odd, let me know immediately."

For a second, Agnes was silent. Then she said, "I'll come myself. No good sending Claire, not just now. They'll know to get you right away if I come here?"

"They will."

Thirteen

IN THE MOST IMMEDIATE SENSE, WILLIAM WORKED alone and had done so for the vast majority of his career. D Branch didn't have so many agents that it could assign two to the same place. When the situation called for out-and-out force of arms, his superiors might make an exception, but they usually sent other men when possible, men who could shoot first and never ask questions. The vast majority of the time, William was on his own.

But he did have superiors, and they were never long from his thoughts nor long out of contact. Even in a place as remote as Loch Arach, William sent regular updates—ciphered, naturally—and received them as well, reading carefully even though most of what the central office told him was happening hundreds or thousands of miles away. Between the laws of magic, demonic power, and the occasional unnatural gifts people demonstrated, action at great distances had always been possible. In the world of the telegraph, the express train, and the steamship, it was all the more likely.

After the night of the demon, William therefore ciphered and sent as exact a description as he could manage, detailed what thoughts he'd been able to assemble about the matter without jumping to any conclusions, and posted an innocent-looking letter to his "man of business in London."

He didn't expect much of a response. The demon had no obvious ties to Germany, Russia, or France, and none of the more troublesome cults had been active in the region. None of them had been active in general, at least since he'd left London. The Consuasori, if not completely shattered, must still have been picking up the pieces of their run-in with him and Smythe a few months before, and the Brotherhood, if William's sources were correct, was in the middle of an internecine conflict that made the Wars of the Roses look straightforward.

When the grocer handed him the usual lavender envelope, therefore, he wasn't surprised. He did notice that it felt thicker than usual and wondered what was going on in the larger world. He hadn't read anything alarming in the papers, but one never did read about the *really* alarming incidents.

William paid for the pound of flour Mrs. Simon had asked him to retrieve, picked up the letter, and turned away, only to have a substantial form collide with his injured arm. With an even more substantial effort of will, he kept his exclamation to a startled "Oooof!" rather than giving voice to the words and tone that would really express his feelings.

"Oh, terribly sorry," said the man who'd run into him. "I do hope you're all right." He spoke with obvious worry, which mitigated the worst of William's annoyance.

"Think nothing of it," William said. "No harm done."

He suppressed the urge to rub his arm. Unlike his coat and jacket, the cuts hadn't turned out to need stitching and were healing without any obvious signs of infection, but he still wore a layer of bandages under his shirt, and the arm underneath them ached devilishly at any rough contact.

"If you're sure—" said the other man.

He was thoroughly average-looking in height, build, and face, with brown hair and eyes. The only things notable about him were the quality of his clothing—sober dark wool that could have appeared in a London bank—and the tense, drawn look on his face.

At the back of his mind, William felt a tickle. He'd seen this man before.

Granted, this was Loch Arach. There weren't many people around. He might even have encountered the fellow at the pub and forgotten about it.

"Of course I'm sure," he said and offered a hand by way of being reassuring. "I don't know if we've met, I'm afraid. William Arundell."

The other man frowned, just for a moment. They *had* met, William thought—or the man had heard a few things about the English tourist with more money than sense. "Ross MacDougal." His accent was subtler than most people's in Loch Arach, less pronounced even than Judith's.

"A pleasure to meet you," said William.

Ross nodded, then glanced at the letter William still held. "Good news from home?"

"I doubt it," said William. "My aunt hasn't looked on the bright side of anything in her life. But she means well, and she never misses a letter. Family, you know."

"I do indeed," said Ross. "My mother and sister are great letter writers. Having me here with them may be a disappointment, at that—one less excuse to pick up the pen."

William chuckled. "I would think there'd be compensations," he said. "How long have you been staying with them?"

"Oh, a month or two," said Ross. "And you? You're Mrs. Simon's guest, if I'm not mistaken."

"For a little over a fortnight now, yes," William said. "She keeps an excellent house."

"Well, I hope we'll have the pleasure of your company for a while yet," said Ross. He hesitated a moment, then turned to the grocer. "Anything for me?"

"No," the man behind the counter said without even needing to check. "Nothing today, Mr. MacDougal."

Leaving them to their discussion, William pocketed his letter and headed off, thinking. Ross made a second recent arrival, though he'd been in the village a while before the first murder. So had Hamilton, granted—and Judith had been at the castle longer than that. And all that speculation assumed the killer had to be an outsider.

Usually, one learned to contact the Outer Darkness

from books or from other similarly inclined black-guards. The world was wide, though, and the forests and mountains of Loch Arach were very old. William couldn't say with any certainty that the killer hadn't gotten the spells from a more knowledgeable ancestor, or gone out into the woods and made a dark pact with a Thing already living there.

There was so damned little he could say for certain. That was very often the case on his missions, but never more so than on this one.

He made his way back to his rented rooms, not seeing either his landlady or her daughter on the way, which didn't surprise him. It was a pretty autumn afternoon, perfect for going visiting and completely imperfect for staying inside and doing chores. That was convenient for him—although he didn't have the luxury of neglecting his.

A small oak desk stood in the corner of his room, complete with stationery, a scratchy fountain pen, and a chair with hard purple cushions. Purple was a general theme in the room. William had stayed in much worse, including places where a bed or even a clean patch of ground was a luxury, so he wasn't inclined to complain, but he still sometimes felt as if he were sleeping on the inside of a giant sugarplum.

In that room, the lavender envelope only seemed appropriate, as did the looping copperplate script on the front and the overpowering fussy floral scent that rose from it. The element of surprise was an agent's best advantage. Nobody would expect a scented letter on lavender paper to come from the central office.

Nor would the letter's contents provide that

hypothetical onlooker with any immediate grounds for suspicion.

My dear Willie, it opened. Despite his familiarity with the scheme, William still squirmed inwardly when he read that greeting, both for himself and for whoever at the central office had to write it. He wondered if "Watkins" did employ an actual maiden aunt.

> *I once again take up my pen to write, in the hopes that this finds you well and enjoying your holiday. We all miss you terribly, but that will hardly surprise you.*

Everything was holding steady back in London. Good. A letter that didn't mention missing him, somewhere in that first paragraph, would have meant that there was trouble and that he should make immediate arrangements to return.

> *I myself am keeping well, though the autumn has brought on my rheumatism, as it always does. Your cousin Earnest has, however, recommended a specialist in such things, who he says was quite helpful to his mother.*

Earnest. The family member mentioned in the second paragraph was always the key to the cipher. William skimmed another paragraph of meaningless news, discussions of more fictional people's health and the repairs being made to a nonexistent town house, and then found the line he was looking for.

I was privileged to attend a lecture on Saturday last, which contained a great deal of thoughtful and enlightening discourse. The topic was vegetarianism.

When the writer mentioned a new discovery or educational experience, he—or she, if it really was a maiden aunt—would skip one sentence, and then begin the ciphered material. William took out his own, more reliable pen, removed a sheet of paper from the stack so that the impression of his letters might not travel through to the sheets below it, and began to work the message out.

MacAlasdairs were Jacobites. Not many other details available to us right now. History gets patchy around then. Sorcerous power definite.

The history of the Risings, real or popular, had never been William's specialty. In his briefing, D Branch had given him a few details: that both sides had used magic, often with massive casualties, and that forces on both sides had, on one occasion or another, dipped into the darker side of the occult. Blood sacrifice, and not of the willing, had been one example. Demonic pacts had been another.

William put down his pen and stretched out his fingers, looking at them and not at the message.

A hundred and fifty years was a long time. Nobody living then would be a problem for him now, but grudges were a more common inheritance than any ever laid out in a will.

And he was English—obviously so.

How carefully had Judith's ancestors handed down

their resentment? How much of it did she still carry around now? And what else might they have passed down along with it?

So far, he'd seen nothing to directly suggest that Judith was anything but what she appeared. He thought of her face, though—tight-lipped and narrow-eyed with suspicion on their first meeting— and then of the snarling creature that had tried to kill him in the woods.

He couldn't jump to any conclusions. But he couldn't overlook the evidence just because he still awoke breathless and hard from dreams of her body wrapped around his.

William picked up his pen again and began to translate further.

> *Will search old records. Family very reclusive since Culloden.*

A new paragraph began, talking about young people today and the failures of modern etiquette. The "end message" code hadn't appeared yet, so William went on deciphering.

> *The demon is lesser, minor pseudo-Goetic. We've encountered it before. You're likely right about the sacrifice and feeding. Someone there is working from a grimoire or learned from one to begin with. This is not folk magic. We advise extreme caution.*

That message, including the royal "we" and the unnecessary advice, was Watkins all the way, no matter how it might have been translated. The man was very fond of reminding his agents that he spoke not for himself but for an entire, if small, branch of Her Majesty's government. In William's more charitable moments, he thought Watkins was probably reminding himself of that too.

We're looking through our files for likely cultists or solo magicians. We will update you when we know more. Meanwhile, make contact with Charles Baxter at the following address.

The letter named a street and number in Aberdeen. William sighed, wondering if his superiors realized just how large Scotland was or how infrequently the trains ran even up in Belholm.

He can explain more in person, and he has additional equipment for you. End cipher.

William skimmed over the last few paragraphs, saw no coded phrases, and tossed the letter into the fire. He felt considerably more satisfaction than usual in doing so, and immediately regretted it.

This was not a hardship assignment. He'd been on *far* worse. The raid on the Consuasori itself had been more dangerous. He wasn't nearly old enough to gripe at an early morning and a train journey.

He certainly wasn't angry at the central office for adding more evidence to support what he'd already half suspected about Judith. That would have been unreasonable.

Fourteen

"Mr. Arundell's going away day after tomorrow," said Agnes, keeping her voice on the low side of conversational, even though Janssen had departed and left her and Judith alone in the drawing room. "I dinna' know that it's *odd* exactly, but I thought you might as well know as not."

"I'm glad you told me," said Judith. "Going permanently?"

She should have been relieved at the prospect—she wasn't at all—but she didn't have time to think much about her reaction because Agnes shook her head.

"For the day. He told me that I shouldna' be expecting him for meals. I asked what'd be keeping him out so long, and he said he'd be taking care of some business matters, so I can only think he'll be gone to Aberdeen, if not farther away."

"If he told you the truth, yes," said Judith.

The train in Belholm went through on its way to Aberdeen early in the morning and came back late at night. If Arundell was leaving the village, that was the only schedule which would make him miss all three meals.

If he wasn't, he likely wouldn't have told Agnes a lie in which anyone might catch him. Folk in Loch Arach might be isolated, but they knew the trains, and it would only take one glimpse of Arundell in the village or Belholm to disprove his story.

Judith smoothed the velvet of the sofa with her fingertips, absently pushing the plush one way and then another. "Keep an eye open while he's gone, will you? And an ear?"

"I always do," Agnes said. "Will you be going into the city as well, then?"

"Yes," said Judith, not at all surprised that the other woman had figured it out. "But nobody's to know, aye?"

"Just hope the castle doesna' catch fire in your absence."

Judith did. She worried about it a little at two the next morning as she mounted Dawn—sidesaddle, as always when she had to ride outside Loch Arach—and pulled her coat tight around her. She worried about the wall that the new stoneworker was helping the elder Jack Shaw to mend, about the Finlays and their stock, and about Mrs. Murray, as well as the host of calamities she hadn't thought of that would therefore occur as soon as she was gone.

Usually she didn't mind, even when she left, but usually she didn't sneak off in the middle of the night. The note she'd left for Janssen left him in charge as always, and he, like the rest of the servants, knew how to keep quiet. However, that wouldn't help much in an emergency.

But she had to go.

On the road, she turned in her saddle as often as she could, looking back at the castle as she had the first time she'd left. Then it had been the middle of the day—a stormy day, granted, but still light. She'd been riding astride and looking for all the world like a stripling boy, and her elation had far overwhelmed any hint of nerves. The whole world had stretched out in front of her back then, filled with promise.

Now she went as a lady, in stealth, to do a job she hoped was a fool's errand.

Arundell could honestly have business in Aberdeen and of a completely innocent sort, as far as Judith was concerned—anything from meeting with a solicitor to buying a new suit to visiting the sort of female "friend" he wouldn't want to discuss with Agnes. That was the best possibility.

The second-worst possibility would be that he'd gone to the city because he needed to, because he had to give way to urges that a small town would notice. Judith had read about the Ripper killings almost ten years ago and more recently about a Mr. Durrant in the States, but that sort hadn't been new to her. War brought brutality out in a few men, or gave them a way to vent what already existed. In peacetime, they would still be themselves, predators more vicious and less honest than her kind could ever be.

Brutality would be bad. Pragmatism could be worse. If Arundell was in Loch Arach for deeper reasons than those he'd mentioned to her—and Judith was almost certain that he was—he might not be working alone or on his own behalf. And if he was connected at all to the killings *and* was serving another, she might be in for a great deal of trouble.

His aura hadn't shown any magical talent. That didn't mean his masters didn't have any.

As Judith rode, the sky over the mountains lightened, although the sun wouldn't be up for some hours yet. By the time she reached Belholm, she could make out the silhouettes of trees and roofs against the starry sky. The town was almost completely asleep, but a few buildings near the train yard had lights in their windows.

Near sunrise, Judith boarded the appropriately named Dawn in the hotel stables, bought her ticket to Aberdeen, and concealed her face beneath an enormous green cartwheel hat, complete with pink silk roses. She blessed fashion, for once, for providing such things indirectly, and Colin for this particular specimen, even though she'd laughed at him when he'd given it to her. Taking no chances, she bought a newspaper at the station and buried her face in it, glancing occasionally over the top to watch the other passengers on the platform.

Two others were women: a tall, gawky girl of about fourteen in plain clothing, probably going to her first place as a maid, and an older woman with a fur wrap around her neck and a weary air. In addition, Judith marked two farm lads, a businessman in a very severe suit—and Arundell, coming into the station just before the train arrived. She held her breath as he boarded and didn't let it out until she'd found her own seat in a compartment behind his.

The train lurched and shrieked into motion, sending

up a cloud of smoke as it pulled out of the station and started on its way once more. Judith gave her ticket to the conductor, took off her hat and laid it on the seat next to her, and leaned her head against the window, studying the world in the cold, blue light of early morning.

The railway wound down out of the mountains and toward the coast. Rocks and trees gave way gradually to fields and houses. Judith couldn't have said whether there were more of the latter than she remembered, or whether she was just unused to towns and even large villages, but she watched with interest as the buildings went by.

It had been seven years since she'd taken the train anywhere, and longer since she'd been to a city. Those times when she had gone out had either been to Belholm to visit the seamstress there, to see livestock bred or inspect new kinds of crops nearby, or to go places one couldn't reach by either road or rail.

Aberdeen was dizzying. People rushed past her on either side: ants in an anthill whose sides were granite rather than sand and whose tunnels were the streets themselves, with the vast flanks of spired buildings rising up and almost blocking the sky. She smelled sea air and engine oil, and the voices of a hundred people flooded her ears, mixed with the complaints of horses and the shrieks of wheels on pavement.

Staggering mentally, she reached both for her memory and for the task at hand. She'd been in cities before—she just had to knock the rust off her memories—and she couldn't afford to lose focus. Keeping a short distance back and trying to become another face in the crowd, she followed Arundell out of the train station.

If such an outburst wouldn't have called attention to her, Judith would have spent the next half hour constantly swearing. The crowds did seem to mask her presence—she didn't see Arundell show any sign of recognition, though he looked around a time or two—but they also made it damned difficult to keep track of her target. Three times, Judith went breathless and cold as she lost sight of Arundell. She could only keep walking the way she'd been going in the hope that he'd reappear.

He did each time, but she knew that was as much luck as it was any skill of hers. She'd been a soldier and a sailor, but never a scout, much less a spy. She walked faster, elbowing her way through the crowd as she saw others doing, but still not daring to get too close.

She did see Arundell turn in enough time to follow, and found herself on a wider street whose occupants were, for the most part, either fashionably dressed or obviously servants. A glossy carriage pulled by a matched set of gray horses sped by, blocking her view of Arundell. Judith did swear then and darted around the back, heedless of the mud spattering her dress.

At first it looked as if she'd lost him. Judith stood with clenched hands in the street, her breath hissing out between her teeth, and felt her heart sink—just before red hair and a fine coat caught her eye again.

Yes, that was Arundell. A slower look confirmed it. As Judith watched him while moving closer through the crowd, he climbed a short flight of steps and rang the bell at one of the better-looking houses, all mahogany doors and polished granite. The door opened, and a butler much more polished and forbidding than Janssen beckoned the visitor in.

That was that, Judith thought as she watched the door shut, at least for a while. No ruse of hers would let her get into a stranger's house, and she was no spirit to slip through the walls, nor did she have any talent for invisibility. Judith leaned against the wall of a neighboring building for a moment, sighed, and then got moving again, looking for a tea shop with a view of the house.

She didn't find one. The best she managed was a small bookstore, where she idled as long as she could before buying two collections of poetry and heading back out onto the street. Fortunately, as long as she tried to keep up with the crowd, walking back and forth made her less noticeable. It also kept her warmer. Even through coat and dress, petticoats and chemise, the wind was enough to make her wrap her arms around herself and shiver.

After an hour and a half, she spied *a* quarry, though not her chief one—a woman in a patterned dress and apron emerging from the servants' entrance of the house next door. "I beg your pardon," Judith said, approaching her.

"Ma'am?" The maid turned, surprised and suspicious.

"Could you tell me who lives in that house?" Judith asked, gesturing to the door where she'd seen Arundell enter.

The maid frowned, but Judith clearly had money and probably rank, both of which commanded an answer. "That'd be Mr. Baxter."

"He's not a new arrival, is he?"

"No, ma'am. He's been there at least these five years that I've been in service. Are you lost, ma'am?"

"No," said a voice behind her: masculine, English, and far too familiar. If Judith's heart had sunk before when she thought Arundell had slipped her watch, it plummeted now. "I don't believe she is."

Fifteen

JUDITH SPUN TO FACE HIM, UNSTEADY AT FIRST BUT catching herself with impressive speed. Under the moss-green brim of her hat, her eyes were wide and her mouth was open. William watched her, waiting for her to explain herself or flee. He doubted she'd attack him in the middle of Aberdeen, but he kept his weight back and his guard up just in case.

"She'd been waiting for me," he said to the maid. "Much obliged for your assistance, I'm sure."

Lulled by the confidence in his voice—*Sound like you have every right to be where you are and do what you're doing,* said the memory of one of his instructors, *and people will believe it nearly every time*—and eager to be on her way, the woman bobbed a curtsy and left.

William and Judith were alone now, the crowds around them anonymous and uninterested. Baxter's house was near at hand with its resources and wards; William thought that gave him the advantage, but he didn't know what Judith might have brought, or indeed, what she might know.

In her face, he read dismay and embarrassment, but

no fear. She stood quietly before him, armored in a dark wool coat and black leather gloves, and waited.

"You've followed me," he said, the only opening move he could see.

"I can't deny it," Judith said, no more ashamed than she was afraid.

"And would you care to tell me *why*?" William asked, lifting his eyebrows in an incredulous look that had intimidated more than one contact in the past.

Instead of backing down, Judith cocked her head. "Would you tell me why you're here?"

"That's none of your business."

"Isn't it?" Her cheeks, already red with the cold air, flushed brighter. "When you come to my village as a stranger, with no good reason for your presence, and beasts start dying in horrible ways? When you stalk about in the wilderness at night and come back with a great bloody wound in your arm?"

The question hit William like a quart of cold water. Damn all small villages and all gossiping landladies—or landladies' daughters. "I assure you," he began, "that I've done nothing against the law. And that means, despite your feudal pretensions, Lady MacAlasdair, that I have a right to take rooms where I will and even to go out at night once in a while if that takes my fancy."

"And I have a right," she snapped back, "to protect my people."

"From *what*, pray tell? I haven't done anything."

"So you say." The city went on its way to either side of them, one passerby even catching Judith with an elbow. If she noticed, she gave no sign, just leaned forward and kept speaking. "If I ask around the other towns you've been to, will I hear about more stock slaughtered? Or will I hear about other deaths? Men? Women and children?"

She *would*, if she asked about any of the towns where William really had been—not that he'd done the killings, but God knew how rumors would travel. He'd already heard vague muttering about a "ghastly accident" in Belholm, which meant they'd probably found the boy, with the signs of his murder gone along with the scavengers who'd reached him first. And the history William had given in Loch Arach had been both scanty and largely false in detail. The combination could be dangerous.

"The stories I've heard," he said, taking the offensive, "are mostly about you, my lady. 'Reclusive,' they say. 'Odd habits.' 'Odd family.' There's even a tale or two about your...excellent physical state."

Judith's lips tightened. "How sweet of everyone," she said. "People do like their folktales. But my family's ruled our lands for years, and I've been at Loch Arach for the last twenty—as you'll know, with all the friends you've been making in the village—without ever a virgin dying on an altar. Not even a lamb. You can ask anyone, if you haven't already."

"Things change," said William. "So do people. Your brothers, for instance. They both married recently, yes? And your elder brother's sired a child—female, but still an heir under Scottish law, I believe? One might say that's a very classical sort of provocation."

"One might," said Judith, every syllable frozen, "tell you to go to hell."

"It's not a command that's ever worked on me so far," William said, "though I suppose you might get your wish eventually."

If she'd been the slapping sort, he thought, his face would be bruised now. Her hands were clenched at her sides, knuckles stretching the leather of her gloves. "You have no right," she began, "and no grounds to accuse me—"

"You accused me first, my lady, if you'll recall."

"Directly, aye. But what do you call all your prying, if not accusation?"

"Curiosity. What are you hiding?"

She smiled like a blow. "The secrets of the Orient, the Fountain of Youth, and the trick of turning lead into gold. Nothing that's any of your affair."

"Then—" he began and stopped abruptly as another pedestrian ran into him. This one was heavier and cursed both of them roundly as he stalked off. William muttered an awkward apology, then turned back to Judith. "See here, the train back doesn't leave for a good few hours yet. As bracing as it is to shout at each other in the fresh air, perhaps we should consider our fellow man and take this to a rather late lunch."

"Somewhere public," Judith said. "And we'll have a table in the window."

"And you have my word that I won't poison you," said William.

Judith chuckled briefly and dismissively. "I wasn't worried about *that*."

William usually liked to be underestimated. From her, it almost felt insulting.

❧

In a restaurant a few streets away, William finally got to set down his briefcase. It was considerably heavier than it had been when he'd left Loch Arach that morning. In addition to more silver bullets, Baxter had passed along another of Clarke's devices, this one a tin circle the size of a dinner plate, studded with pearls and glass beads in arcane patterns. Carried, he'd said, it would let William follow the traces of magic, as well as see in the dark. Clarke had a genius for both magic and metalworking; sadly, it did not extend to miniaturization.

William would take what he could get, and that included news. There wasn't very much, but what Baxter had told him was alarming. Interrogating the Consuasori brothers D Branch had captured in August had revealed that at least five of the cultists had gotten away, and two of the society's grimoires had gone with them. If the missing material matched what D Branch had acquired, there could be plenty of trouble in the future.

He ordered wine with lunch. He needed something of the sort—and he didn't want to risk anything stronger. Not with Judith sitting there looking like an empress in the middle of gilt fixtures and velvet draperies, and not speaking a word until the waiter arrived. Then she ordered, not bothering to tell William what she wanted but speaking directly to the waiter, who looked startled but clearly dared not object, though his eyes met William's in silent sympathy.

If Judith noticed or minded, she gave no sign. Hands folded in her lap, posture book-on-the-head perfect, she waited silently. William didn't think she was sulking. She wasn't the type. She was, he suspected, biding her time.

Once the waiter left, William struck first. "You do realize," he said, "that the first death occurred before I arrived?"

"Before I met you, aye," she replied, parrying without any sign of effort. "And before you took rooms with Agnes. That's not quite the same, is it?"

"Do you really think I'd be skulking around the woods with my baggage?"

A line formed between her dark brows. "I don't know what you'd do."

"But it's not likely, is it?" he pressed her.

"Most things that happen aren't very likely. It's not very likely that one of my people would go mad all of a sudden."

"You think it's the work of a madman, then."

"What else would it be?"

"Do you think I'm mad?"

"You don't act it," she admitted. "Mostly. But it's not always so easy to tell."

At Judith's request, they'd been seated beside a wide window. Outside, the sun was already setting. Winter was coming on, and the days up in Scotland were particularly short. People walked past, most of them not even glancing at the window. William heard laughter from other parts of the restaurant, footsteps on the carpet, and the soft, muffled chime of metal on china. Comfortable sounds. Civilized sounds.

He sighed. "If you had any real evidence of your innocence or my guilt, you'd have shown it by now."

"Aye," Judith said. "And the same's true for you, is it not?"

"So far," he admitted. "So perhaps we should both call a halt to investigation for the moment."

"A temporary truce?" Judith smiled, arching her eyebrows.

"For reprovisioning and tending to the wounded. I think we can each count on our dignity on that score."

Her laugh was low and throaty, and she tipped her head back a little with it, so that William found his eyes following the lines of her long neck down from the hollows behind her ears to where her skin disappeared under the green velvet of her dress.

The waiter saved William's dignity. Appearing with wine, chicken, and baked herring, he forestalled any conversation—and gave William a moment to figure out what to say next. That usually wasn't difficult, but today was not proceeding at all according to the usual standards, even for him.

"Is this your first time in Aberdeen?" he finally asked and waited for a reply that he was sure would be at least partly sarcastic.

Instead, Judith simply shook her head. "But it's been a great while. 'Reclusive' isn't far from the mark. There's enough at Loch Arach to occupy me most years. More than enough at present."

"In the absence of accidents and mysteries, what do you do?"

"Keep the castle running. The village as well. I've no doubt they'd get along without us, but I like to imagine I help. I breed horses, and I see to the lines of cattle on occasion, and we've an orchard—apples, mostly, though I'm thinking of starting plums next year. And my brother Colin wants me to think about electricity," she added, pursing her mouth in affectionate dubiousness. "And then I read in winter or the evening."

She spoke offhandedly, lightly, but William saw the real interest in her face, the animation that filled her posture and her gestures when she spoke of her plans and Colin's ideas. It cost her a little, he thought, to keep herself to a mere summary, and he found himself smiling at her with real goodwill. "It's not just duty with you, is it?"

"I don't know," said Judith. "It's a strange word, aye? There's a part of the world, even if it's a small one, that I can maybe make better. I like doing that. Building. I don't know if it's my duty or not. I stopped thinking of those things long ago."

William remembered a small estate in the Lake District and his uncle striding the lanes, nattering cheerfully about crop rotation and plowing, a pipe in his mouth. It was a strong memory. He'd tagged happily along as a boy, more intent on the large dogs that accompanied them but aware of his uncle's voice in the background, of a feeling that here was a stable point in the universe.

"It's possible to think too much sometimes," he said.

"'So sharp you'll cut yourself.' That's how my nurse used to put it—also a long time ago. And generally she was talking to Colin, not me." Judith looked across the table at William and leaned back, assessing. "So, then—are you a recluse by inclination, or is Loch Arach a novelty for you?"

Outside, the sun sank farther down the sky. Perhaps that was what made their table seem lighter and warmer.

Sixteen

By the time they'd finished their meal, it was full dark. Judith had barely noticed sunset fading to twilight, or twilight fading to night. When she stepped outside again, at William's side, she reached, alarmed, for her pocket watch.

"Don't worry," William said. "We've still an hour until the train leaves. Night comes on fast here at this time of year, doesn't it?"

"Aye," said Judith, "and it's darker in the cities. That is, there are more lights, but the sky's darker. It's a bit unsettling after so long in the mountains, I suppose."

She wanted to believe that unfamiliarity and surprise had been the foundation for her dismay. She knew better. Talking with William, she hadn't been paying attention to the time, and she'd lingered, laughing at his stories, talking poetry (he'd read Kipling's latest volume, which she badly wanted), and surreptitiously glancing at his broad chest or watching the sure way his hands moved. Walking beside him now, she felt the magnetic pull of her own desire and stuck her hands in her coat pockets so that she couldn't do anything foolish like take his arm.

The city *was* dark, and the artificial light, at least for her, only made the streets and the crowds more confusing. With a week or two, she might have learned to be at ease. Just then, she wished she could change form and fly out, leaving the whole dank stone maze of it behind her. Judith squared her shoulders and walked along. Lunch didn't mean she could trust William, and even trust wouldn't mean she'd let him know how uneasy she was.

He stopped at a street sign and pulled a map out of his pocket. "I think," he said, "that we've taken a wrong turn."

"Ah," said Judith. Evidently he wasn't familiar with Aberdeen either. She found that comforting, petty as the reaction might make her, and bent more cheerfully to trace streets with her finger. "Aye, we should've gone right there."

"But it looks as though there's an intersection this way," William said, pointing.

The whole thing was confusing. Navigation was considerably easier from the air. "Might as well try it," Judith said and straightened up to start walking again.

At first, the new route was fine. Then their second turn took them into a narrower street, one rife with even more smells than was usual for a city. The turn after *that* put them in an alley.

"Ah," William said, frowning.

Then, from the soot-stained sides of the alley, shadows emerged and became men. Judith counted five: big fellows, all of them, and at least two openly carrying long knives. She let her breath out through her teeth and stepped back.

"It's all right," William said, putting a hand on her arm. Oh, good—he was going to try to be protective. This day was going *wonderfully*. He turned to the men. "Very sorry to disturb you. We'll just be on our way."

Protective and diplomatic. Even better.

"Don't move," growled one of the larger men. "Don't run. Don't scream. You'd better not scream. Nobody'd hear you. Nobody'd come anyway."

Even from a distance, he reeked of drink. His eyes were glassy, and he grinned when he spoke in a way that Judith didn't like at all. Neither did she like the way the others were looking at him, taking their cues from his behavior. On their own, sober, any of them might have been reasonable. Right now, she could feel the avalanche building.

The men would probably catch up quickly if she and William tried to run. The alley was dark, and the leader was probably right. She'd never known most people in cities to intervene, and the local constabulary didn't take much interest in a neighborhood like this one. She wasn't armed. She didn't know if William had brought whatever weapon he'd been reaching for out at Finlay's, or how skilled he was with it if he had. And she was wearing skirts.

She sighed, held still, and decided to try a little diplomacy of her own. "I'm sure we can settle this peaceably. Just leave us enough money for tickets home, aye? We'll hand over the rest."

The leader shook his head. "Won't need money when we're done with you. Won't need to go home either," he said. Judith didn't recognize what cue he gave, and he didn't speak, but she heard footsteps behind her.

Fine, then. *Fine.*

She whirled, caught the man's outstretched hand as he tried to grab her arm—they *always* tried for the bicep if you were a woman, devil only knew why— and used his body as a pivot for her own. Her elbow smashed into his jaw with all her weight behind it. His head snapped sideways with a cracking sound: his jaw, not his neck, for he yelled in agony and staggered back, clutching the side of his face.

There was no time to see William's reaction.

"Are we finished—" she started to ask.

Then the leader roared and rushed forward, and the rest followed his lead. It *was* an answer, just not the one Judith had wanted. "I did my best," she muttered, not sure if she was speaking to William or the robbers or her own conscience. Then she gave herself over to the moment.

Fighting, for her, had always been a diminished form of hunting. She didn't transform, she couldn't fly, but she operated almost entirely on instinct. A century of experience and training didn't alter that—it just made the instincts more effective. On a bone-deep level, she knew when to duck and when to kick. She could anticipate the thrust of a knife and step nimbly to the side, then throw a punch that knocked her assailant back into the stone wall behind him.

Even as she fought, she heard a gunshot and another scream. When she could spare a glance, she saw William, back to the wall and gun in his hand, and one of the men writhing on the ground. A pool of blood spread from the man's side.

Human blood had its own smell: sweeter than an animal's and richer at the same time. Judith knew it very well, as well as she knew the sound of gunfire, the smell of powder, and the feel of flesh giving way before her fist or her foot. She broke a man's wrist, took the knife he'd been wielding away from him, and slashed his fellow across the chest with it. That was familiar too. He made gasping noises and fell.

She stepped forward and caught one of his companions. The man struggled. He wasn't screaming anymore. Judith locked one of his arms behind him, yanked him toward her, brought the knife around—

No, this is not then. This is now. This is not there. You don't have to do this.

—and reversed the blow, slamming the knife's hilt into the man's temple hard enough that he slumped to the ground.

Nobody was moving. Not enough to be a threat, anyhow. She registered the thrashings of the men on the ground: feeble and disorganized, neither foe nor—she reminded herself—prey. Her ears caught moaning but no footsteps. She let her vision expand.

It had all happened very quickly. Such things always did. William was still standing and alive. Three men, including the leader, were lying on the ground. Another crouched against the wall, clutching his bloody leg. The last had pressed himself into a corner and was staring at them, petrified.

"You have five more bullets, don't you?" she asked, loud enough for the remaining robber to hear.

"Four," said William, more calmly than she would have expected and with a completely expressionless face. He pointed to the man with the bleeding leg. It looked like a wound to the kneecap, nasty.

"Ah. I didn't hear the shot." That happened sometimes. God knew they'd all been making enough noise. She looked coldly over the man in the corner. She did everything coldly right then. That was how it went. "I think we can go now, don't you?"

"Yes. Quite so."

This time William did offer her his arm, and she took it: all part of the act. He could probably feel that her fingers were shaking. He would doubtlessly misinterpret that. The knowledge made Judith cringe inside, but it was a useful error. She would let him make it. She'd exposed too much of herself already that evening.

Carefully, they made their way back toward the main streets and didn't speak until they were some distance from the alley. "We could tell the police," said William reluctantly.

Judith shook her head. "No point to it. Their own people will find them. Or their enemies." She shrugged. If you ran with wolves, you got bitten in the end. She hadn't noticed whether the leader had still been moving when they'd left, and she couldn't say she cared very much one way or another.

Men died. Nobody could avoid that. They died when you tried to keep it from happening, and they died when you took the chance. The important thing was not to make it a certainty. Not anymore. She drew her free hand across her mouth, wiping already-dry lips with cold leather.

She knew that William was watching her. Before he could ask if she was all right, or how she'd learned to fight like that, she went on belatedly. "Besides, the police would ask questions."

"And you're not fond of those."

"Are you?"

He sighed and shook his head. "Let's find the road."

They went carefully this time, and slowly despite the later hour, retracing their steps back past the short-cut, down the street where they'd taken a wrong turn, and farther back in the other direction. All around, buildings and people cast strange shadows in the glare of lights: candles, gas lamps, maybe even some of the electric torches Colin had been talking about. There was no moon in the city, no stars.

Soon enough, Judith thought again, she'd have to get used to all this once more. And there would be more *all this* to get used to. It was the way of the world.

Now the light, the noise, and the smells struck her even more powerfully. Her blood was up after the fight, surging through her veins like the tide. She could feel the energy still singing in her muscles, quickening her pace, and every nerve was tense, ready for more action. William's arm was an anchor in a world of chaos, but his closeness was far from calming.

She kept looking at him. Not looking to make sure he was still with her—for a mercy, she was sure he could keep up with her at least on this ground—but just *looking*, noticing the brisk way he moved through the crowds or the way his red-gold hair blew back in the wind. Desire crept through her body like a hot stream.

Walking, it was all right. Walking, she had a way to work off the tension and other things she had to attend to. Even the streets of Aberdeen were no real challenge that way, aside from overloading her senses, but the journey to the station kept her busy enough. It was too loud for either of them to talk, which helped too. Without words, she could keep from acknowledging anything between them, particularly what had happened the last time they'd walked together for any length of time.

They reached the train with little time to spare, but ready cash was a great persuader, and the conductor politely hustled them into a compartment just before the engine started. That was when the real trouble started.

On an evening in the middle of the week, the train was not particularly crowded. Deferent to the presumed wishes of a presumed wealthy couple, the conductor gave them a compartment to themselves. Judith couldn't fault the man. She could only sit across from William, her heart racing faster than any healthy woman's would have just from sitting still, her ankles crossed in a proper pose that made her only more aware of the fullness and warmth gathering in her sex.

He crossed his legs as well—unthinking posture or an attempt to conceal his own arousal?

Judith turned away and looked out the window, watching the streets become fields and the fields grew farther apart. She thought about retrieving the novel from her bag, but she realized that William would suspect she was avoiding him if she did and also that she couldn't concentrate. She felt each bump and sway of the train too keenly, and the friction only built the pressure between her legs.

"You fight very skillfully," William said after a while. His voice was faintly rough.

Judith wished she hadn't noticed. "Two brothers," she said, not looking at him. "You learn to handle yourself."

"Do you?"

"Aye," she said and snapped her head around just long enough to glare at him. She was not discussing her training, she was not telling him the truth or anything close to it, and she wasn't letting her gaze linger on him, particularly not on his legs. Men wore much looser trousers these days than they had when she'd been young, but the way he was sitting, she could still see the outline of his thighs and notice the firm muscle there.

She cleared her throat. "You're a fair shot yourself."

"My uncle taught me," he said, which was probably as much a lie as anything she'd said, unless his "uncle" had also taught him not to bat an eye at either men who tried to kill him or women who…fought very skillfully.

"Compliments exchanged, then," she said. "Chivalry satisfied?"

"Oh, that wasn't chivalry," said William. Judith had to look back and found him smiling slowly. "But I could continue the compliments if you want."

Judith felt his gaze like a glancing caress on her breasts before, being a gentleman, he snapped his eyes up to meet hers.

That was worse. Those blue eyes were small oceans

of lust, so deep and dark that the mere sight left Judith breathless.

Maybe she could have held out against her own desire, even at that moment. Seeing his, she knew herself overmatched and surrendered.

"Oh, what the *devil*," she snarled and crossed the compartment.

Seventeen

Even on a jolting train, Judith moved with the speed and grace of a striking snake, just as she'd fought in the alley earlier. One minute she sat across from William, all coiled tension; then she was bending over him, her slim hands pinning his shoulders back against the seat of the train, her lips hot and fierce against his.

Another man might have been more wary. The woman had followed William to the city, her family had at least one secret, and he was far from certain that she was innocent where any of the recent deaths were concerned. Added to that, she'd just fought like a damned Amazon, leaving three men with broken bones and perhaps killing at least one. *Brothers* did not teach a woman those techniques, nor did they give her either the speed or the almost offhand strength she'd displayed in those few minutes.

Nor had William missed the expression on her face at the very end, the way she'd just barely pulled the knife back. Her lips had been drawn back from her teeth and her green eyes had fairly glowed. *Tyger,*

tyger, William had thought, his own blood singing with the aftermath of a successful fight.

Another man would have tried to keep her at a distance—a man who hadn't held all the lean strength of her in his arms, a man who hadn't spent the last few hours watching her face change with anger and humor, and wondering what it would look like in passion, a man who hadn't heard her talk of duty and pleasure. *A man with more common sense,* Clarke would have said.

But if Clarke had worked in the field, it had been before William had ever joined D Branch. He was a long way from the reckless schoolboy glee that could surface on the other side of fear. Judith hadn't been the only one to fight and maybe kill, and if William had read exhilaration in her face, it had probably been there in his as well.

He'd certainly felt it afterward. He'd managed to distract himself somewhat on the way back to the train. He'd managed not to think more than once or twice about finding *another* alley, one where he could pin Judith against a wall, shove her skirts up, and bury his sudden and insistent erection between her thighs.

Civilized and horrified as the mind might be at a distance, the body rejoiced in its own survival. William had come to terms with that years ago.

Now he knew that Judith had as well.

And if he did have cause to be wary of her, then at least he was keeping her occupied.

He let her take control for that first startled moment, lips opening to her darting tongue. Then he wrapped his hands around her waist and pulled her down into his lap. She went more than willingly. Her fists clenched on the shoulders of his jacket, her legs parted around his body, and then she was strad-dling him, a welcome and torturous presence against his swollen sex. Her skirts fell around them both in a cascade of green and white.

It was a very short distance from her waist to her breasts, particularly once William had pulled her close. Just a quick motion of his hands and he was cupping them, feeling where they rose soft above the irritating barrier of whalebone and cloth. Judith hissed against his mouth, and for half a second he wondered if he'd hurt her, but she arched backward, thrusting her breasts into his touch, wordlessly asking for more.

Well, not *asking*, really. The lady wasn't much for asking. He had a brief notion of trying to make her ask—trying to make her beg, in fact—that made him feel like the train had left the tracks. Then she started rocking against him, little motions of her hips that swiftly fell into a complementary rhythm with the swaying of the train. Her lips left his as her head fell back.

The view was astounding. Judith's long, slender neck arching backward above her out-thrust breasts, her eyes half-lidded with desire, and her mouth slightly open, lips swollen and dark. As William watched, she ran the tip of her tongue around those lips, then caught one between her small white teeth, biting back a cry.

William quickly abandoned the idea of trying to make her do anything. He abandoned any ideas that required patience, planning, or any more mental activity than it took to thrust back upward in response, mimicking through too many layers of clothing what he really wanted. That got a moan from Judith—a low, throaty sound that went directly to his cock.

Wanting to hear the noise again, he slid one hand down from her breast, running over the curve of her waist and hip to find the edge of all her skirts and petticoats, and slip underneath them. There was no corset between his skin and hers there, no buttoned-down-the-damned-back dress guarding her body, only the thin silk of her stockings where they stretched taut over her thighs. Stroking upward with his fingertips, he heard another moan and felt the rhythm of her hips speed up, spurring a matching urgency from him. Even in indulgence, he tried for some self-control, but that was rapidly becoming an impossibility.

Further testing him, Judith dropped her hands from his shoulders to his chest, then down toward the waist of his trousers. There she found that she couldn't reach lower without moving away. She made a small, frustrated sound in her throat that made William laugh and ache at the same time. He sympathized. Then he found himself making the same sort of noise when she did move away, his body protesting even as he knew it was only a necessary step on the way toward better things.

The train lurched around a corner. Their car tilted, spilling Judith back against William. The contact wasn't graceful this time, and her head knocked solidly against his chin. He felt the impact and winced, but he was kissing her again before she could apologize, unable to resist when she was practically lying on top of him, lithe and warm and eager. She reached for him a second time, and as she searched blindly for the fastenings of his trousers, her fingers brushed over the rigid length of him until he was almost lost to all sense.

Almost. Not quite. As the first button gave way, William tore his mouth from Judith's and caught her wrist. "Wait," he managed, half breathing the word. "I've nothing on me."

She frowned, perplexed. "Nothing?"

"Preventives. French letters—" He hesitated. Surely she knew. She behaved like a woman of the world, and her actions of the last few minutes were more evidence of that. Still, a gentleman's upbringing made him pause and wonder how to go on.

"Oh," she said as he was still searching for words. An impatient shake of her head sent her hair tumbling around her shoulders. "Don't worry. I can't have children."

It was so tempting to believe her. She sat in his lap with a hand at his groin, her breasts heaving with every quick breath and her face flushed entrancingly. Every inch of William's body told him to take her word for it.

"No," he said, both to it and to her, and he pushed her hand away. He had no reason to believe that she was telling the truth—even if she thought so, he'd known more than a few people about whom the doctors had been wrong in that area—and a child would be even worse for him than for another gentleman. Blood connections were always dangerous.

He half expected Judith to try again and steeled himself to refuse, but she left her hand where he'd placed it. Catching her breath, she sat unmoving except for her free hand, which twisted the fabric of her skirt back and forth.

William recognized the struggle. He knew it well, and also knew that neither of them had to win it entirely. Before Judith could speak again, he wrapped one arm around her waist, steadying her on his lap, and pushed her skirts up again with the other hand. She'd turned sideways slightly, the better to reach his buttons, and the position gave him access too. It was quite easy to slip his hand up her thigh and trace his fingers over the opening of her drawers.

"Oh," again, but this time it was desire and relief mingled. She arched up, seeking his touch—and at the same time, her hand slid between them again, returning to her prior task. Her fingers moved with even less finesse than before, often going still entirely as William stroked her, but before very long the buttons opened.

William didn't want to close his eyes. He wanted to watch her. But he was overwhelmed: cool air and then a warm, firm hand closing around his shaft, soft heat and wetness beneath his fingertips, the smell of pine and smoke and female arousal. He couldn't do anything but lean his head back, let his eyes close, and lose himself in the moment.

Neither of them had the time or the inclination for gentleness. Judith was wet and hot around his fingers, stiff beneath his circling thumb, and her hand slid up and down his cock with sure, steady pressure. William held on to his control by a thread as she started rocking her hips again…and the thread started to snap when she flung her head back and her whole body went tense for a second. In the next instant, she was climaxing around his hand, and he couldn't hold back. He thrust into her grip again and again, until pleasure crashed through him and blotted out all sense of time or place.

⁂

They had no time to linger. William was still collecting himself, breathless and boneless, when he heard footsteps outside the compartment and a knock at the door. He pulled his hand back to his side, while Judith yanked down her skirts, but the door, thank God, did not open. He only heard the conductor's voice outside: "Belholm, next stop," and then more footsteps as the man moved on, impatient to get to his other duties.

A hasty bit of work followed: cleaning, rearranging, and otherwise trying to make themselves look like they'd just spent a placid journey being completely respectable. Of all the women he'd known, Judith possessed the most impressive facility for putting her hair up neatly without maid, mirror, or even stable ground to hand. William didn't say it aloud.

He didn't know what *to* say. He half expected Judith to warn him again that nobody would believe or care about any tales he chose to spread, or question his motives. That had been insulting, but William thought he might prefer it, since now she didn't speak at all. She barely even looked at him, concentrating on her dress and her hair.

Preoccupation? Shame? Anger? He couldn't tell.

"Have you a way of getting back tonight?" he finally asked as the train pulled into Belholm station.

"I left a horse in town," she said. She sounded surprised but not affronted, much to William's relief. More reassuring still, she went on, "You're not likely to find the ride comfortable, though. Nor would he be very inclined to carry two people our size. What will you do?"

"Take a room in the town and walk back tomorrow when it's light." He smiled at her. "You don't have to tell me that I don't know the road as well as you do, and I don't much enjoy broken ankles."

"Good," she said. She stood up, fastening the last button on her coat. Her hair was tidy under the hat, the wool coat concealed any rumpling of her clothes, and the only signs that she'd recently been writhing in his arms were her swollen lips and flushed cheeks. "Have a good night, then," she said as the conductor opened the compartment.

"And you," said William, and he watched her leave. She walked into the darkness as if she were meeting an old friend.

Eighteen

THE FIRST FROST HAD COME AND GONE—NOT EARLY enough to interrupt the harvest, but severe enough to put a decisive end to it. The day of the festival was windless, cold, and bright, with the suggestion of brittleness that always accompanied clear days in the winter. Judith gave orders to lay on extra wood and to build the fires in the hall well before dinnertime. When she left the castle doors, the smell of smoke was heavy in the air. It was a familiar scent, and one she usually let pass without thinking. That day it reminded her of the year marching on, as so many had before.

This year's Harvest Maiden was carrot-topped Mairi Murray, who rode atop the corn-laden cart in her blue-and-pink-sprigged Sunday best, with a crown of pink and purple heather atop her flowing hair. Claire, one of the few girls who'd stood no chance at cutting the last sheaf, seemed to be content enough with her lot. In sky-blue muslin and with the dignity of coiled and pinned hair, she followed the cart with the other girls her age, walking at a pace sedate enough to give all the local boys a good look. Caring much less for making a show, the younger children thronged around the outside, laughing and shoving in their own private exchanges.

Judith chuckled to herself. She'd been one of those children once. She remembered plum cake and singing. She'd generally contrived to lose her bonnet in the melee, much to the dismay of her mother and various nannies. Girls now didn't have to be bothered, lucky little things. Braids were much more convenient.

The equivalent of Claire's crowd had been present back then too, but Judith had never been one of them. Adolescence hit the MacAlasdairs hard: not only did one's body change, horrifying enough, but one had to adjust to and control the urge to transform into an entirely new creature. By the time she'd learned proper control, she'd also learned that she was different—and her childhood friends had moved past her, some into marriages and families of their own, others into service. None had remembered her very well.

Mortals worked that way. She'd left shortly after learning to control her shape. She could still feel her mother's kiss on her forehead. The day had been autumn, and the smell of smoke had been the same.

Then the cart was inside the castle gates, and Judith came back to the present to play the role that had been hers for twenty years. As the singing stopped, she stepped forward, smiled, and took the bound sheaf of corn from Mairi's hands. Judith spoke a few words, none unusual and all good-natured, stepped back to laughter and cheers, and watched the crowd explode into the castle grounds.

At moments like this, it was hard to believe there weren't very many people in Loch Arach. They seemed to be everywhere, from elderly women walking around together in the sunshine to babies gurgling cheerfully in their mothers' arms. The gardens held couples and would-be couples; the pond, under the stern eye of Janssen, was a source of wonder and winter-groggy amphibians for children of a certain age.

Judith walked through the crowds, speaking to some people, not interrupting others, noticing who was there and how they looked. Mrs. Murray wasn't there, of course, though her husband was laughing with some of the other men. Old Hamish was getting around nicely; she'd heard his hip was paining him in cold weather, but either it wasn't too bad or the ale helped. Gillian Gordon and her family were admiring the flowerbeds—at least Judith could see Gillian herself and her mother, and her son riding on his father's shoulders, but where was Ross? She spotted him a little distance from the rest of his family, smoking and gazing at one of the castle walls.

He didn't look very well. His face was drawn even at a distance, and he held his shoulders tightly. Judith wondered briefly if he'd had bad news from London, or if living in close quarters with his family was just proving hard on his nerves. He wouldn't have been the first man to feel that way.

"Lady MacAlasdair?"

A voice cut into her thoughts. She turned to see one of the other new faces in the village: the mild brown eyes and soft features of Dr. McKendry's friend Mr. Hamilton.

"I wanted to say how very much obliged I am," he went on when she greeted him. He spoke like a university man, she noted, but his accent was still strong. "It's awfully good of you to play hostess to all of us like this."

"Oh," she said, "it gives me a chance to talk with people. And it's nice to celebrate *something* before winter comes and we all huddle inside for months."

"Aye, McKendry's been telling me grim tales. I don't entirely think he expects me to live out the winter."

"I'm sure you'll *live*," said Judith, laughing. "I'm just not certain how you'll feel about it. I hope you don't mind spending a good deal of time indoors."

"If it keeps my mind on my research, so much the better."

"Oh? Are you a scholar?"

"A surgeon, actually. I've just been stricken with the urge to experiment—a hazard of the profession."

"You can't tell me you've set up a laboratory here," said Judith, lifting her eyebrows. The thought that a surgeon might want to experiment on animals turned over uneasily in the back of her mind, like a monster stirring in restless sleep. Surely Hamilton could get all the mice or guinea pigs he wanted legally.

"A small one, yes. At the moment, I'm rather keen on theory. I had a good deal of practice in Fife."

"Practice doing what, if you don't mind me asking?"

"I'm experimenting with blood transfusion. Dr. Blundell did some marvelous work thirty years ago, but there are still so many advances to be made—and so many puzzles to figure out. For instance—"

Just as his eyes were beginning to gleam, he stopped himself. "But it's no subject for a lady. I'm sorry. And, oh, there's Mr. Arundell. My dear fellow, do come join us."

Hamilton's relief at avoiding an awkward subject was palpable. Judith could only hope her unease at the situation was much less so. "Good evening," she said as William approached. "I hope you're enjoying yourself."

A number of inappropriate ways to go on promptly popped up in Judith's mind, everything from *You know how much I like to see you…enjoy yourself* to *And if you're not, you can always enjoy me.* She bit the inside of her cheek. This would have been a wonderful time to be a pure, innocent miss who knew nothing of innuendo, but she was two hundred and thirty years old and had been a sailor or a soldier for most of that time. She knew a filthy way to interpret every third word in the English language.

"Oh, yes," said William, and he smiled slowly at her. There was the innuendo again, only he didn't even need words. What question was he answering again? "Reminds me of my own youth. Fewer smuggled firecrackers, though."

The festival. Enjoying himself. Right. Judith gave herself a firm internal shake, which with any luck would dislodge her mind from her loins for a while. "Don't say that too loudly," she said. "People will get ideas."

"And McKendry doesn't need the work," Hamilton agreed, then gave William a curious look. "You grew up in the country, then?"

"Yes—Sussex. And my chums and I went to the odd fair or two when we were at school."

"With permission?" Judith asked.

William smiled innocently. "Sometimes."

She had to laugh. "*Official* fireworks might not be a bad idea next year, at that," she said, remembering nights in Shanghai with a shared bottle of rice wine and colored flowers exploding overhead. "Assuming they won't scare the horses into a year of fits."

"Or cause an avalanche," said Hamilton, casting a wary eye toward the mountains.

"No need to worry there. These stones are old and settled." And if they weren't, Judith didn't say, she'd know well in advance. That was one of the things she and her ancestors had always kept an eye on—both with patrols in dragon form and with magic—in one of the north-wing rooms where the servants didn't go.

"I'll take your word for it. I'm a city lad myself. I have to admit that this much nature unnerves me from time to time."

"Not an unreasonable point of view," said William. "Any patch of earth or sea probably has a few surprises left, and they're more than likely unpleasant to us tiny occupants."

"On that," Judith replied, "we're agreed."

The crowd around them took on a new purpose and headed for the doors of the castle, gawky boys approaching girls with their hands in their pockets and elderly women taking their husbands firmly by the arms. Judith could guess what they were about, and she knew for certain when she heard the first few notes of "The Duke of Perth."

"If you'll excuse me," she said, "the dancing's starting. They'll expect me in the first set—and it'll warm me up a bit."

&

Thinking back later that night, Judith couldn't say when she'd realized William was watching her. After the second dance she shed her cape, finding the wool of her dress plenty warm enough by then, and maybe she'd glimpsed him as she'd hurried back from the coatroom. Maybe she'd seen him in the corner as she turned to face a new partner. Maybe, and she didn't like to think much about the possibility, she'd been looking for him the whole time.

At first he was just standing and holding a glass of ale. He and Hamilton had apparently taken their conversation indoors, and McKendry had joined them along the way. The next time Judith glanced over, as she took Andrew Stewart's arm and proceeded down the line, Gillian Gordon had joined the three men. McKendry was using her to demonstrate turning while the others laughed.

Ross, Judith noticed, was neither in the group nor the dance, nor drinking with Gillian's husband, Ronald. She hoped he was doing the gentlemanly thing and squiring his mother about. Mrs. MacDougal wasn't as young as she had been, and Gillian could use a change of society.

The next time she saw William, he was standing across from her and holding out his hands. Judith blinked. The music left her no time for surprise, and many years of practice carried her forward before she was even conscious of moving. "Feeling adventurous?"

"Always," he said, flashing her a grin. "Dr. McKendry said this was one of the simpler dances. And—when in Rome…"

"I'd not have liked the Romans overmuch, I think," said Judith. William's hands were warm against hers, not as callused as many of her tenants' but enough so to increase her suspicion that he was no gentleman of leisure. "But aye."

They separated, circled, and came back together. He was a little off count, clearly new at this, but not bad. He'd also taken off his greatcoat in preparation, and it was a grand thing to watch him in motion, even while she took petty satisfaction from his errors.

"You don't underdo hospitality, do you?" he asked, looking around at the garland-hung hall, then toward the door to where the tables were beginning to fill with silver-covered dishes.

"I don't give many parties. There's no point in going halfway when I do." Judith wound a figure eight around him, came back, and watched him do the same. "You catch on quickly."

"We had to learn the quadrille when I was a boy at school. It's not very much like this, but it helps a little."

Another figure parted them, to the tune of a fiddle and many stomping feet. Judith stepped toward William; they took arms and walked down between the rows of dancers. She wondered for a second if people would talk, but she felt no particular gaze on them. Most people, she thought, would just see Lady MacAlasdair being hospitable to the newcomer. She hoped so, at least.

"Besides," said William quietly, "as unexpected skills go, I think mine pale in comparison to yours."

"Brothers. I told you."

"They must have been extraordinary brothers." They took hands again. William looked down at her, his eyes bright and razor-keen.

"They were," said Judith, smiling thinly. "Are. In many ways."

"And—"

The door burst open before William could go on. Through the crowd, Judith glimpsed Young Hamish, alternately pale and black-streaked.

Before he opened his mouth, she knew what he was going to yell.

"*Fire!*"

Nineteen

IN AN INSTANT, JUDITH DROPPED WILLIAM'S HANDS and crossed the room, slipping nimbly between the now-frozen people on the floor until she stood at Young Hamish's side. "The store?" she asked, her face sharp with focus.

"Aye, m'lady. Started in the chimney, I think."

William headed toward the two of them as the rest of the ballroom came out of its paralysis. Movement and sound returned, though muted: whispers and murmurs, uncertain moves toward the door, and more decisive gatherings in a corner.

"Anyone inside?" Judith asked.

"No, m'lady. They're all here." Sure enough, Old Hamish was struggling out of his seat in the corner, with the assistance of one of his fellows. His son—Middle-Aged Hamish?—and his wife were making their way through the crowd, which parted for them.

Judith nodded once. Now beside her, William heard her let out a quick breath. It barely qualified as a sigh, and she didn't produce another one. Rather, she turned to the assembled villagers. "The grocer's is aflame." She raised her voice to be heard over the muttering, which died down quickly, but she didn't shout.

"Finlay, take four men and go get the pumper to the loch. I'll need ten men to start work with buckets while they're gone. You, you, you—" she continued, pointing to young men and one or two sturdy young women, including Claire's friend Ellen.

"And me," said William, stripping off his jacket. A bit of scarring aside, his arm was as well as it ever had been, and he'd carried much heavier things than buckets in his day.

He'd expected Judith to argue with him or at least to look surprised, but she just nodded. "Follow the others."

❧

Loch Arach had a well in the center of the main street, bordered by low stone walls and covered with a slanting blue-tiled roof. It looked much like any other well in any other rural village, and William hadn't given it much notice before. Now it was the center of his and everyone else's attention—that and the flames and black smoke rising from the grocer's roof. All eleven of them kept glancing that way as they approached the well, and William would have bet that the others were asking themselves the same questions he was.

How fast are the flames moving?
Will we make it on time?
Will the fire spread?

"For a mercy," Ellen said from a few places in front

of him as they waited to fill their buckets, "there's no wind."

"Aye," said the black-haired youth standing beside her, "and those trees are all bare. The dry leaves would ha' caught like paper, and then the whole village would be like to burn. We've a chance as it is."

"We've a chance," echoed Ellen, and the pump worked steadily in the background, like a metallic heartbeat.

Years had passed since William had pumped his own water, but the knack of it, thank God, came back quickly when he stood at the well. He filled his buckets and followed the others back toward the store. No longer in a line, they went as fast as they could without spilling the water, spurred to even greater speed as they got close enough to start coughing from the smoke.

It was bad.

As Young Hamish had said, the chimney had caught first, and the flames had spread quickly to the wooden shingles. By the time William reached the store, half the roof was alight and flames were coming out of the upstairs windows. The smoke formed a dense, black cloud. He had to draw close to see that ladders leaned against the house, and men at the top were throwing buckets of water onto the flames. Two people stood near the base of each ladder, handing the men buckets from William's most recent comrades.

It might have been helping. He couldn't tell through the smoke.

He neared the bottom of one ladder. "Here," he said, holding one of his buckets out to a figure there.

She turned and he saw it was Judith, with the sleeves of her dress rolled up and her skirts kilted to the knee.

Neither of them had time for surprise or banter. She took the bucket and handed it up with one hand, using the other to support the ladder. After a second, she held out a hand for the other bucket. From above, William heard grunts of effort and splashing—but mostly the crackling roar of the flames eating away at the building.

On his way back to the well, he wiped sweat from his forehead and realized that he hadn't seen any on Judith's face, though she'd been far closer to the fire than he had, and passing buckets up the chain didn't exactly seem like easy work. She was wearing wool too, and ladies' fashions called for several more layers than men's.

It was a quick moment of curiosity. Mostly, he was too busy to think.

When William got back with his second load of buckets, Finlay and his crew had returned. With them had come the pumper: a vast iron tub mounted on wheels but carried on long wooden shafts, with a hand crank and a hose attached to it. Men were passing the hose up to the top of Judith's ladder, and an older, stouter gentleman was turning the crank with steady speed.

As William watched, the man at the top of the ladder sprayed a gout of water onto the chimney itself, sending smoke hissing up into the air. The flames seemed to have died down—and a cheer from the ladder confirmed that as the man turned the hose on other parts of the roof—but William knew there was still a great deal more to do.

Back and forth he went. He lost count of how many times. The water splashed onto his legs, and the wind felt like ice against the wet patches on his trousers, even as the rest of him sweated. Waiting for the pump, he rolled up his sleeves, which helped a little bit. Now their task was endurance rather than haste. The first few buckets of water, and particularly the pumper's spray, had stopped the fire's rapid spread, but killing it would take a great while. The fire broke out hydra-like in one place as soon as the men had stamped it out in another.

From time to time, William's awareness broadened enough to take in other details. Other villagers had come down from the castle. Many—too old, too young, or generally too frail to be helpful—stood at a distance and watched. A few others acted. As William held a bucket with one hand and waited for the man on the ladder to finish with the second, he heard a woman clear her throat nearby. Turning, he saw Claire Simon holding out a cup of tea.

"It clears your throat a bit," she said without any trace of hesitance or infatuation. The teapot was in her other hand, and neither cup nor pot shook at all. William smiled his thanks, took the cup, and tossed the tea back in three swallows. It did help with the smoke, and the warmth sank into him, giving him new strength. He passed the cup back to Claire, who went on to the next man in line, just as her mother and some of the other village women were doing at other ladders.

Nobody really spoke otherwise. Words slowed one down and weren't necessary—one knew what needed doing, did it, came back, and did it again. Passing a group of the spectators, William did see one old man catch his eye and nod in grim approval of the outsider making good. He probably didn't do that to any of the local men. They didn't need anyone's judgment.

William became so used to the sound of the flames that it was odd when they began to die down, and he frowned, not comprehending what had changed and why. Then he saw the men at the pumper picking up the shafts again, and the man who'd held the hose coming down the ladder.

"Roof's out," said a voice, a man who'd either seen William's puzzled face or was commenting to a general audience. "They'll be going 'round in force tae the windows now."

Indeed, the men were moving the pumper around a corner of the store, and a small crowd was going with them, carrying buckets and ladders. The roof smoldered above, a sullen black ruin. Two chunks of it had fallen in. As if a reminder that nobody was out of the woods yet, a tongue of flame licked out of the upstairs window.

William followed as well, found the tub full when he reached the pumper, and went around to the next ladder, joining two or three others. Over to one side stood the Connohs, blanket-draped and surrounded by concerned neighbors. A gap between people showed their tearless, stunned faces.

"They'll rebuild," said Judith's voice, close at hand. "I'll see to it. Hand over one of those, will ye no'?"

Neither her voice nor her expression allowed for chivalrous refusal. William passed her a bucket and inwardly confessed himself glad to be shed of the extra weight. Judith took it without complaint or apparent effort. William reminded his pricked vanity that she hadn't been carrying water the whole time, but it didn't do much good. She looked nearly as tired as he felt. She also looked relieved.

"The danger's past?" he asked.

She shrugged. "Not if we stop now. But aye, there's no chance to it anymore. 'Tis but mopping up from here on in." Coming from her, the term struck William as odd, but his mind was too fatigued and smoke-clouded to produce a reason why. "You all made a fine job of it. I'll say as much up at the castle later—over food."

"The praise is nice, but the dinner's more alluring just now," William said.

Judith laughed. "Aye, I think you'd have company in that sentiment."

She was looking forward as they walked, focused on the ladder that was their goal. So was William, but he was closer to the building. It bought him half a second as he saw the flaming bit of wood—a scrap of furniture or windowsill that their efforts had dislodged—plummet through the cold air. It was still burning when it hit Judith's bare arm.

"What?" she asked, sounding more annoyed than distressed. Before William had time to move, she batted the debris away with the bare fingers of her other hand, just as she might have flicked off a troublesome insect. It landed on the ground, where William immediately poured half the contents of his bucket onto it, then trod the smoking black remnants into the dirt.

After that he looked up, his heart going still in the aftermath of danger. At least Judith wasn't screaming yet. "Are you all right?" he asked and looked immediately toward her arm.

The skin there was smudged with ash. He couldn't tell anything for sure. But he would have expected blistering or at least redness. As far as William could see, Judith's arm looked as it always had: slim, muscular, slightly darker than fashionable—and completely uninjured, as were all of her fingers.

"Oh." She followed his gaze and gasped. It sounded overdone to William, and the relieved smile she gave him looked shifty. "I must have brushed it off before it could burn me. Thank God for absentmindedness, aye? And reflexes."

"Yes, quite," said William.

He did give thanks, despite himself. He thanked God for whatever had left Judith whole and unhurt instead of writhing with charred flesh. He just didn't know what that had been.

Twenty

IT HAPPENED AT SUNSET.

Sunset had never been Judith's favorite time of day. Even at its prettiest, the sight of the sinking sun still made her feel twitchy. It was too red, too angry, at once too much like blood and too much of a reminder that, whatever else the sun might be, it was also fire greater than even she or any of her family could control or withstand. Even with the sun so far away, she couldn't be entirely easy with that knowledge. It was doubly true now that she'd known enough of war and magic to be sure that the future would produce at least *one* damned fool who'd try to bring that power to earth.

Her mother, sorceress that she was, had told Judith once that sunset was one of the between times, neither quite one thing nor another. There was great power in those times and places, Riona had said. Doors to other worlds opened more easily. That hadn't helped Judith's discomfort.

Dawn was another one of those times, but she'd mostly seen dawn on early watches or after a night of revelry when weariness or drunkenness, or both, had distracted her. Now she simply slept through it—being the lady of the castle had its privileges—and at sunset she distracted herself with tasks or books.

The day after the fire, sunset found her on the road, walking back from the village where she'd been calling on the Connohs in their new lodgings. The store was going to take a while to rebuild and even longer to be habitable, rather than just a place to store and sell groceries. Meanwhile, the family was living with Young Hamish's married sister, and the accommodations didn't look *too* cramped. They'd resisted all of her hints about finding a place for them in the castle. After a while, Judith had admitted defeat.

This sunset was of the sullen red-and-gray winter variety. Brittle grass and browning heather brushed the sides of her skirt. Hard dirt crunched beneath her shoes. Cold wind knifed through her coat.

Eyes watched her.

The feeling came from nowhere, and she could see nobody around, only barren fields to each side and behind, and the castle and forest ahead of her. Yet she was completely certain of the scrutiny.

She knew words in Latin that let her see hidden things: spirits, auras, and lines of magical force. As their mother had done, Stephen called it "invoking the Wind that Parts the Veil." Colin talked enthusiastically these days about energy and magnetism. Judith knew and cared only that it worked. She stopped in her tracks, a tall, dark woman standing alone in the midst of late-autumn desolation, and said the words aloud.

The world clouded. Grass, heather, trees, and houses

all became misty and insubstantial. As far as Judith could observe, her own aura was as it always was: bright green, shot through with streaks of glimmering silver. She didn't spend long looking at that this time. Other things caught her attention.

Literally, "things" was the first word that came to mind. Little, six-armed rat-things—just looking at them hurt Judith's eyes. Six of them lurked around her in a rough semicircle, any one of them staying perhaps ten feet behind her. If she hadn't been looking, she might have missed them, even with magical sight. She hadn't—and her stomach clenched at the thought that these miniature horrors could have been following her for a good month now. If they had been, they'd kept more distance. Now they'd grown bold enough and perhaps strong enough to attract her attention.

The longer she looked, the more nauseated she grew. The rat-things had nasty-looking teeth and sharp claws at the end of each arm—now the wounds on Finlay's dead sheep made sense—but they weren't a physical danger. They were clearly spies or scavengers, not killers. They weren't harmless, though. By their very presence, they caused damage, not directly to people or things but to the fabric of the world nearby. There were no exact words for what they did, but rough synonyms came to Judith one after the other.

Fray.

Tear.

Twist.

Corrupt.

Rot.

She remembered Shaw Senior telling her that he'd

checked his ladder before starting work. She remembered Agnes talking about Murray's horse suddenly going vicious—and she wondered just how the fire had started at the Connohs' store. Things went wrong with these creatures in the world, and although Shaw's injury had happened while she'd been in the castle and therefore in close proximity, the others had been farther and farther away. The effect was spreading.

She turned and started back toward the castle, moving at her same unhurried but purposeful speed while her mind whirled. Odds argued against the rat-things being natural, which meant they'd been summoned for a purpose. That purpose might include spying. Tactically, it might be best to let them keep watch and pretend she had no idea they existed—but she couldn't let them stay in the world, not with the damage they were doing.

How to get rid of them? Assuming their master wasn't already seeing through their eyes—Mother had said it was damnably hard to ride along with a demon, and that people who did usually couldn't even fake sanity for long—she didn't want to risk even one getting away to bear tales.

The wind picked up again. She barely felt it. The demons were tagging along behind her, maintaining a steady distance. Judith glanced back briefly to confirm this, then looked quickly forward again. Watching the creatures move was even worse than looking at them in the first place.

Could she take all six of them? In a fight, yes, almost definitely. But if one ran, she might not have the reflexes to catch it. Small things were fast and slippery.

She'd learned that hunting rats on her first ship and had spent twenty years with a scar on one arm to remind her. She had the instincts of a soldier, not a predator.

Not in human shape, at least.

When a narrower path branched off from the main road to the castle, Judith took it and headed toward the forest. At this distance, she could make out individual trees rather than a single dark mass. The still-green bulk of pine and fir surrounded the leafless branches of the other trees. Protective, she thought, but perhaps she was just looking for protection.

She was also looking for concealment. The trees would function admirably in that regard. That much was not subjective.

Still walking without haste, Judith crossed the first line of trees and immediately went off the path, ducking between trunks and dodging undergrowth. She did look back once in a while, making sure that the rat-things were still following her, and she took an easier route than she might have otherwise. Although she hadn't been in the forest in a few weeks, she knew almost every inch of it from the ground and the air alike. She couldn't count on the rat-things being good at navigation.

They did keep up though, and without any apparent effort or distress on their part—although she didn't know what either would look like on such creatures. Whether natural or as abnormal as they were, their senses were good, as were their speed and mobility. Abstractly, Judith found that alarming, but for her purposes just then, it was the best thing she could have hoped for.

Gradually, the trees around her became larger and older, and the ground beneath them clearer. With the thick leaves overhead cutting off their sun, the plants in the undergrowth had died out. The soil they left was thick, dark, and moist. It had rained yesterday, too late for the Connohs' store but at least in time to help Judith.

This was the most ancient part of the forest. Her ancestors had gone to the nearer portions for wood throughout the generations, and villagers had even hunted in there when there was no danger of disturbing the MacAlasdairs in their other forms, but this part had never known a woodsman's ax, and she doubted if anyone on two legs had ever hunted there.

Judith spied her destination ahead: a huge clearing, dark with the shadows of the old trees that circled it, but clear for yards around. She knew the place from many seasons and many years. Her first real hunt had begun there—she and Stephen tagging along behind their father—and many others had followed.

Now she was alone. The prey was unworthy, inedible, and *wrong*. But it would be a hunt nonetheless.

She stepped into the clearing. A squirrel fled at her approach, scurrying for the safety of a pine tree and chittering alarm to any of its fellows who might be listening. Judith thought she heard an extra note of agitation in its call. No animals found her presence pleasant, even without the accompanying rat-things.

The creatures followed her as she'd hoped. First they lurked at the edge of the clearing. Then, as she moved farther in, they came. They seemed to maintain a fairly consistent distance. Whoever summoned them had probably given them specific orders, since they didn't look that bright.

Judith calculated. She wanted them as far out in the open as possible. They were maintaining formation. To get them all out from under the trees, they'd need to be roughly in the middle of the clearing, but no more.

The farther off from England, the nearer to France.

She'd been gun captain for a few years out in the Pacific. Now, as she had then, she sighted the spot she wanted. This time, she wouldn't be depending on half-grown boys with shot and powder. She walked, stood, took a breath—and transformed.

It was a full-body shiver. It was a moment when she saw double and felt stretched. From the outside, she knew, it took no more than a few seconds, but it always felt longer. Then she was the dragon.

The rat-things were even smaller now, and they hadn't moved. Either they were stunned by the transformation or they didn't have the wit to know they were in danger. Judith rumbled her satisfaction.

She inhaled and thought *control* at her gullet, where the force was already warming her chest. Judith and her brothers had inadvertently tested these trees in their youth, and they'd proved very sturdy, but there was no reason to take risks.

Now the rat-things were shifting, growing wary. It was time.

Judith swung her head and spat fire in an arc that ran from the last creature on the left to the one in the middle. It was a thin, whiplike stream of flame, which crackled out and caught the rat-things just in the center of their chests. The shrieking hum that emerged from them overwhelmed pride at her precision. It went all through her and made her back teeth hurt. The smell was putrid too. She reared her head back and snarled.

The other three rat-things bolted. Two headed back the way they'd came, while one broke sideways. Judith grabbed that one with her jaws, careful not to bite—there was *no* part of this thing that she wanted to eat—shook it sharply, and dropped it unmoving to the earth.

Meanwhile, the other two had hit the tree line. Quick little buggers; she had to give them that. Judith sprang up, let her wings give her momentum for a second or two, and then dove sharply. The ground shook as she hit it, throwing the rat-things onto their backs. She snaked out a foreleg and ripped through them with her claws. They felt liquid, as if they'd been rotting for a long time already, and they shrieked like their companions. If they hadn't been dead already, Judith thought darkly, she'd have killed them again for that. *Nothing* needed to make such a noise.

She wiped her claws on the soil. With any luck, the things' blood wouldn't do much harm, but she'd come out and purify the place later to be sure.

She turned back to the clearing and the burnt bodies there. None of them were moving. All were dissolving into the air, in fact, and to her relief, they didn't seem to be doing any more damage to the world with their deaths. A stray patch of pine needles *was* smoldering, though. She stomped on it with one clawed hind foot, grinding until the smoke went up; then she tossed dirt over everything.

This was her place. She would take care of it.

Twenty-one

ONE ADVANTAGE OF FINDING TROUBLE IN ISOLATED farming villages was that people actually went to bed. Sunset itself was a touch early, but even by that time most of Loch Arach's residents were getting dinner on the table, shutting the livestock in for the evening, or otherwise settled in their own homes. Nobody would suddenly go out to catch a show or attend a dance. A good many of the younger generation chafed at these conditions, but for William, they meant there were fewer people to ask inconvenient questions.

Waiting until full dark, sadly, would make Mrs. Simon or Claire wonder where he was, and William already knew they didn't keep such speculation to themselves. Late afternoon was the best compromise, he'd decided. If everything went as he planned, he'd be back well before dinner. If he did encounter one of the villagers, he'd just say he was out to look at the sunset. He was sure no local boy could have passed off such an explanation, but he was an outsider and strange.

Clarke's silver medallion would be harder to

explain. That was why William kept it tucked inside his coat and didn't take it out until he found a secluded copse of trees halfway between the village proper and the castle. Then he knelt, placed it on the ground, and said the Enochian phrases that Baxter had passed on to him. A low humming, not unpleasant, filled his ears as the medallion attuned itself. He waited, almost holding his breath in the hope that nobody would stumble upon this, the most crucial and most obvious stage of his task.

Without interruption, the humming ended. William bent and picked up the now-quiescent silver disk. He saw a faint glow in the heart of the multicolored glass beads—maybe refracted sunlight, but then again, maybe not.

The rest of the disk's power had little room for debate. His vision snapped from one level of reality to another with the immediacy of putting on spectacles. Rocks and the outlines of houses looked far away and faded. Plants had a faint glow about them, stronger in the pines than the other trees and weakest in the dying grass.

Off near the main road, six leprous-gray trails ran in thin lines, back to the village and on toward the castle. Of everything in the new landscape, they stood out the brightest.

He headed out to join them, glimpsing flickers of russet light around his own body as he moved. The whole experience was rather fascinating so far. He wouldn't have minded lingering, if he hadn't had his duties to think of—and if he hadn't been looking at the gray trails. As he got closer, they seemed to squirm beneath his vision. He thought *infested* and then *dissolving*, and didn't know which one was right. He thought of the rat-things he'd seen near Finlay's and dropped his free hand to touch the butt of his pistol.

A short distance ahead, another trail joined them. This one was green, of a shade that looked like it had been vivid when it was new, and thicker. Like the gray lines, it went forward toward the castle.

William's chest tightened.

Either the green thing was Judith and the rat-things had attacked her or were stalking her in preparation, or;

The green thing was Judith, the rat-things were her allies, and she'd met them here for reward, assignment, or punishment, or;

The green thing was a third party altogether, and whether it was fighting or allied with the rat-things, both of them were headed toward the castle for some reason.

Every possibility involved Judith and danger. While he was laying the possibilities out in his mind, William was already following the trails, breaking into a light jog that he knew he could sustain for a while and keeping his gaze well ahead to make sure nothing would bring him up short. He almost stumbled anyhow when he saw the smaller path branch up ahead, and that all seven of the trails turned there.

Not the castle then, but the forest. In some ways, that was a relief; in others, anything but.

As he jogged onward, the trails got brighter, and William knew he was catching up to the things that had made them. They hadn't been in a great hurry.

From what he'd seen of the rat-things, they were speedy little devils when they wanted to be. He was glad of their lethargy on this occasion. He was in decent shape, but not as young as he had been, and the trails got harder to see once he entered the forest. There, they competed for his attention with the auras coming off trees and the brighter sparks of birds and small animals. None of those left tracks the way that his quarry did, but immediately at hand, anything living and mobile could easily drown the traces out.

The ground was also horrible for running. That had been true when William was following an actual— though narrow and bumpy—path through the forest, but far too soon the tracks veered off through the woods themselves. He swore when he saw that— quietly, so as not to alert any of his targets that might be in hearing distance, but intensely profanely.

Nor did his sentiments change once he got started. Forests were all well and good in poetry, or as places for lovesick men and deposed kings in Shakespeare, but real forest floors held both roots and rocks, cunningly hidden under carpets of pine needles—slippery pine needles, at that. Real forests had plenty of undergrowth to catch at his coat and trousers, briars to whip across his arms like little bloody needles, and birds to screech practically in his ear when he was trying to duck under branches. He hit his head the first time that happened, with a *thud* that made him wonder why he'd bothered trying to be quiet in the first place.

He was still keeping up with the tracks as far as he could see. He knew it almost for certain when he heard the sounds up ahead of him. First were a *snap* and *fizz* like a struck match; then a shrill buzzing sound that rang in his ears and called to mind horrible hours in the dentist's chair. When a great beast snarled, drowning out the drill sound, it was almost a relief.

Almost.

The wind shifted toward him, and the scent it brought made him struggle not to gag. Smoke mixed with the sweetly rotten scent he remembered from the demon that had attacked him, flooding his nose and throat. His eyes watered. It would make sense for the rat-things to smell like the other demon, he thought. It would make no less sense for the larger creature to smell that way too, if it had come from the same place.

With sweat icy on his body, and tense from bones to skin in the instinctual response of a naked ape sensing a huge predator, William slowed down. He tucked the medallion under one arm, slipped his silver-loaded gun into the other hand, and moved quietly toward the noises. The trees gave him good cover. Most of them were far larger around than any man, even him, and their leaves let barely any light in. This part of the forest was very old.

The thought was not comforting. It brought to mind sailors' tales of krakens and sea serpents, the ancient beasts of the deep, giant bones buried in the American West, and Bible verses that he'd learned in childhood. *There were giants in the earth in those days.*

As counterpoint to the verse, a great weight landed on the ground up ahead. The forest floor actually shook beneath William's feet. With his hands full of objects he didn't want to let go of, he caught himself on a tree with one shoulder, cursing again at the impact. He kept the profanity silent this time. He was too close for any untoward sound.

Ducking around another tree and behind a third brought him to the edge of a great clearing, where the last rays of twilight came to earth. He didn't need that light, not with the medallion, but even without it he would have seen enough to freeze him, openmouthed, in his tracks.

A dragon stood at the opposite end of the clearing.

Training and practice let him calculate and observe even while he quietly gibbered. Dragons were sleeker creatures than they'd appeared in the stories of his youth, apparently. The one in front of him had the four limbs that had distinguished the knight-gobbling sort from their counterparts of Chinese legend, and no whiskers. It was a rich, shimmering green, covered with scales the size of his hand, and a sharp-looking ridge ran down from the top of its head to the tip of its lashing tail.

That was quite a distance. By his shocked estimate, the dragon was at least twenty feet at the shoulder and probably triple that in length, and the furled wings on its back might have covered the clearing. For all of that size, there was a certain grace about the creature, the sort of disconcerting nimbleness he'd seen from tigers.

It slashed out with one foreleg as he watched, aiming for something in the tree line. The light shone briefly on claws like kukri knives. For an intense, horrifying moment, William wondered whether he should try to help the dragon's prey, for all of the three or four minutes his life might last doing so. Then he saw the bodies on the ground.

Three were horribly burned, which explained the smell. The fourth unmoving creature lay in the middle of the clearing. No human being could survive with its body at those broken angles, and apparently some demons couldn't either. All four of the bodies were rat-things. Their trails were fading, and so were their bodies, slowly dissolving into air and earth. William focused and saw two other trails leading to the tree line, toward the place where the dragon was fighting.

The dragon's claws made contact with a *splortch* like overripe fruit hitting a wall. William got a very brief glimpse of one of the rat-things, mouth open in angry pain, and then that damned buzzing noise, the demons' death cry, hit him again.

If he hadn't had any other reason to object to those creatures being present in his world, the sounds alone would have done it. He leaned against the tree and wished he had a hand with which to clutch his head.

He heard the dragon exhale and saw it retreat from the tree line, wiping its claws on the soil in a strangely dainty gesture that, on second thought, seemed practical. Who knew what kind of poison lurked in the rat-things' blood? And if he'd never thought of dragons as particularly forethoughtful, he'd also never thought much about dragons at all, once he'd left the nursery. D Branch didn't know everything, and it didn't tell its agents everything it did know.

The dragon turned. A long, curved horn came up from each side of its head, William saw. Its face was narrow and pointed, and its eyes were comparatively huge, as well as a striking shade of greenish-gold. As he watched, those eyes focused on a patch of ground near where the burnt rat-things were fading—a patch that was sending up a few faint plumes of smoke.

With a quick, sinuous motion, the dragon slammed one forefoot onto the smoldering earth and twisted it, grinding out stray sparks the way a man might crush a cigarette end. Then it flipped loose dirt on top of all the bodies, even as they faded. It was quick and precise about the whole business, much more agile than William had thought—and far more systematic. He watched with eyes that felt about the size of dinner plates.

If he survived, he'd deliver a report that would have Watkins buying him dinner at any club in London.

Cleanup concluded, the dragon stood in the center of the clearing. William waited for it to spread its wings and fly away—Amy Finlay's "giant eagles" were suddenly much clearer—but instead it coiled around itself, tucking its tail neatly under its chin. Perhaps it was the pose, but now it looked much smaller than sixty feet.

Then it shimmered like a mirage. There was a moment of color and light that William couldn't fully translate as the dragon shrank and shifted and became a bipedal figure, a shade less than six feet tall, in a skirt and shirtwaist. Black hair made a neat bun at the back of her neck. Claws became long-fingered hands. The eyes were smaller, but the color was the same.

Judith MacAlasdair stood in the middle of the clearing, looking around her with the distaste of a woman who'd just completed some unpleasant household chore.

Suddenly, she frowned. She turned. Those green-gold eyes focused directly on William.

Twenty-two

THE EVENING JUST GOT BETTER AND BETTER.

Judith still had the faint taste of rat-thing in her mouth, and her head had started to ache, an unsurprising result of hearing the demons' death cries. Several unpleasant ideas were circling her mind and getting ready to perch. Most concerned why the little monsters had come, why they'd been following her, and how much of the recent destruction was her fault.

Now William Arundell was standing at the edge of the clearing. She didn't know how much he'd seen, but the way he was staring let her know that it had been more than enough. And he had a pistol leveled at her head.

"I don't want to," he said. "But I'll defend myself if you make me. The bullets are silver."

There was no question in his voice, no uncertainty that silver would hurt her or that she knew it. In his other hand, he held more silver: a flat disk that glittered with gems and shone with magic to her sight.

"What are you?" Judith asked.

"Human," said William. "Which makes one of us, doesn't it?"

"I'm not *not* human," said Judith.

The silence of a winter's night filled the clearing. Each of them stood staring at the other. *Standoff*, Judith thought, remembering American stories. Silver could kill one of her kind. In dragon form, if the shooter missed the head or the heart, it would usually take more than one bullet. From her memory, though, William was an excellent shot, and she'd transformed only a minute ago. She doubted she had the energy to do it again for a while, not after the fight.

With any luck, he didn't know that.

William cleared his throat. Without moving the gun or taking his eyes off her face, he asked, "Did those creatures attack you?"

"The other way around. They were following me."

"And so you struck first."

"I'm sorry, were they friends of yours?"

His mouth twisted in distaste. "Hardly. I'm simply trying to get a sense of what happened."

"Why?"

"Wouldn't you?"

"Not if it wasn't my concern. You haven't explained how it's yours."

"I want to find out what's happening here," he said, "and I want to stop it."

"A couple of minor demons and a few dead livestock? Why is that worth your time?" She drummed her fingers on her hip. "You're clearly not an amateur. I'll give you that. You can't really be up here because you think that whoever's responsible *might* switch to humans."

Judith watched William's face as she talked. It was a careful blank. "So," she asked, "who's died already?"

William visibly weighed his options, then sighed. "The peddler I'd mentioned. Actually, a boy down in Belholm. I don't know his name. He visited a friend of mine. Afterwards."

"Your...friend of a friend?"

"Yes."

"When?"

"A month ago. More or less."

"How do you know the killer was from here? Or that it wasn't just a fight gone bad?"

"I saw the body," William said and then after another short hesitation, "and I saw tracks. Magical ones. They led in this direction."

"And you heard stories about a strange village with a stranger lady." Judith felt her lips curve into a thin smile. "Well. I can't deny I'd have been suspicious in your shoes."

He didn't apologize, which was wise. She'd been sincere. An apology would have meant that William thought she was stupid, or at least irrational. "If it helps anything," he said, shrugging one shoulder, "I'm fairly certain now that you *aren't* the killer."

"Oh?"

"Whoever killed the boy used his death to summon the demons—the things that you just killed. You wouldn't have needed to kill them if they were yours."

"If only I'd thought to slay demons in front of you weeks ago," Judith said dryly. "We could have avoided so *many* misunderstandings."

Although his gaze never wavered, William

visibly stifled a laugh. "Proper introductions are very important."

"I'll have to study my etiquette books again."

"Do your people have many rules of etiquette?"

"Scots?" asked Judith, widening her eyes. "Of course. We're not barbarians, you know."

"Dragons."

"What makes you think we're a people? I could just be a witch."

William chuckled. "To begin with, you're very well-preserved, even for the age you claim."

"Clean living and a pure soul. Or possibly a pact with the devil. Take your pick."

"So were your parents, from what I've heard," William went on, ignoring her riposte. "And nobody's quite sure how old your brothers are, nor what happens in the north wing of your castle. In fact, one or two of your servants seem quite unable to discuss the matter. I've never heard of spells that would let one take inhuman form, and"—his eyes traveled over her, for once without heat—"you're not wearing the sort of jewelry that would be a focus for any kind of powerful shape-shifting. That means your…other shape…is likely to be natural, and the odds are good that it runs in your blood. Besides, your family's sorcerous ability is a matter of historical record."

When he mentioned Colin and Stephen, Judith lost the urge to play. She listened to the rest of his evidence with numb lips and a cold face. "Whose records would those be?" she asked, her voice dropping. "Your master's? I was thinking it very generous of you to spend all this time working on behalf of a poor boy's ghost or a little village in the middle of nowhere. But as I said, you're no amateur."

"I'm not new to magic, no," he said. His eyes were narrow again, and the look of a decision in progress was back on his face. "That doesn't mean I have a master."

Judith snorted, dragon-like. "You're not new to magic. You're not new to firearms. You can find 'historical records' concerning my kin. You're carrying a whopping great chunk of magical craftsmanship, and you sneak off to Aberdeen for secret meetings. You're working for someone, Mr. Arundell. Who is it?"

She watched him as he thought of what to say. For the most part, he didn't look that impressive. The trip through the forest was no easy one, particularly for a mortal who didn't know where he was going. Burrs and briars had attached themselves to William's coat; his trouser cuffs were muddy; and there was a clump of pine needles in his hair. By appearances, he was in far over his head—until one got to the pistol and the expression on his face.

Not new to magic might have been quite an understatement.

At last, William shifted his weight slightly. "See here," he said. "If you give me your word that you won't try to damage me, I'll put the gun down. We're both reasonable people. The person at work here probably isn't—and we both want to see him stopped. Or her. We could be far more effective together."

"If you're not the killer," said Judith. "You said you're fairly certain I'm not. I didn't say any such thing about you."

"Why would I have told you about the boy if I was?" William pointed out. "You almost never go to Belholm. Odds are you'd never have heard."

There were possibilities—that he knew someone else was going to tell her and wanted to get there first, that he was telling her so that she'd think they were on the same side because he had a larger plan—but those options all seemed too complicated to be likely, especially now. Besides, she only had to give her word.

"I won't hurt you," she said. "I swear it."

"By the stars and the sun."

She hadn't intended to lie, but she curled her lip anyhow when he asked for the oath. He *was* good, and she didn't like it. "By the stars and the sun," she said, "I promise that, unless you try to kill or do grave bodily harm to me or mine, I will make no attempt to harm you."

Judith felt the bindings settle about her, constricting the dragon part of her nature. She'd never been certain whether the oath would bind her as fully as it would one of the real immortals—she hadn't taken it more than three times in her life—but it would assuredly hinder her.

With a nod, William returned the pistol to his coat. "When I said I wasn't a policeman," he said slowly, "I was telling the truth. Just not all of it."

"You were misleading me? Imagine that."

"Let's not throw stones at each other's glass houses, hmm?"

"Fair," said Judith. "Speaking of houses—" She looked around indicatively. It was almost full dark. That wouldn't be a physical problem for her, but she wasn't angry enough with William to make him stumble into trees more than necessary. Nor did she want the village discussing how they'd both disappeared for hours at nightfall. She was glad she'd worn old clothing. Transforming was hard on a new wardrobe, when the magic didn't recognize clothing as part of her, and she could only imagine the reaction if she came back with William at her side and her shirt in tatters. "Can you explain while we walk?"

"Glad to," said William.

Seeing in the dark didn't seem to be a problem for him, it turned out, but he still didn't know the woods nearly as well as she did. They went in silence until they reached the main path, and it startled Judith a little when William spoke again.

"There's a branch of the government that concerns itself with magic and, ah, otherwise unknown beings."

"Monsters," said Judith, rolling her eyes in the darkness. "I won't start crying if you say it. I won't slap you either."

"You don't seem the slapping kind."

"No. No point in hitting if you don't break bones." Brothers didn't count, and that had all been years ago. And she'd at least bloodied Stephen's nose back then. "Go on. I take it you belong to them."

"I wouldn't put it that way."

"I'm sure you wouldn't. And?"

"The boy's ghost contacted one of our other agents. He'd felt the person who killed him using that death to make contact with the demons and thought that someone ought to be told. He was a brave young chap, it appears, and a keen one. Whoever he was."

There was genuine regret in William's voice. Judith had heard its like a thousand times. On occasion, it had come from her lips or her pen.

I regret to inform you, madam, that your son…

In sympathy, she reached toward him, only to think better of the impulse at the last second and pull her hand back. If William noticed, he was well-mannered enough not to show it. Judith cleared her throat. "And you tracked the killer here. More or less."

"More or less," said William. Looking down the path, he laughed ruefully. "I confess I had thought this was going to be a much simpler affair."

"That's how it usually goes, isn't it?"

"Quite so."

The sky was dark now, and the haze from earlier lingered, hiding both stars and moon. Judith let her mind sort itself out, shunting surprise and confusion off bit by bit until it could get at the important questions and the really disturbing truths.

"Very well," she said. "What do you know about this killer?"

"Not much. I didn't see a face or a very defined shape."

"I didn't know you'd seen anything at all."

"It's a spell. And a fairly new one. I couldn't entirely explain how it works," he said, holding up a hand.

She grinned. "Don't worry. I'm not my brother Colin. I wasn't going to ask. So—"

"Tall and thin. As I said, the shape wasn't very clear—that is, when I suspected you, I thought you'd been wearing a large coat, perhaps—" He cleared his throat, and she half saw, half felt him glance toward her breasts.

Inconvenient memory brought with it an even less convenient surge of lust. "Let's take it on faith that I'm not insulted," she said roughly. "Did you use the same spell at Finlay's?"

"With similar results—and I saw the demons that time." He paused, then added, "I went back after our encounter. At night, as I suspect Mrs. Simon was good enough to inform you. There was a larger demon in the forest as well."

At Judith's sides, both her hands curled into claws. She drew in a rippling, half-snarled breath through her teeth. The rat-things had angered her, but they'd not been large enough to count as real trespassers. A bigger demon…in her territory…and threatening William… That was a different story entirely.

"What became of it?" she bit out.

"Ah—dead," William replied. He sounded startled, and she could see the whites of his eyes for a moment, but he didn't shrink away. "As you've seen, I'm not in the habit of wandering about unarmed."

"Wise," she said, the urge to defend subsiding. "As far as the killer goes, I can only tell you that Stewart's cow was the first such killing I've heard of, and I hear of most things in Loch Arach. But I take it there's a reason our man—or woman, I suppose—wants to summon demons here."

"Yes," said William. "I was hoping you knew."

Judith shook her head. "Offhand? No. I'm sure I can think of reasons. Perhaps my brothers can as well. I'll let you know once I've spoken to them."

"Thank you," said William. Once more, he hesitated. Then he looked soberly at her. "Judith," he said slowly, "you know I can't *not* report what I've seen, don't you?"

She hadn't thought of it, but hearing the words brought no sense of surprise and a leaden feeling of inevitability. "Nay, I don't suppose you could."

"You're not going to say anything else about it?" he asked. They were close to the castle now.

Judith shrugged. "Is there aught to say on the matter? You've my word not to harm you already. 'Tis unlikely I could find the words to sway you. Raging against what is and cannot be otherwise has never been to my tastes. Besides," she admitted, "I'd like as not do the same were I in your shoes."

"Ah," he said. "I—appreciate that."

"Glad to be of service, Master Arundell."

Wisely, he changed the subject. "If I may say so, you speak—differently sometimes. Just now, for instance. It's not only sounding more Scottish. The words are different too."

"Oh," said Judith. She hadn't been conscious of the slip, but thinking back, she could hear it in her own speech. "It's how people talked when I was young. One goes back in times of strain."

"Yes, quite," said William. "I'm sure I've done it myself."

She saw him struggling between etiquette and

curiosity. As they came to the fork in the road, one lane leading to the castle and the other to the village, Judith smiled. "A hundred and eighty years ago." Sixty seemed quite young to her in retrospect, though she hadn't thought so at the time. "Good night, William."

Twenty-three

As he walked back to the village, William began to try to compose a report in his head.

> Lady MacAlasdair not the killer. Actually a dragon, as is family. Unsure how this happened. Possibly all several hundred years old. Relevance to case unknown. Just thought you should be aware of situation.

It didn't sound good. Nothing sounded very good in the terse phrases that most easily lent themselves to ciphering, but William discovered that he couldn't even think of a long and flowery version that suited him particularly well.

> Dear Sir: A further development has come to my attention and recommends itself to your probable interest. Lady MacAlasdair—

No.
On the face of it, the news was as probable as several

NIGHT OF THE HIGHLAND DRAGON

other incidents he'd written up. In Belgium, an eyeless little thing made of clay had tried to kill him with a pair of garden shears. After he'd shot the homunculus and its master, and put a torch to the man's cellar-slash-"laboratory," William had reported the incident quickly, faithfully, and in detail. Watkins had asked questions, but none about the basic strangeness of the matter. Basic strangeness was what D Branch dealt in.

But—dragons. It sounded so very nursery tale, as if the next thing to happen would involve a poisoned apple or a good fairy.

For all he knew, it might. William shook his head, and then stopped.

Even lost in thought, he made a habit of keeping his eyes and ears open. That was especially true on the open road, and doubly so in his current time and place. He'd distinctly seen movement up ahead of him. He turned his head and spotted a human figure walking toward him.

"Hallo?" William called, trying to sound like a nervous traveler. The medallion was safely tucked away in his bag, but it still lent him some virtue. His vision in the cloudy night was as good as it would have been with a clear sky and a full moon. He rested one hand on the silver-loaded pistol in his pocket. "Er—"

"What?" The voice was male, with an educated version of the local accent, and irritated. "Yes?"

"Sorry," said William. "Just a touch jumpy in this darkness."

With both of the men walking forward, the distance closed rapidly. William recognized Ross MacDougal, in a warm coat and hat, with a basket on one arm.

His face looked pale, but that could have easily been the light.

He gave William a tight smile. "I can't say I blame you. It's one step from wilderness out here." Ross looked from William to the road that stretched beyond him and frowned suddenly. "Are you coming from the castle?"

"Oh yes," said William, surprised at the other man's expression. "Wanted to drop by and offer my assistance, naturally, with this dreadful fire business. And to see what provisions are being made for food and mail and so forth. I thought the lady would know, if anyone did."

"Oh aye," said MacDougal, his expression reluctantly easing. "Did she?"

"I don't know," said William. If the man disapproved of William calling on Judith, it was best to make the story as innocent as possible. "She was busy. I left a card with her butler and waited for a while, but a man has only so much patience. Particularly at suppertime. I'm impressed by your self-discipline, if you're coming out now."

"I don't mind about supper as much as some," said Ross with a faint chuckle. He gestured toward the basket. "My mother set her heart on sending some of her preserves up to the castle, and I think a loaf of bread as well. As if they don't have enough—but you know how women are, I'm sure."

"I've a passing acquaintance with the breed," said William. "Though not of mothers for some years. It's good of you to take the trouble. Especially as she sent you so late."

Ross glanced away. "Ah. Well," he said, "I'd meant to come earlier, and indeed I had started before the sun went down. But I ran into business in the village, you see."

From the way he was acting, *business* was likely to mean one of the female inhabitants. William chuckled. "Quite understandable. And I'm sure everything will taste just as good in the evening."

"If they're busy up at the castle," Ross said, "perhaps I shouldn't intrude on them."

"Oh, I don't know. Lady MacAlasdair might only have been avoiding me." William smiled and made a self-deprecating gesture. "Englishmen aren't very popular with a few people in these parts. And even if she is busy, the kitchen servants likely won't all be, will they? I'd imagine you'd at least be able to hand the goods over, and they might give you a cup of tea as well."

"That's a cheerful thought," Ross said. "You're disposed to be very helpful, Mr. Arundell, from everything I've seen. Do you have any intention of making your visit permanent?"

"Oh no," said William. "Charming place and all that, but I don't know that I could spend very long away from London."

"You must have been able to stay in the better sections," said Ross, pursing his mouth. "But I'll not deny those are quite nice. Will you be staying the winter, at least?"

"You know, I'm not sure," William said and fought back the urge to sigh. Spending the winter on a Scottish mountaintop had not been in his plans when he'd first arrived. Now it wasn't such a grim prospect—and that was a bad sign in itself. "My plans were never fixed. It depends very much on what news I receive from home, I suppose."

"Oh," said Ross. "Well. I'd best be getting on, lest we both end up missing our suppers. Good evening to you."

"Good evening," said William, and he walked on.

Only a few minutes after he'd started walking again, he regretted leaving Ross behind. Not that he was so very attached to the other man's company, but talking to him had been a distraction. Once William was alone, his thoughts started circling once more, producing and discarding drafts of a letter, interspersed with images of Judith.

In dragon form, naturally, she'd have been a sight to remain with him for his whole life, even if he hadn't known her at all, and perhaps a sight to trouble his sleep as well. Although she'd counted herself among the monsters, she hadn't looked like the horrors William had encountered before. Once he'd gotten past his shock, he'd found her to be rather majestic, an unsettling description when he thought about it. He suspected that Watkins would find it even more alarming than he did.

Formally, after all, D Branch was loyal to only one source of majesty.

Watkins wasn't a man to act rashly, William told himself. None of them were. And D Branch was also small and widely stretched. The Germans were making noises on one flank—though he doubted that would come to anything, one had to make the appropriate countermoves to ensure it didn't—the colonies were restless in several directions, and cults were springing up like mushrooms after bloody rainfall. Nobody was going to send an army up into the Highland mountains after a family that had, for at least a few hundred years, shown every sign of living as peaceful and productive British citizens.

And D Branch had known *something* about the family for a long time.

Unfortunately, that only argued more strongly that the MacAlasdairs had gone to not inconsiderable effort to keep the details secret. For the most part, they'd succeeded—and then William had come along.

Well, it wouldn't be the first time William had uncovered traditions their practitioners would have preferred to keep secret. It wouldn't, likely, even be the action he felt the most guilt over on his death-bed. He'd taken oaths to D Branch when he'd been inducted. Even if those oaths hadn't had magical force behind them, he would have taken them seriously. This was his job. This was his duty. If it had always been pleasant, *he* would have been paying *them*.

The lights of Mrs. Simon's house came as a relief. So, in its own way, did her shocked look and Claire's curious one, and the prompt-but-not-too-rote reeling off of the explanation William had devised, similar to the one he'd given Ross. With the light revealing the state of his clothes and hair, though, he added another touch. He'd followed a deer into the forest, on a whim, and had gotten well and truly lost before managing to locate the path out.

"You were lucky," said Mrs. Simon, shaking her

head. "I dinna' think there's anyone but the MacAlasdairs and their gamekeeper as know all the paths in that place, and perhaps no' even them." She clicked her tongue, a wordless commentary on the foolishness of even middle-aged men from London, and then changed the subject. "I've kept your supper hot for you. You're no' so late as all that."

"Thank you," he said and managed a smile. "If it wouldn't be too much trouble, I'll have it in my room. I've a letter that urgently needs writing."

"Aye, of course," she said, frowning. "No bad news from home, I hope."

"News," he said wearily. "I hope it's not bad."

Delay never improved anything. Once William reached his room, he sat at his desk and put down the evening's events in blunt, stark detail, neither omitting nor trying to disguise anything that had happened. At the last, he stopped, chewed on the top of his pen until he started to taste ink, and then added:

> *She guessed that I was going to inform you of her identity. As far as I could gather, she isn't angry about this and will make no effort to prevent it.*

She wasn't happy either. Judith had faced him with over a century's experience in accepting circumstances, and probably at least that much knowledge of the way men and their institutions behaved. Acceptance, and even expectation, didn't preclude resentment.

You've my word not to harm you already. Had that been the only thing keeping her from violence there on the path? Had his pistol been all that had saved his skin earlier? Tactically, professionally, William had thought it might have been, and had used every safeguard that came to hand against an unknown force. He didn't regret it.

But as a man, the possibility that Judith might seriously have wanted him dead made him weary and bleak, as if the color had drained out of the world around him.

He put his report into code, adding the first paragraph with the keyword and the last for pure disguise, folded it sharply, and sealed the envelope. The sound of paper against paper was too quiet. It should have been harsher: a slammed door, a dropped glass, a slapped face.

Dinner was outside his door when he finished. Writing, he'd heard the footsteps but not investigated, and either one of his hostesses had been tactful enough not to interrupt. A small tray held a covered dish that smelled of mutton and onions, as well as bread and tea and even a few iced biscuits. William had to smile at that last touch. Mrs. Simon's motherly instincts extended further than she would admit.

He wondered how far they'd go if she knew his real situation. The people of Loch Arach seemed very loyal. Even the servants who couldn't talk about the north wing hadn't really acted as though they wanted to, or as though the restriction particularly bothered them. Mrs. Simon was one of Judith's friends, as far as she had any in the village—or among mortals. William supposed it would be hard for beings like her to get attached to those with only human blood.

Food was waiting for him. He carried the tray over

to his desk, careful of the newly sealed letter. He ate mechanically and well; it did help. By the time he was done, the pain had receded to a gray dullness and a vast tiredness that spread all through his body. He told himself that it would recede further still, and that he knew his duty. He thought that he wouldn't be able to get the letter out first thing, in any case. He'd have to go down to Belholm with it, or at least find Young Hamish's temporary lodgings and ask whether he was still taking the mail.

He let sleep take over, soothing away shock and worry alike for a time.

Twenty-four

WITH THE HOUSE MOSTLY DARK AND THE SERVANTS safely busy or abed, Judith opened the door to the north wing. Beyond lay a short hallway with three rooms opening at equal distances from each other. The walls and floors were unadorned stone. It was safer that way. It was also colder, particularly as there'd been no fires in the place for a hundred years or more, and despite her thick wool wrapper, Judith shivered as she walked.

On the left was a solid iron door, massive and older than Judith. She kept it oiled and polished every month, just as she swept and dusted the other rooms with her own hands—servants didn't come into the north wing. Of everything in the castle, the upkeep of that door and the room behind it was most important. The large chamber, lined with silver runes and warding gems, was where the adolescent MacAlasdairs learned to control their transformations, and where Stephen had secluded himself while his curse had lasted.

That chamber wasn't Judith's destination that evening, and neither was the one on the right, where a vast inlaid table changed to show the condition of the land and the weather. She opened the middle door, a solid but more modest polished oak, and stepped into a plain stone room whose bare floor stretched away in all directions from a circular pool two feet wide. At the near edge, as a concession to flesh that at least *felt* mortal, she'd placed a green velvet cushion.

Shelves on one wall held old books and other devices, many of whose powers Judith herself was unclear about. A few swords and axes hung in brackets opposite them, and a circle with more inlaid runes occupied one corner of the room, but Judith's concern that night was for the pool. She lit the candles in their sconces, letting the smell of smoke and beeswax fill the room and begin to calm her nerves. Even she, least sorcerous among her family, knew that magic was best done with a steady mind.

After a few breaths, and after making sure she'd closed and locked the door behind her, Judith knelt on the cushion and rolled up her sleeves. The pool glimmered beneath her with a silver gleam that would have been out of place for any real water she'd ever seen. She'd never known where the "water" came from. It didn't rise or fall with the weather, as a real pool would have. Her father hadn't known either. Time swallowed knowledge, even for her bloodline.

Judith reached down and placed her palm against the surface of the pool. It was warm, and it gave at her touch, but her hand took a moment to break through. "Judith Mary MacAlasdair, daughter of Andrew Marcus MacAlasdair and Riona of the White Arms, seeks her kinsmen's aid and counsel."

The formality helped this time. She rarely used the scrying pool because she always felt the cost afterward, and particularly since Stephen's curse, she wasn't fond of magic. Just then, Judith welcomed her annoyance and her unfamiliarity with the ritual words.

This was going to be a hideous conversation.

The water wrapped itself around her fingers, gripping her hand with more-than-human strength. To either side, it clouded and colored. Stephen appeared first, on her right, with a thick dressing gown belted around him and his red-black brows drawn together in anticipatory worry. He was right—if Judith was using this means of communication, the situation was no common one—but if the same thought had occurred to Colin, he didn't show it when he appeared. He had his shirtsleeves rolled up and his collar unbuttoned, and he held a glass of wine in his free hand.

"A few weeks of our company and you're already missing us this much?" were his first words. "You're a pinnacle of sisterly affection, Judith, truly, but I'm afraid I can't oblige you. There *might* be worse fates than Scotland in winter, and yet none spring to mind."

"Might be worse fates than having you eating our supplies too," said Judith, "but I'm as puzzled as you are."

"What's gone wrong?" Stephen asked. "Are you well?"

"Aye, so far," said Judith. "But there've been a few things you should both know."

Quickly and bluntly, she sketched out the events of the last month. She included William's role working for a mysterious branch of the government. She talked about his visit to Aberdeen, although she did not even hint at kissing him, much less what they'd gotten up to on the train. Neither Stephen nor Colin was the sort of overprotective idiot one too often found among mortal men, and none of the three of them were under any illusions about the others' innocence, but there were things one did not discuss with family.

By the time she was finished, Stephen's mouth was a thin line. "So he knows everything."

"Not everything. He knows what I am. He can hazard a guess about what you two are. And has."

"Wonderful. By God, Judith," Stephen said, every atom the exasperated elder brother, "when I think of all the time and effort I spent—and you just let—"

"'Just let,' like hell," she shot back, drawing herself up to her full height. The pool wouldn't *show* that, granted, but it made her feel better. "The man followed me magically, which I'd no notion he could do. I'd transformed because I had to. He walked in on me at a bad moment, aye, and I'll hear not a word from either of you on *that* score, thank you very kindly."

"She has a point, Stephen. Not her fault you got a pretty girl for your intruder and she's stuck with some awful chap from Whitehall." Colin's silver-blue eyes glimmered with amusement, even now. "And I'll admit, of the three of us, I'm the most complicit in my own unmasking, grabbing at young women on balconies and so forth. Still, can't complain."

"Neither can I," admitted Stephen, allowing himself a slow and contented smile. Then he was back to sobriety, sighing. "But that's a far different situation from a government man. What are we to do about that?"

"Nothing *to* do, from what Judith's said." Colin shrugged. "Unless you want to kill him before he can get word out, Ju. I can't say I approve entirely if you do—seems a rotten thing to do to a chap just for doing his job, but I'm not there and you are. So—"

"*No!*" The answer tore itself from her throat, completely bypassing her damned brain. From the looks on her brothers' faces, it sounded just as vehement out in the air as it did in her ears. Bloody *hell.* "No, I gave him my word I wouldn't hurt him. He was holding a pistol on me," she added in a feeble attempt at justification. "And I don't just kill people."

In the past, she had. Or at least she'd killed for worse reasons than to protect her family, and the people in question had, despite uniforms and a degree of training, been far less able to defend themselves than William Arundell was.

This is not then. This is now. This is here.

Also, the idea of hurting him made her feel like being sick.

"No, we don't," Stephen said, his voice stern. It drew her back to the present moment, and she gave him a grateful smile. Let him think it was for supporting her on the principle.

"I said it seemed rotten, didn't I?" Colin sighed and sipped his wine. "Don't read me a sermon—I'm glad to fall in line with the *no bloodshed* policy of the new administration. And I might add that I saw this coming."

"Government agents and demons?" Judith asked.

"Well, thank you very much for warning me, Cassandra, I'm sure."

"Not *specifically*. But the world's smaller than the two of you are used to. It gets smaller every day, and people develop new forms of evidence too. There won't be much room for secrets in a decade or two," Colin said, "even on remote mountaintops."

The notion should have shaken the walls around her, even the floor beneath her feet. She'd never thought about not having to hide what she was—or about not being able to. Judith licked lips gone suddenly dry.

"We've not always been completely secret," said Stephen thoughtfully. "Father used to tell me that, when he was a young man, there were those in the Queen's court who knew of him and of other magical creatures. And the folk of the village knew us better back then, he said. At least a few of them. It was different after James, and more different still after Culloden."

Judith nodded, remembering a few of her own early years. "Things get lost," she said. "It's not a bad perspective. Particularly since, as Colin said, there's nothing we can do to keep William from reporting."

A thought began to take form, but it wasn't solid yet. She let it alone. Such things developed in time, or not.

"What about this other man? The killer?" Stephen asked.

"Could be a woman," Colin pointed out. "Nasty piece of work either way. Particularly as they've clearly gotten their grimy hands on some sort of magical knowledge. Might be best if we came in to help."

"Not a damned chance," said Judith before he'd finished talking. "Best thing we can do is spread all the possible targets out as far as possible. Plus, the two of you have civilians to look out for."

"We're all civilians, really," said Colin, "even you now."

"We still know what we know," said Judith. She liked Mina and Reggie, and she knew from stories that they were good in a pinch—but they hadn't been trained to fight either demons or men. "And your wives are mortal—even Mina can't heal like we do or stand up to as much damage—and Stephen has a child. No. None of you get within fifty miles of Loch Arach."

Being a reasonably kind sister, despite what Colin had said in their youth, she would never let on that she saw relief warring with concern on both their faces, and in serious danger of winning out in Stephen's. "There's truth in that, aye," he said, "though I'll not sleep easy until you've found this…person."

"If it helps," Judith said dryly, "I don't think I'll be sleeping all that well either. But it's not been so long since I risked my life for a living, and I doubt this sorcerer could threaten me much in a fair fight. It's only a matter of digging the rat out of his lair—and whatever Mr. Arundell's faults, he's likely had more training in *that* than any of the three of us. Now that he's not applying it to me, with any luck, it'll point him in the right direction before long."

"He's got to be good for something, after all," said Colin. "Like, *mmm*, thistles, I believe?"

"You're a foolish city lad, Colin MacAlasdair," Judith replied. "And he's a good man. Takes his job seriously—and it's a serious job. If he hadn't exposed us, we'd all think very highly of him."

"I don't think highly of anyone who takes things seriously," said Colin with a grin. "Matter of principle, that. But I'll admit he's probably quite admirable, considered from a remote and lofty vantage point."

"I hope so, for all our sakes," said Stephen, "and that his masters are as well. Is there anything more, Judith?"

She shook her head. The distance talking was beginning to drain her now, sending lassitude throughout her whole body—like being drunk without the giddiness. She stifled a yawn, incongruous to the situation and subject though the urge was. "Everyone well at your ends?"

"Aye," said Stephen. "Anna's walking now. We may need a faster nanny."

"Just wait until she flies," said Colin cheerfully. "We're keeping in one piece, Judith. And I'll let you go so you can say the same."

They said their good-byes and departed, leaving Judith kneeling before the pool. It took considerable effort of will to get herself to her feet, and she thought that it might not all be magic. The day had been full of activity, and high emotions took their own toll.

Around her, the castle was very dark, very large, and very empty. She walked back to her room and listened to her own footfalls echoing down the winding hallway.

Twenty-five

"NOTE FOR YOU, MR. ARUNDELL," SAID CLAIRE, handing over the envelope practically as William stepped in the door. "Ben brought it just now. Ben Murray," she added, when he looked blank. "He's one of the footmen up at the castle."

"Oh?" William asked. None of his sudden interest showed—not the way his heart sped up, nor the twin thrills of hope and dread that ran through him as he took the note. Any half-decent agent would have been able to hide those things, and he was far more than that. He felt them all the same. "I'm much obliged to you, Miss Simon."

He didn't open the envelope in front of her, obliged or not. And curious or not, Claire was too well-brought-up to ask or even to look disappointed when William vanished into his rooms. Her interest was plain, but William didn't think it was the same interest she'd displayed when he'd first arrived. At sixteen, Claire was likely as keen to know about an intrigue as she was to be a part of one herself.

There was no address on the front of the letter, only

his name, and the hand was a round copperplate, more
florid than he would have expected from Judith—until
he recalled that she'd likely learned to write back
when George the Second was on the throne. The *s*
in "Mister" was just a touch elongated, now that he
looked closely.

With the note in his hand, he spared a moment to
wonder: good news or bad? *I've found out who the killer
is, go to work* or *On second thought, leave this place or I'll
have you beheaded?* There were plenty of ways for a
woman as smart as Judith to get around an oath.

After making inquiries, he'd given his report to
Young Hamish that morning. The Connoh family had
set up temporary shop out of their lodgings, mostly
selling papers and taking in mail. The report would go
out tomorrow. He couldn't do anything about it now,
even if he'd wanted to.

He flipped the paper open.

The words ran smoothly in the same hand that had
addressed the envelope, black ink on thick parchment.

William:

> *If your crowded social schedule permits it, I would
> welcome your company for dinner tonight at seven.
> Send a reply by Claire. The excuse for a walk will do
> her good, and Agnes will thank you for the respite.*

> > > > > *Judith*

Not a death threat: if she intended to poison the
soup, she wasn't going to warn him about it. Nor did

she seem to want him gone immediately. The note revealed only that much. There were any number of reasons—businesslike, friendly, and hostile—that she might want to talk with him.

She had used both of their first names. William allowed himself to think that was a decent sign and to smile before he sat down to compose his reply of thanks and acceptance, showing his hand no more than she had done. He would go in as an agent to an unproven power, not assuming alliance, friendship, or more.

"Please tell your mother that I'll be away for dinner," he said when he handed Claire his reply.

"You will? At the castle?" she asked, round-eyed, and then caught herself. "Begging your pardon, Mr. Arundell. I dinna' mean to pry."

"No harm done," he replied with a smile. And there was no harm in telling her—she was a bright girl, and the conclusions were easy to draw.

Judith must have known that, he thought as he watched Claire half run off toward the road. She'd been the castle's lady for generations, and Mrs. Simon's friend for all of Claire's life. She would have predicted that Claire would guess, which meant that the dinner would be public knowledge in Loch Arach by the next morning.

That was another piece of evidence against her doing him any harm at dinner. William doubted that all of the villagers were constrained, magically or otherwise, not to talk about visitors who disappeared after paying a visit to the castle. Odds were that she was planning to let him walk back out again, and probably even in his right mind.

He washed, shaved, and dug evening clothes out of the back of his wardrobe. He'd had them unpacked and pressed when he'd first arrived, just in case, and now was glad he had. Mrs. Simon wasn't around to do it on short notice, and even if Loch Arach had been large enough to offer replacements at the last minute, he was particular to certain tricks his tailor had. The cut and fabric of the coat, for instance, were perfect for looking distinguished while hiding the presence of a gun at his hip. Small charms sewn into the lining of the shirt warded off food-borne enchantments of the mind and body, and there were small sheaths in the shirtsleeves for flat knives.

Ordinary tailors might make gentlemen. D Branch's tailors kept them alive.

William snapped on silver cuff links, made certain his tie was crisp and correct, and peered at himself in the cloudy mirror over the dresser. Everything was in place. All the armor was polished, the horse saddled, and the lance sharpened. Outside, the sun was halfway down behind the mountain, and the clock on the wall said that it was half past six.

He walked out of the boardinghouse and briskly up the road toward the dragon's lair.

❧

Janssen met him at the door, his own black coat and white shirt freshly pressed and his young face schooled to comic formality. "Mr. Arundell," he said, as if neither of them had seen the other in shirtsleeves, covered in ash and sweating, just a few days before. "May I show you into the drawing room, sir?"

"Yes, of course," said William with equal formality.

The castle felt different as he entered. The only changes he could identify offhand were the blazing lights along the hallway and the background noises that told him servants were busy in the rooms out of his sight. Both could merely have been products of the difference in time. It was evening now and had been earlier when he'd visited before.

More than that, and more nebulous, was the feeling that ran through the place, one of patient anticipation, of waiting to see—something. William wondered whether the servants themselves were aware of that, whether even Judith was, or whether the castle itself was waiting. After centuries hosting a family like the MacAlasdairs, the place could have a will of its own.

Then again, everything he felt could have come out of his own head.

That had changed enough over the last few weeks.

There was a fire in the parlor. Finding a seat, William folded his hands in his lap and stared at it, clearing his mind and calming his nerves with every carefully steady breath. He kept his eyes on the leaping flames until he heard the door open. Then he turned to greet Judith—and couldn't even think of looking anywhere else.

In their acquaintance, she'd almost always dressed well, but he'd never seen her dressed formally before, never witnessed on her the results of such time and care as ladies spent even for dinner in company. Secluded in Loch Arach, William had almost begun to forget those customs.

Now he remembered.

Judith stood in the doorway, a faint smile of greeting on her face. Plaid taffeta, green and blue and red, rose in a narrow skirt to her slim waist, then clung to her full breasts before fading to thin bands over her shoulders. Gold net took up the dress then, in long sleeves and a high neck that might have been modest if they hadn't been nearly transparent. On her left hand, the emerald ring caught the light and sent back green fire. Matching earrings nearly glowed against her neck. Her hair was twisted up, smooth and elegant, and held in place with gold pins.

If she'd had her hand on a dog or a child, she could have been a portrait: *Lady MacAlasdair*. If she'd had a throne, she could have been a queen—or a goddess.

Then she grinned at William, which didn't dispel the impression completely, but at least made her look mortal again and approachable. "Full battle kit for both of us, aye?"

"Diplomatic regalia, I'd rather think."

"Diplomacy's just war of another sort," she said, but without sharpness. "But the food, I vow, will be a damned sight better."

It was. William's experience of Scottish food had already given the lie, for the most part, to the bad jokes he'd heard in London clubs, but Judith's cook far outdid the pub food and even surpassed Mrs. Simon—though, granted, the woman probably had more to work with. He ate soup and beef and herring, all with excellent wine, though he only allowed himself to drink a little. Despite appearances, he was on duty.

While they ate, the conversation was not of anything

significant. Footmen were still in the room, removing plates or bringing over more servings, Janssen appeared to pour wine, and there was no privacy to be had. They spoke of racing and the theater and politics, of how the Connohs were doing after the fire and how Shaw was recovering, and even a little of their pasts, though neither of them revealed much. None of it was important to William's goals, but he was too absorbed to be impatient. When Judith stood up to end the meal, he actually felt like protesting.

As he'd expected, she invited him into the drawing room. The evening wasn't over and probably wouldn't be for a while yet. But it would, he knew, turn most decidedly toward business, and he couldn't help regretting that.

Regrets didn't matter. Neither did his desires. He didn't let himself voice either, even inside his own head. He smiled and followed Judith back to the drawing room.

"I assumed that you drink brandy," she said as a footman opened the door and William saw a carafe and two half-full glasses on the table inside. "With just the two of us, it'd be a wee bit awkward separating the women and men for it as usual."

"I do," he said. The notion made him smile. It also reminded him that they were the only two people in the room, once the footman had closed the door behind them, and brought to his mind a sharp awareness of how improper the situation was. His pulse began to speed up, and it was an effort to speak evenly. "And you? Cigars as well?"

She laughed and seated herself on a couch, relaxing

against the cushions. Had she been less alert, the pose would have been extremely languid. "Both, in my day. I generally keep to drink these days. 'Tis passing hard to get cigars up here—most of the locals stick to pipes, and I never acquired that habit."

"I can't imagine you with a pipe." He *could* imagine her with a cigar in one hand, lounging just as she was, and the mental picture had a surprisingly immediate physical appeal. William sat down quickly.

Judith took one of the glasses but didn't drink. She didn't speak either, only looked from him to the liquor, as if she was reading its dark ripples for signs. Perhaps she was. Shadows from the leaping flames, stirred to fresh life in the fireplace, danced on the thick carpet between them.

"So," she finally said. She looked up from the untouched brandy and met William's eyes. All humor had left her voice now. It wasn't solemn or hostile, but completely businesslike. "You've this organization of yours. I know you can't be telling me everything, but I do want to know more. And I want to know what you can do for us."

Twenty-six

WILLIAM FROWNED. JUDITH DIDN'T THINK THERE WAS either displeasure or surprise in the look. More, he was sorting through what he knew, determining how much he could or should tell her—and perhaps how much he should ask in return. "I can think of a number of places to start," he finally said. "What do you want to know?"

And the ball returned to her side of the court. She found that she was enjoying the exchange, both for the challenge of question and response and, to her surprise, for the relief of telling William the truth. She had been honest with so few people about who she was. With this man, it felt welcome rather than dangerous.

Of course, that itself was a danger.

"You said your people 'concerned yourselves' with magic and monsters," she replied, drawing herself back toward caution. "To what end?"

"The defense of the realm, of course."

"Of course," said Judith dryly. She took a sip of her brandy. "Defense of what part of it? Against what?"

"Defense of the people and their lawful rulers," he said, startled that she would even have to ask, "against either their personal enemies, as in this case, or the enemies of the nation."

Judith chuckled, and the sound was low and dark even to her own ears. "When I was a child, *we* would have been the enemies of your nation."

"Are you now?"

"I couldn't speak for everyone in Scotland, nor even everyone in the village," Judith said, "and I certainly don't know what everybody in England thinks of us, but I doubt it. Those of us who want independence try to get it at the ballot box these days and by shouting in Parliament. 'Tis less bloody, most of the time."

"And what do you think of it?" William asked, eyes keen and blue.

Judith shrugged. "If it comes in its time, I'll be happy enough. If it doesn't—we're not badly treated here. I'm not the political my father and sister were. One king or queen is as good as another, provided they keep to their place and that place is far from me. London's far enough." She shifted on the couch, taking the reins back. "But so are the nation's enemies. Who are they now? The Russians? The Germans? Or are you being traditional these days and hating the French?"

"All three and more, should they move against us." With a small *click*, William set his brandy glass down on a small table. "If you're old enough to be cynical about the ways of nations, you're old enough to know why I'm not ashamed to say that. We don't seek conquest anymore—"

"Not on *this* continent," said Judith, and she saw him wince.

Nonetheless, he continued. "And the enemies I've encountered, generally speaking, have either been the foes of all natural life or have dealt extensively with those foes. For the most part, they've also been subjects of Her Majesty, nominally speaking."

"Which is why you're here."

"Which is why I'm here, yes. I don't believe we're dealing with a German agent or a rebellious Irishman."

"For one thing," said Judith, "the accent would have stood out a wee bit." She sighed. "If your targets are mostly like this killer of ours, I can't fault you. But what would you do with my family? We're far from completely human, but we're thinking beings, and we're not acting against the Crown. Would you press-gang us into your service or exile us from your borders to be sure we never become a threat? Will you, in fact?" She caught his eyes. "I assume that your superiors know already, or will very soon."

"Yes," he said unflinchingly, "but I don't know."

"At least you're honest about it," she said and didn't say *now* or *about that*. Glass houses and all.

William rubbed his forehead. "To the best of my knowledge," he said, "and bearing in mind that I doubt I know everything we do or have done, we've never forced anyone into service. That's a good way to wind up with a traitor in your midst, and spells can't cover everything. You would know that, wouldn't you?"

"Hmm?" Judith asked, caught off guard by the rapid change of subject.

"Your servants can't talk about certain parts of the castle, can they?"

"Some can't."

"How many?" William's face sharpened. "In fact, how many of the villagers still have their own, uninfluenced minds?"

"Almost all," Judith replied coldly, all the more so because the question did make her squirm a touch inside. "Nobody who works in the castle can talk about certain parts. It's no harder an oath, I'd wager, than what your own masters demand. And, like you, they take it voluntarily."

"And overlook being asked. Just like their families overlook the 'giant eagles,' or how well-preserved your family stays—or, I suspect, how much you look like a…great-aunt?"

"Great-grandmother," said Judith with a tight little smile. "And aye. They do." She straightened her back and lifted her head. "There've been no clearances in Loch Arach. Nobody loses his farm because we're wanting a flock of sheep or a patch of land for hunting. Nobody starves in a bad winter, and fewer perish of disease or illness than might if we didn't make it worthwhile for doctors to abide here. We've a good school and scholarships for any lad who passes the exams, and I believe by the standards of London, I treat my servants very well."

Knowing that he'd be unable to deny any of it, she flung the words in his face. William let them come, gave them due and thoughtful consideration, and then nodded. "And all you ask is…"

"Loyalty. And the ability to overlook a few things

now and again. Human beings are quite good at that, and we're all eager to do it in one area or another." She reached for the brandy again. "I saw London, William. I saw a fair few cities, in fact, and I fought in a war or three. The civilized world lives and breathes willful blindness."

He didn't try to deny that either, but smiled wry acknowledgment, and then said, "Where you're concerned, it might not be able to for very much longer."

"That's what my brother said. That's why I'm talking to you. And I still wait upon an answer to my question."

"To the best of my knowledge," William repeated slowly, "we've never forced anyone into our service. That said, we've also never before encountered anyone with…" He hesitated and found, to his credit, perhaps the most tactful words that existed to describe the MacAlasdairs. "…so much clear nonhuman influence. Not anyone inclined to discourse, at least."

"Not anyone who didn't see you as a meal, you mean," said Judith.

"Or building materials." He grimaced in memory.

That allusion didn't match any race Judith had heard of, but she hadn't made a comprehensive study. "How old are you?"

"As an institution, I take it? In our current form, around forty years. If my memory serves, and if my superiors were being honest with me, we more or less organized ourselves after the Crimea. Before that"—he spread his hands—"efforts here and there. Mostly scattershot. I'm given to understand that Cromwell and his crowd set us back considerably—and the first of the

Stuarts wasn't much help either, though I'm sorry for any offense that gives you."

"None at all," Judith said with a snort. "We've had no reason to be fond of James up here—and particularly not in my family. He was before my time, but my mother had a number of hard names for the man, and she a soft-spoken lady by custom." She smiled at the memory, then moved on. "Are you in the army's command? Scotland Yard's?"

William shook his head. "I'm no policeman. And the Yard doesn't get along very well with us, in truth. The honest ones are, I suspect, *too* honest to approve of covert activities."

"Soldiers are a more practical lot," Judith agreed. "Mostly."

"Mostly." Sensing, as she did, that they'd more or less crossed the Rubicon, and that the ground, if not precisely safe, was less deadly, he relaxed and eyed her contemplatively. "Do you speak from experience?"

"Aye. I was a navy man most of my life, but I spent a bit of time in the army as well. Though that was mostly in the colonies. America, I mean."

"A navy 'man'?" he asked, and his eyes dropped just for a second to her breasts. She felt the gaze as if he'd brushed his hand across her bodice, and her nipples stiffened. Evening dress was good for camouflage; she was lucky that way.

She shrugged one shoulder, making the motion slow and fluid, and smiled at him. William shifted in his seat. Good. The score was even again. "I'm no great sorcerer," she said, "and I couldn't make very much difference in my appearance, but if I dress the part and act it, I've enough magic to cover any slight flaws. From the stories I hear, there were plenty of women who managed it with only trousers and a little binding. Once your mates are your mates, nobody really cares very much."

"I'd imagine a few of them would care *too* much," William said.

"Scum is scum. It'd be the same for a pretty boy. I had a few other advantages," she added, remembering the gunner's mate on her first ship. When she'd broken his jaw, there had been a few comments about how she was stronger than she looked; then they'd gone ashore and he'd vanished. Not everyone had the resources Judith did. Lynn would be one less problem for those who didn't. She studied William. "You'd have been an officer, I'd think."

"I would have, had I gone into the regular forces. My parents hated the idea. They didn't have any other children, and my mother couldn't bear the idea of me going off for years at a time, to say nothing of getting shot at. But I wanted to serve," William said, affectionately amused by his past self. "My uncle offered me another way. He was an…esoteric sort of scholar, you might say. Knew a few of the right people."

"It hardly kept you from getting shot at," Judith said, "from what you mentioned before."

"No. But my parents never knew I was in the line of fire, and that was the important thing. They died thinking that I analyzed reports for the Home Secretary." He took another sip of his brandy. "For that matter, I'm surprised you weren't an officer—of the two of us, you're the one with the title."

"It wouldn't bear close inspection. Neither would I. And they care more about background for officers, or they used to. It was easier to be just another boy who'd run off to sea."

"Oh," said William.

Curiosity was clear in his face. Judith saw a thousand questions there. But she didn't see fear or hate, or what she now realized she'd dreaded more—a come-look-at-the-freak sort of condescension. Instead, what lit his eyes and parted his lips was interest—maybe even wonder—and her body responded, going soft and wet and a little light-headed.

No. Not yet. Business first.

She swallowed. "So," she said, "what happens once your superiors get your report?"

"I hope they'll deal with you and your family in a civilized manner." William paused. "In fact, I'll give my word that, as far as it's in my power, I'll make certain that they do. But I'd be lying if I offered any guarantees."

"And you never lie?"

"I try to avoid it, when possible. It causes complications."

"Truth is easier to remember," said Judith. She got to her feet, waved William back to his seat on the sofa as he started to rise, and walked over to the window. Pushing the drapes aside, she looked out.

A wide expanse of black met her eye, the castle buildings and various trees darker shapes within. She could barely make out a few points of light off in the village. It was funny how far away half an hour's walk could look.

Judith turned back and saw William watching her. "Tell them," she said, "that my family is very old. We've seen a great deal—my father's father was a legionary in Rome. And though knowledge vanishes with the generations, we've still enough of it, and enough power, to be good allies."

She didn't say, *Or bad enemies*. It was in better taste in a bargain to let the man across the table draw his own conclusions.

"I will," said William, and then he did get to his feet. He was a strong figure, all height and broad shoulders, with the ruddy glint of his hair contrasting with his black wool coat. He was probably armed— he'd have been a fool if he wasn't. It did not detract from his appeal. "And we can work together in the meantime against this threat to both of us?"

"Aye," said Judith. "We can. Which leaves me with only one more question."

"Oh?" he asked, and he must have sensed the shift in her demeanor, for his mouth softened, a sensual smile curling around the corners.

As she'd been wanting to do all night, Judith stepped toward him and held out a hand. "There are many ways of sealing an alliance," she said, "and we've a more pleasant option than most. The view from my window is very fine, if you'd care to see it."

"Oh," he repeated, his voice dropping, and he kissed the back of her hand. "I most certainly would."

Twenty-seven

JUDITH LACED HER FINGERS THROUGH WILLIAM'S AND led him out into the hallway. Only years of practice allowed him to note his surroundings in the journey that followed. Otherwise, he would have walked through the hall and up the stairs like a blind man, seeing only the slim curves of Judith's body, hearing only the rustling of her skirts, feeling nothing but the touch of her hand on his and the resulting waves of lust running through his body. The temptation to get lost in such sensations was almost overwhelming as it was.

He did see stonework and tapestries, lamps in brass sconces and pictures on the wall—landscapes, and studies of fruit and objects, but no portraits. He glanced at doors and was reasonably certain that he could find his way back out if he needed to. Even with Judith a scant few inches away, and with the promise of much more to follow, he didn't forget the possibility of danger.

That awareness did nothing to shift his mood. Rather, it heightened his arousal. He'd been to bed with dangerous women before, even with women who might have tried to kill him—best to assume, he'd learned early, that *everyone* might try that—but never had he felt the risk so close at hand. Power walked beside him, and mystery, and those things drew him to Judith just as much as full breasts and bright eyes.

By the time they reached the top of the stairs, he was aching with desire. Several times he quashed the urge to pull Judith into a corner and kiss her. He'd seen no servants, and the halls weren't well lit any longer, but he knew great houses, and he knew people who were adept at not being seen. If Judith was waiting until the bedroom—well, she had to live in the village. He didn't and, knowing that, held himself back.

If Judith didn't go in for public display, neither did she seem worried. She led William onward with a faint smile and a smooth, unhesitant walk, the posture of a woman who'd long since known herself in her own place and capable of commanding anything around her. At that moment, William knew that included him—if not entirely, at least more so than he would have expected. If she'd bade him to kneel at her feet in the dark hallway, he would have done it. As the image came to mind, he drew a deep breath through his teeth and almost wished she would.

She didn't turn, but glancing back, she caught his gaze, and her smile deepened. "Almost there," she said. Her eyes were the dark green-black of the trees outside, shadowed with desire, and her lips curved, ripe and welcoming. "This place is betimes larger than I'd have it be."

"I was just thinking," William said, "that we should have met in a cottage somewhere."

Or he should have taken her in the drawing room—laid her on the couch and pushed up her skirt—but although the thought made his cock pulse and strain against his flies, he knew it wouldn't have been right. Much as he wanted Judith, and as half-jokingly as she'd said it, this *was* the close of an agreement and the beginning of an alliance. A degree of ritual was appropriate.

Besides, there was a certain torturous pleasure in anticipation.

Judith's bedroom was an island of sea-colored brocade and velvet, with a massive canopied bed that might have come from the century before. The sound of the closing door shut out time as well as the world outside. This was here and now, and the world stilled in anticipation.

"I'll need your assistance," Judith said, her voice low and silky. Almost touching him, she turned, showing a row of jet buttons down the back of her dress. "Women's clothing these days. 'Tis a wondrous thing that anyone manages to roger a lass."

"Some of us," William responded, "are patient men."

To his surprise, he found that he spoke truth. Yes, he hungered to touch her. Yes, he was breathing quickly by the time his fingers undid the first button. But he waited. He was careful. His awareness narrowed to each small, black oval, and each one undone was a drumbeat in his brain: *one* and *two* and *six* and *seven*, and his heartbeat matched the rhythm.

At the end, he brought his hands upward in one smooth line over Judith's corset, tracing her spine and making her shiver, and then pushed the silk to each side. It fell away from her shoulders, and her body, emerging, shone golden and sleek. She made a throaty sound of appreciation, then took matters into her own hands, stepping unhurriedly out of the cloud of taffeta and linen. A few quick motions at the front of her corset, and it too opened and fell away, leaving her naked save for jewelry and silk stockings.

"My God," said William, or he thought he did. Sounds definitely came out of his mouth, but he couldn't have sworn they were anything as organized as words. Forgetting gentlemanly behavior, he stared.

Naked, she lost neither dignity nor power. Judith made no move to cover herself. Her breasts, full and round with large dark nipples, were bared to his gaze, as was the triangle of black hair between her thighs. She set one hand on her hip and smiled at him, and William thought of classical statuary, of goddesses and queens, and also that he might actually die of lust.

"You're not very efficient," she said. "You could have started undressing minutes ago."

"I was appreciating the moment," he said, and this time his mouth did manage to shape words. All the same, his hands were quickly about their business. He might have popped a button or two in his haste, but he didn't care.

Judith watched, eyes filled with anticipation. When William undid his trousers and his cock finally sprang free, she ran her tongue slowly over her lower lip, and his previous statement about patience almost became a complete lie. With an immense effort of will, he managed to get himself free of his clothing.

She stepped into his arms then, her whole body naked and warm and vibrant against his. William kissed her slowly, learning again the feel of her lips and tongue, the taste of her mouth, and before he was done, he knew that her earlier calm had been at least partly show. Her nipples were hard against his chest, her breasts rubbing against him with every increasingly quick breath, and her hands locked at the middle of his back, holding him tightly against her.

When William finally pulled away, it was only to take the few steps to the bed. He led Judith this time, one arm around her waist, and she went eagerly with him. Side by side they tumbled onto the blankets. Already William was cupping Judith's breasts, and while panting, she was running her hands over his chest and sides, slow movements that nonetheless spoke of restlessness. So did the motions of her body—the small, involuntary circles of her hips and the way she pressed her breasts into his hands.

He was no less overcome. The world had truly narrowed now. He was barely aware of the bed he lay on, only that there was a surface. He did know that his breath was fast and hard, that he groaned as Judith's long fingers skimmed over his nipples and her hot mouth traced a line down his neck, that every time she writhed against him, the friction of her smooth thigh against his erection made him shudder with pleasure.

When Judith reached lower, William found some vestige of willpower and grasped her wrist. For a second, she gave him a puzzled look, black brows slanting together, swollen lips beginning to part in a question.

"My turn this time," he said.

For once in his experience of women, he knew he didn't need to worry about either hurting or overpowering his partner—even in human form, he knew there was strength enough to Judith—but chivalry still gentled his touch as he nudged her over onto her back and rose above her. He allowed himself only a fleeting and far too tempting moment of lying flush against her, feeling her legs beginning to part around him, and then slid lower, taking one of her nipples in his mouth as he'd wanted to do for, oh, ages now.

Judith moaned, deep and long. Her fingers threaded through William's hair, tugging a little but mostly just urging him onward as her body did, her back arching as he circled his tongue. Her own hair spread out on the coverlet, a black cloud around her flushed face. By the time he switched to the other breast, her head was tossing back and forth, her lower lip between her teeth in some attempt to at least quiet the sounds she was making.

It was not inordinately successful, that effort, which made William smile even as he took a firmer grip on his willpower. He didn't think he'd ever been so hard, so hot and full, so desperate to be inside a woman.

With a last attempt at patience, he stroked up her thighs, feeling the sleek firmness of muscle beneath the smooth skin. Judith parted her legs easily at his touch, and William cupped her sex, relishing the feel of soft hair and then—*ah*—incredible wetness, and the way her hips instantly strained toward him. With his mouth still on her nipple, he felt her chest rise as she sucked in a breath, and felt with all of him the sudden desperate tension of her body.

"Now," she said, and her hands left his hair to catch his shoulders, urging him back upward. "Now would be good."

Judith's voice was fierce, but still one step from demanding. Demanding was, William thought, still too close to begging for her tastes. He had a vague idea of testing that particular line, but Judith's hands were insistent, her legs open below him, and he abandoned any thought of playing that game. *Next time*, he told himself silently.

He'd prepared for many circumstances when he'd dressed. The French letter was in the pocket of his trousers. William made quick work of putting it on, then positioned himself over Judith, the tip of his cock just at the entrance to her sex. Then he thrust forward, Judith wrapped her legs around him as she cried out, and he didn't think any longer about a next time, or about teasing this time, or about anything remotely civilized or abstract. All was sensation. All was urgency and welcome, and Judith's eyes wide and green below him.

He had just enough self-control left to listen to her body, to find the rhythm she'd started and to match it: slow and deep at first, each parting and rejoining like its own separate act, and then faster as Judith arched up against him, taking his rod deeper and rubbing against him at the same time. She'd abandoned any effort to be quiet, and her cries and moans sounded in his ears like rockets, wearing away at his self-control one after another.

When her climax hit, she screamed against his shoulder, and her thighs tightened around his flanks just as her sex tightened around his cock for the first time. She was, William learned, powerful *everywhere*.

He felt himself starting to spend a moment later. He drove hard and deep into Judith, her body still shaking around his and urging him on to greater heights of rapture, until the final waves passed over him and he collapsed.

Twenty-eight

IT HAD BEEN A LONG TIME.

Judith turned on her side and stretched, feeling the pop of muscles in her back and thighs, the faint soreness between her legs. She grinned up at the ceiling. The bed felt softer beneath her, the silk brocade sleeker and cooler. It had started raining sometime during their interlude, and she heard the drops pattering against the windows. Carnality also was a transformation, and the aftermath of all such things made her more aware of her body. She'd missed it.

Absently, she reached out a hand to William's chest. Considerate, he'd rolled off her a moment after he'd reached his peak, before his elbows could give out under his weight. Now he lay on his back, staring upward in the same contentedly stunned state from which Judith was beginning to emerge.

She hoped so, anyhow. Men weren't exactly *opaque* at moments of passion, and she was fairly sure William had enjoyed himself, but both pride and her own pleasure made her hope she'd done well by him. And it had been a long time.

Judith trailed her fingers through curls of red hair, felt the warm skin and the smooth muscle beneath them. "They keep you in good fettle, your masters," she said, smiling again. "Or is this all by way of recreation?"

"Hmm?" William chuckled, the vibration thrumming up through Judith's fingertips. "Rather a combination, I suppose. The work requires fitness, and after so many years at it, I can't really imagine being any other way. Though I suppose I'll have to, eventually—once the knees give out and the rheumatism sets in."

"And what'll you do then?"

"Find a nice rocking chair and a pipe, I suppose. Give young men hell and tell them that hardship's not a patch on what it was in my day." He looked down at Judith. "I don't suppose you've ever had to worry about it."

"Not for a century or two more," she said. "We do get old, in time. We're human enough for that."

"Oh," he said. "I hadn't thought to ask—and I certainly don't mean to be impolite—"

"Half," Judith said, "or less. My mother was human. A witch, but human. And not even my grandfather could remember any of us who was pure dragon. The blood of the other side runs strong, 'tis all, when it's present." Before he could figure out the implications of what she'd said and go tense and polite, she added, "You're very strategic-minded, and I approve, but I meant what I said in the train. We *can* interbreed, but it takes effort."

"That must be rather convenient, in its way."

"Very," said Judith. "For me, at least." There was

no point pretending she'd been a virgin; he already knew otherwise. "But then, I'm not the heir and don't have to worry about producing one. Fate be praised."

"And yet," said William, stroking a hand down her shoulder and over her arm, "you're the one who minds your family's estates."

"I mind Loch Arach and the castle. My brother handles the finances and the city business. There's more than what you see here, same as with any family like ours." She smiled against the pillow, letting her eyes drift shut for a second and enjoying his touch. "Though I suppose it's less metaphorical for most."

"Less physical, certainly. Most of us are more than the face we show."

"Most of us show different faces for different company. Varied, but perhaps not so layered as you'd like to think," said Judith. She forced her eyes back open. "I can't be falling asleep like this, you understand. Things still to do tonight."

In truth, she hadn't expected to find sleep so tempting or so easy. Her mind held no memories of this kind of easy contentment after a tumble, or of the desire to let herself melt into the bed and her lover's arms—but she'd been younger then and had been in ships or army camps or the sort of inn where the mattress made noises independent of any human or half-and-maybe-less-human movement. Different circumstances, Judith told herself, and different results.

William made a languid but affirmative sound. "And they'll be missing me down in the village, I suspect."

"Oh, I'm afraid the rumors will already have started," said Judith, forcing herself up and onto her feet. The dinner dress was a lost cause, unless William was a good hand at both buttons and laces—and asking him to dress her seemed too intimate, far more so than the reverse had been—so she took a nightgown and a wrapper from the closet. "I hope you don't mind."

"I'd resigned myself when I came up here."

"And yet you did come," said Judith. She pulled on her clothing and watched William dress, admiring the play of muscles in his arms and back. "Queen and Country, old boy?" she asked, trying to imitate his accent.

He turned, startled, in the process of fastening a cuff link. They watched each other briefly in a silence gone suddenly heavy. Then William smiled. "Among other things," he said, "at least when I thought you were only offering dinner."

"I hope someone gives you a medal, then," said Judith. Dressed, she kissed him quickly and then opened the door. "The rain's stopped now," she said after a moment's silence to confirm it. "I'll show you out. I told the servants to take the night off after we went to the drawing room. They'll still gossip—but there won't be proof, if that matters to you."

"It doesn't to you," he replied, a curious smile on his long, lean face. "Or so you said."

"No, I said hearsay doesn't," said Judith, and she didn't answer him further.

In all her years at the castle, she'd been discreet, as much out of habit as from fear of any real consequences. Out in the world, unusual license made people talk, and the last thing she—or any other member of her family—had ever wanted was to become the subject of speculation. Questions in one area too easily led to questions in others.

But that was the wider world. Loch Arach was hers and her family's, and different. And soon enough she'd be gone, first to England and then to some imaginary grave in the city, victim of an invented fever. Once word of the evening got around, those future rumors might take on a different hue, might delve into what she'd *really* died of and why she'd truly left, but that wouldn't be so bad. Questions about a living woman were dangerous—gossip about a dead one diverted attention, like a magician's trick.

All the same, she didn't particularly want to answer questions—or even to see them in anyone's eyes—more than necessary. So she said a polite and proper good-bye to William as they approached the castle doors, then let him slip out without risking anyone outside seeing her dressed for bed. Judith locked the door behind him, then turned and considered the things she still had to do.

She couldn't think of any. The tasks existed, she was sure of it—she hadn't been lying to William earlier—but they hovered just out of her memory, irritating and elusive.

The castle was empty. She'd been very thorough about giving the servants the rest of the evening off. Part of her had remembered the train ride and hotly anticipated the possibility of the night progressing as it had, while more tactically, alert to the possibility of danger, she'd wanted to get rid of potential casualties or witnesses. Judith hadn't thought it likely that William would try to kill her—if nothing else, he'd fall under considerable suspicion—but there were other possibilities, and if violence had broken out, at least there would have been no targets save her.

Instead, there'd been talk and pleasure and the growth of the trust that had started building between them back when they'd fought off the robbers together. Judith didn't regret any of it; she also hadn't thought that the aftermath would leave her feeling so much at loose ends.

"Well," she said to the dark and silent hall. Absently, she twisted her hair into a knot behind her head and began to walk up the dimly lit staircase and back to her bedroom. Whatever she had yet to do would doubtless make itself known to her in time. The evening had gone well. There was no point in fretting.

"You've been stirring your tea for five minutes together," said Agnes. "I dinna' think the last three have improved matters any. What's fashin' ye now?"

"I couldn't say," said Judith, which was the truth on many levels. She shouldn't tell Agnes that she'd taken William to bed. She couldn't tell her about his allegiance or her family's secrets or the negotiations they'd held, nor could she pinpoint just what was troubling her, other than the feeling that she'd taken a step forward and was still waiting for her foot to hit ground. "Sorry. Bad company this morning."

"Perhaps I'm just no' who you're hoping to see." Agnes grinned and lifted her eyebrows.

Here it came. There was no point postponing the fatal moment. "You think I'm here after Arundell."

"Not completely. I'm no' saying you're visiting me under false pretenses. But I know well he came back late last night, and Claire says he'd been up to the castle. 'Tis your own affair, my lady, of course—but if you were here to see him, he's above stairs. Reading a letter, he said."

"I wish him joy of it," said Judith, though under the table, her fingers worried little patterns on the wool of her dress. "We had an excellent dinner. I wanted news from London—my brothers are damned poor correspondents—and he was good about providing it."

"He's fair useful for that purpose," Agnes agreed, "though what he mentions of concerts and music halls and such is like to drive half the young people here away before too very long."

"If it wasn't Arundell, it'd be something else. That's how the young are."

Agnes made a noncommittal sound. Below it, Judith heard a man's footsteps approaching, and her fingers had tightened on the teacup and fabric before the door opened. She turned, made herself smile naturally, and met William's eyes.

He smiled back: quick, polite, discreet. Good. She should have known. He was a professional. She hadn't been his first woman. Both of them knew how to conduct themselves. Judith watched him cross the room, remembered how he'd moved above her the night before, and fought back a shiver. "Mr. Arundell. Good morning. Agnes was just worrying that you'd lead all our youth to perdition."

"I'll do my best to avoid it, Lady MacAlasdair," William replied. "If it helps, I give you my word that

I've never learned to play a pipe of any sort. Only the piano, and it's rather difficult to lead children under a mountain with one of those."

Laughing with him warmed her as much as lusting after him did. It was both a relief to Judith's nerves and another sign of danger. It was also not a phenomenon she had the chance to think about for very long.

More footsteps sounded outside. These were light and hurried: Claire, running. There was nothing out of the way about that—sixteen was a running kind of age—but the last few weeks made every sound and flicker of light an omen. Judith was tense, getting ready to rise from the table, even as the door burst open.

"Mother—" Claire's face was white, her blue eyes huge in contrast. If she saw either Judith or William, she gave no sign. Infatuation and awareness of rank were nothing to her right now. She was a child in that moment, and the only person who mattered was the one who'd mattered most from the start. "Mother, the most horrible thing has happened."

Twenty-nine

ALMOST AS FAST AS JUDITH HAD MOVED IN THE CLEAR-
ing, Mrs. Simon was out of her chair and across the
room, wrapping her daughter in her arms. Claire
pressed her face against her mother's shoulder and
started to cry. Between her sobs and the position,
William couldn't hear much of what she said, but
whatever it was made Mrs. Simon start, her own eyes
widening and her mouth going thin. A look at Judith
showed a similar expression on her face, but with less
shock and more suspicion in it.

When the broken word "bodies" reached William's
ears, he understood why.

Mrs. Simon pulled back, though she kept her hands
on Claire's shoulders. "Calm yourself a moment,
quine," she said. The word was obviously an endear-
ment, though one William had never heard before.
"You'll need to tell her ladyship. 'Tis the sort of thing
she ought to be knowing."

As if Claire were ten years younger, Mrs. Simon
took out a handkerchief and wiped her face. As if Claire
were ten years younger, she submitted without protest,

though she did blow her own nose. William looked away and kept silent. The girl would look back on this with enough mortification as it was. Just now, she didn't seem to know he was in the room. She only looked at Judith when her mother spoke, and that in a sort of daze.

"I—" she began, her voice choked with tears. She cleared her throat, snuffled, and started over. "Mairi and I were going down to her house. And we cut through the graveyard. We—we'd done it before. Everyone does. It's shorter that way, and there arena' so many brambles, and a few folks walking about isna' like to disturb the"—she gulped—"dead."

"I shouldn't think it would, no," said Judith. "Nobody'll be angry with you, Claire. Just go on."

Claire nodded. "We saw the earth had been tossed up. And we thought that was odd, since nobody's died. We thought perhaps an animal'd been at the place. So we went over to see—I thought maybe we could tell the minister how bad it was—and it was *awful*. And not an animal at all. They—somebody— somebody dug up the graves. Two of them, and they broke the coffins open, and we could see the bodies. And one of them, it was like he was staring at us, but he didna' have any eyes—"

The last word came out as a wail, and Claire buried herself in her mother's arms again.

William's first feeling was relief. Whatever might have happened to expose them, the bodies were still in the churchyard and not, for instance, up and walking around. Claire's mention of disturbing the dead had steeled him for the worst. Desecration wasn't that, but it was bad and had the potential for worse.

Almost reflexively, he turned to look at Judith. She met his eyes, her face grim, and nodded. "I'll go and have a word with the reverend."

"He"—Claire sniffled—"knows. He came out when we screamed, and *he* screamed, and then he fell down and we ran for the doctor and he's still alive but—"

"Evans is in his seventies," Judith said to William. "A good man, but—spirit, flesh, so on. You did well, Claire. I'll see to it that this is set right." Her voice itself was a pledge. As quickly as she'd turned to Claire, she looked back at William. "Mr. Arundell, may I impose on you? It's not a scene I wish to walk into alone."

"Of course," said William. Even in the midst of his alarm, he heard the real offer of cooperation underneath her words and the trust there, and rejoiced in it. After all, Judith MacAlasdair, who'd spent more years in armies than he'd spent walking the earth, would hardly be in need of male support to go and look at a body or two. "I'll go get my things and be down directly."

Once they'd left the house behind, Judith glanced at the bag William had retrieved. "More preparation?"

"One never knows."

"In this case, one knows a little too well," said Judith. "Or at least suspects."

William had gone to services on the occasional Sunday, keeping up an image of respectability for Loch Arach that he'd never bothered about in larger cities. He'd spoken with Evans only briefly. The old man did not appear to concern himself much with things of this world, and what he'd been able or willing to say about either the village or the MacAlasdairs had been vague and not helpful. He'd been gentle and amiable to all appearances, and when William saw Dr. McKendry coming out of the parsonage, he hurried forward with almost as much interest as Judith herself did.

"He'll be all right," said the doctor, not waiting on Judith's question. Her face was expressive enough when she wanted it to be. "Only a shock—but that's no joke for a man of his age. I've told him to rest for a few days. You'll have heard what brought it on?"

"I heard," said Judith. "Have you seen it?"

"No. Neither do I want to, unless you feel I'll do any good. The graves disturbed were older, I hear, and I dinna' think medicine's of much help there any longer—but if your ladyship desires—"

Judith shook her head, one quick motion like the stroke of a knife. "No. Take care of Reverend Evans. Tell him I'll handle matters. Tell anyone else who asks too. I don't guess there's much chance of keeping this quiet, is there?"

"Not hardly," said Dr. McKendry.

"Aye, so I'd thought." Judith sighed. "Mr. Arundell will be helping me have a look. They're doing wonderful things with investigation in London now, I hear. If you have a moment, send a few strong lads with shovels round in about an hour. We should be done then."

"I'll pass the word. Good day, Lady MacAlasdair. Mr. Arundell."

"Good day," said William. Judith was already striding toward the graveyard.

The older part was right up near the church, but the graves in question were a little distance away from that, set apart from the clumps of families. Before he could see the headstones, he spotted the graves themselves, dirt piled up in rich brown hills. He heard Judith hiss breath in through her teeth.

"Anyone you know?" William asked quietly.

"I'm not sure yet. But—if I had known them, it didn't end well." She closed her eyes for a second, as if that would aid her memory. "It's harder to tell now, with the graves more crowded together and so many of them worn down. But I'm fairly certain those men were hanged."

"Oh, hell," said William. She was probably right. When they drew close enough to see the gravestones, he noticed that they were plain things, with only the dates of birth and death on them and no words of comfort for anyone—not absolute proof that they'd died as criminals, but further evidence.

Both coffins were open—smashed with a heavy implement, likely a shovel. Only a skull stared out from one of them, while thick wood hid the rest of the body. The other corpse was, well, fresher—buried more recently and in a sturdier coffin. The man still had a face left, ravaged though it was. The grave robber had been more thorough in this case. The whole top of the coffin was gone. The body lay plain in William's view. William looked down the length of the probably-not-a-gentleman and found what he'd been dreading.

"The left hand is gone," he said. Only the two of them stood in the graveyard, but he spoke quietly anyhow. The spirit of the place demanded it. "Do you know if he went to the grave that way?"

"Let me think." She read the name and dates on the gravestone over, tapping her index finger against her lips. "Sixty-eight. I was here—I recall the trial. Murder, it was, and a shocking case. His own wife and daughters." Judith spoke slowly and without emotion, a woman describing a dream. "We sent to the Queen for permission. Have to, these days. Ryan. Aye. Brute of a fellow. And we buried him with both hands. Which means someone took one. Why?"

"I couldn't say for sure," said William, "but I've heard a legend or five. Things you can do with a dead man's hands—walk through walls and the like. Criminals' hands in particular. I wish I knew more theory."

"So do I," said Judith. "Colin would be helpful about now. Never tell him I said that," she added with a faint smile. "So—a necromancer. Wonderful news."

"You already knew he summoned demons."

"Aye, well, I'm not saying I'm *shocked*." Judith stepped back and looked at the graves, hands on hips and lips pressed tightly together. "When I get my hands on the bastard—but then, we'll need to know which bastard it is."

"A new one," said William, looking down at the muddy ground.

"What, we've got *two*?"

"No. Someone new in town—or at least someone who does more indoor work than most." He gestured. "See, there are footprints here. All around the graves, I'd wager, though you and I and the girls might have disturbed some of them. Man-sized, though not a man with very large feet or a vast stride. More importantly, they're from shoes, not boots."

"Evans wears shoes," said Judith. "But if he'd been digging up graves last night, he'd be in one now."

"And I don't get the impression, from what either Claire or Dr. McKendry said, that he came this close to the graves themselves. We can check, but—no, he's not a likely suspect. That leaves McKendry, though he's hardly young himself, his friend Hamilton, and me." William smiled. "And I'm touched that you didn't think of me immediately when Claire came in."

"I saw your face," said Judith with a shrug. "'Twould be a hell of an actor who could look so surprised—and so displeased. And if you'd done this, you'd not have been nearly so messy about it or have pointed out the footprints. Besides"—she gestured to Ryan—"it rained on him, and rained hard. When it was raining last night, I was with you."

"And here I was thinking that you trusted me blindly."

Judith turned to him, her smile friendly and predatory at once. "Never blindly. Not anyone. Not even myself. But aye, I trust you."

It was the wrong time and place to reach for her. It would have either been irreverent or patronizing. William kept his hands at his sides and simply looked, meeting her eyes for a long minute, before turning reluctantly back to business.

"Whoever it was," he said, "he must have had to leave in a hurry. Otherwise he *wouldn't* have left things in such a state. There might have been a witness—or the nearest thing to one."

"Not Evans, or he wouldn't have been so shocked. At that, if anyone had seen, word would have gotten around long before Claire and Mairi stumbled in here."

"Unless they didn't see. Our grave robber might have been easy to scare off. If you'll keep watch," William said, thanking his better angels that he'd thought he might be going out again and had therefore brought his bag, "I can try to find out more."

Judith nodded. "Shout when you're done," she said and turned toward the gates of the graveyard. "There's nobody who'll see you from outside, and nobody who'll get past my watch."

She headed away from him, her feet making soft noises on the damp earth. William watched as her figure grew smaller. Then he put down his bag, bent, and retrieved the silver chains. He focused his mind as he'd been taught, and before long was barely even aware of Judith's presence.

Barely. There was a feeling of safety that he hadn't experienced before. Maybe it was just because he had a lookout this time, or the sanction of a woman who was as close to the authorities as anyone in Loch Aràch was going to be.

William doubted it.

Thirty

THE AUTUMN WIND DID AN AMAZINGLY GOOD JOB OF cutting through two layers of wool and three of cotton. Judith wrapped her arms around her chest and shifted her weight, hoping that William's bit of magic wouldn't take very long—and that it would be useful. In front of her, the road stayed empty; nearby, the stone frames of the church and the parsonage were small and gray against the mountains' darkness. The smell of wet earth was strong, though not as strong as it had been by the graves themselves, and now she couldn't even smell a trace of flesh. It had been faint to begin with. The bodies had been old.

So far she'd not had to turn anyone away from the graveyard. Word would naturally have gotten around by now, but respect would keep most people away, particularly with news of the vicar's sudden illness.

Poor Evans. She should have sent for an assistant—and eventual replacement—long before, Judith thought. When she'd first come back, that duty wouldn't have slipped her mind, but until Claire had mentioned his collapse, she hadn't thought of his real age. She still remembered him taking up the post: an endearingly homely man, a little past sixty, with curly blondish-gray hair, a full beard, and a plump middle-aged wife. He'd come back around the same time she had. Judith didn't remember him as a boy—her visits then had been brief—but she knew he'd been born in Loch Arach, kin to one of the Welshmen who'd been her mother's people, and then left to attend a university.

That was how it worked now. When she'd been a girl, most people had died without going more than twenty miles from the place they were born. Strictly going by the numbers, she supposed that most of them still did—but it didn't feel that way. Prosperous men sent their sons away to school. Some even sent their daughters these days. Youths with less money took matters into their own hands. They did as she'd done, despite her wealth, and joined the Queen's service, or simply ran away and found a trade out in the wider world. The railroads made it easier. The papers made it alluring.

A few came back for good. She had. Evans had. More stayed gone, and if they returned at all, it was only on a fleeting visit. Take Ross MacDougal—a name and a source of infrequent letters for ten years, and then back with his family, as much a stranger as kin now. He'd be leaving soon, no doubt. Winter in the mountains was no easy stretch, and he'd never acted like a man who'd come to stay. Running from a disappointment wouldn't make a man linger past snowfall, and neither would the desire to show off his fancy new clothes.

She caught her breath, the air cold in her throat.

Fancy new clothes, she mused, and thought of London and of dates. A shape began to emerge out of them: not yet anything clear, but a patch that might be fog or might be a coastline. Judith stood and thought some more. When she heard footsteps coming up behind her, she whirled, expecting William, eager to speak and to listen.

She made herself wait. Theories should always wait on facts. "Anything?"

"Not much." William sighed. "Though it's as we were thinking. A light went on in the window over at the vicarage, and our man grabbed tools and ran. And it was a man, or at least man-shaped. That's all. Without recent death, there isn't as much of an echo to pick up. That isn't to say I'm longing for murder, of course."

"No," said Judith, not paying much attention. He hadn't found any new information; therefore, it was time to put together what they did have. "I'd forgotten about someone," she said. "When we were talking earlier."

"Oh?"

She nodded. "Ross MacDougal. He's a local lad by birth, but he went down to London about ten years back. Did well for himself, by the way he dresses, and—" She stopped, because William was staring at her, mouth slightly open. "You've heard of him?"

"Respectable-looking chap? About so high"—he sketched with a hand—"with light hair?" When Judith nodded, he said, "We met. Twice. The first time was in the store, before it burnt down. Nothing more than small talk there, but I thought he looked distracted. And I thought that I'd seen him before. Back in England."

"Would that mean anything, if you did?"

"It might. Not that I've any single nemesis plotting my downfall," he added with a quick smile that immediately subsided back into his look of serious thought, "but the men we...handle...run in packs. Cults, mostly. Secret brotherhoods. I wonder sometimes—but that's not relevant. He and I might have encountered each other before under less pleasant circumstances."

"Or at a gentleman's club," said Judith, playing the contrarian now.

"Or that. Or shared a compartment on a train. So— nothing to hang a man on. Not yet. But the second time—" He paused, and she saw his shoulders stiffen beneath his coat. He took her hands between both of his and looked soberly into her eyes. "The second time he was going to see you."

"Was he?" she asked, not alarmed but beginning to be wary. The shape in the distance was beginning to look more like land—and a rocky coastline at that. "When?"

"The night I...walked in on you. In the forest. I met him on my way back. His mother had asked him to bring a basket up to the castle, he said, and he said too that he'd gotten delayed. He never saw you, I take it."

"No, but he wouldn't have. He knows the cook well. He'd have left it with her, if I wasn't there, and I'd imagine it might have slipped her mind. I could believe his mother sending things up to the kitchen.

She used to be my housekeeper. Poor Elspeth," said Judith. "If we're right—damn. She's that proud of her boy these days."

"'A policeman's lot is not a happy one,'" William quoted, but he was mocking neither her nor the situation, she was sure of it. The only humor in his voice was very dark indeed. "He didn't seem at all glad to see me. But he could have just been out of sorts. It wasn't a very pleasant walk, I'd think, particularly for a man used to hansom cabs and the Underground."

"You would know," said Judith absently, still thinking of Elspeth—and Gillian too. It'd be a hard blow for the whole family, were Ross the guilty party. No harder than Hamilton's guilt would be for McKendry, maybe. She scowled down at the rock wall of the graveyard.

"Not as much as you might think. Most of my work hasn't been in cities. But"—William squeezed Judith's hands lightly, drawing her out of her thoughts—"we have no proof of anything yet. Nothing odd happened to you after his visit, did it?"

Judith shook her head, then laughed, short and sharp. "Nothing I didn't bring on myself," she said, looking up at William until a twist of his lips showed that he'd taken her meaning. "So—it's down to those two. Hamilton's a medical man. And one who experiments. He'd *mentioned* blood, for which the dead couldn't be much good, but his research could have led him in other directions. He wouldn't be the first surgeon in want of a corpse or two."

"What good would demons do him?"

"What good would they do Ross? Or anyone?"

She rubbed her forehead, trying to think. "They were following me. Spying on me. Both men would have heard stories enough about us—Ross when he was young, and Hamilton once he came here. I suppose Hamilton could have been curious. Scientific-minded and all. Ross isn't."

"Wasn't," said William. "Ten years can change a man."

"Aye. And he could have other reasons. Blackmail, mayhap. Or sorcery. We have"—she hesitated and then settled on a vague enough response—"a few enchantments running, and we are what we are. If he's learned magic, he could want more power of that kind. There's no way of knowing."

Either of her brothers would have done better, she thought. Colin knew magic and all the games of society, and Stephen lived in London, dealing daily in power and intrigue. She'd been a soldier and a sailor. She was a landlord—landlady—now. The water was up to her neck, and she could barely find the bottom with her toes.

But this was her village and her duty.

"The thing to do, I suppose," she said, "is to see where Hamilton and Ross were last night. Though if we start asking after either of them, whichever one it really is will get wise quickly."

"Right," said William. "And we don't have much time regardless." He looked back over his shoulder toward the opened graves. "I don't know precisely what our man's planning—spells themselves aren't my forte—but I do know that anything involving a criminal's body is likely to be very drastic and very bad."

"Worse than demons?"

"Could be," said William. "We'll split up, if you're amenable. Each ask about one suspect. That way, we stand a chance of finding out what we need before word gets back to the culprit himself."

When he'd asked her to keep watch, Judith hadn't thought anything of the request, too concerned with the desecration and the magic being worked behind her to think of emotional matters. Now, while she considered logistics, a small thought slipped in behind the more practical workings of her mind: *He trusts me.*

She had no leisure to be glad, or to worry that she was. "I'll talk to the MacDougals," Judith said. "They know me. You take McKendry. We'll meet at the church at noon, aye?"

"Aye," said William, and then he smiled. "That is, yes."

"Don't worry," said Judith. Figures were coming down the road now: the requested brawny lads with shovels. "It takes a few years more to go native."

She headed off, first to meet the approaching crew and then to have what she didn't doubt would be a series of increasingly unpleasant conversations. Behind her, though, she knew that William smiled, and matters seemed a shade less bleak.

Thirty-one

As in any other village William had stayed in or passed through, the well-to-do citizens of Loch Arach clustered near each other, particularly when the source of their income was something other than farming and thus required neither fields nor barns. Dr. McKendry's low stone house was, therefore, only a short walk from the parsonage and the graveyard. Had Judith not assigned their tasks and given good reason for her decisions, William would have felt that chivalry bound him to protest giving her the longer journey.

He didn't think it would have done much good, but he would have had to speak.

He pushed open the gate and walked through the small garden, now bare and brown except for the solid green darkness of the hedges. Smoke rose steadily from the chimney above him. The smell was comfortingly normal in the face of his morning's activities and of what still lay ahead.

The maid who opened the door for him was named Edith, he knew now, and she smiled in recognition when she saw William. "Come along inside," she said.

"He'll be wanting to see you. They both will—but 'tis quite a morning the doctor's had."

"So I saw," said William.

"They're saying someone's been robbing graves." Edith looked back over her shoulder at him, her eyes large and round, and William noticed that she was only a few years older than Claire. "Is it true?"

"Not completely. But—yes, someone's dug up a few." She'd find out soon enough. "Only criminals so far. And only the older graves."

That was another facet of the mystery, wasn't it? Did the hand have to be old—yet not so old as to be skeletal—or had Loch Arach simply not hung a man in a while? He paged through books in his memory, all the grimoires he *had* gotten notes from: Solomon and Abramelin, Agrippa and Parkin. They offered information, but too much of it. He would have given his *own* hand for a quick way to contact the central office and the men there, scholars rather than field agents, who knew substantially more than the quick summaries and scattered methods he'd learned.

Seated in a small, blue-papered parlor and waiting for "the gentlemen," William kept thinking while—he hoped—his face remained outwardly serene and pleasant. Only fifty years ago, people had thought dead men's hands would cure illness or take away growths. Hamilton was a surgeon. That might not explain the livestock or the demons, but men of science did experiment on animals, and maybe Hamilton had called the creatures up to see if the spells truly worked. It wouldn't have been the first time.

Or maybe—

"Mr. Arundell," said Dr. McKendry, coming in with a tired smile. "Michael will be down directly. He's finishing up an experiment just now, and these things are tricky business. One misstep and a week's work is ruined, or so I hear."

"I wouldn't want to disturb that," William said, wishing that politeness would let him say otherwise, or that he knew enough to be definitely rude. "I wanted to pass along Lady MacAlasdair's thanks for sending those young chaps up earlier, and to see if you'd had any word about Mr. Evans. I'd like to stop in and extend my sympathies."

"Happy to do what I can, of course. Shocking business." McKendry settled himself into a leather-covered chair and opened a cigar case, offering one first to William, who declined with a shake of his head. "As for Evans, only what I told you before. He's not likely to be up to company until tomorrow at least. Did you find anything over at the cemetery?"

"Mostly the obvious," said William, reserving the hand and the footprints for later necessity. "The grave robber worked in the rain—an enterprising scoundrel, we have to give him that—which means he was at it around nine last night, or half past. I don't suppose either of you saw anything? You're tolerably nearby."

Dr. McKendry shook his head. "I wish I could help you, lad," he said, "but I was dead to the world by then. The curse of age, as you'll know in time. A troop could have marched past my window without me knowing."

❧

"My lady." Gillian Gordon turned wide, surprised eyes on Judith, and Judith herself felt slightly off balance. She had expected a formal meeting, not a chance encounter outside the barn. Nonetheless, here Gillian was, a pail of milk in each hand. "Were you coming to the house?"

"Aye," said Judith. "Not disturbing anyone, I hope."

Gillian shook her head.

Beneath the remnants of a harvesttime tan, her face was red, especially around the eyes and the nose. Wind or weeping? Judith couldn't tell.

"No, it's always a pleasure," Gillian said, though her voice said that the words came from politeness and not true feeling. Judith wished she *had* only come on a social call and had the luxury of taking the hint.

"Let me help you with those, at least," she said, reaching out a hand for the milk pails. The brisk combination of speech and action had served her well as a soldier and did the same now. She had a pail in each hand before Gillian could think to object. "Your beasts are still giving well, I see. A good sign for the winter. But you should have an extra hand, so close to term."

"Och," Gillian said with a faint and effortful smile and a pat to her stomach, "I'm an old hand at this by now, m'lady. Besides, Ronald's taken wee Ronnie out with him—and that's half my troubles put to rest—and Mam's watching the little one. A bit of milking's restful in its way."

"Glad you feel so," said Judith. "Cows have never been overly fond of me. But I'd think you might find the house a bit crowded these days too. Or perhaps you've more patience with your brother than I have with mine."

At that, Gillian flinched. "Oh," she said quickly and too lightly, "Ross is out so often, he's never a bother. Not to say he's not attentive."

"No, of course not," Judith said and glanced toward the house. "But I'd imagine he wants to catch up a bit, after being gone so long. Is he in now?"

"No," said Gillian, and the tension in her body wound tighter. "He went on a walk a wee bit ago, and he's not been back since. He—"

Judith slowed her steps, pretending to take extra care with the milk pails. "Hmm?"

"He and Mam had words."

"Your mother's always been one for speaking her mind," said Judith, letting herself smile a little. "And it's hard to come home again once you're grown. My father and I had some rows that practically shook the foundations."

"Oh, there's that, but—" Gillian looked off into the distance, chewed on her lower lip briefly, and then shrugged. "I don't know. It might only be as you say, m'lady. It's just… Ross is so high-strung these days. And it's not that he misses London, I think, for he hardly ever speaks well of it—says it's a dirty place, full of horrible people."

"Worse than I've heard of it," said Judith, "but it's no place I'd live myself. Some of us just aren't made for life around crowds. Perhaps he's thinking of coming back."

"It could be," said Gillian, who apparently took no

pleasure in the thought of it. She shook her head. "But I shouldn't be telling your ladyship my troubles, nor keeping you out here in the cold when you've come all this way. Let me manage the door for you, at least."

With a milk pail in each hand, Judith assented easily, if not gladly. Nothing could have made her glad to enter the Gordons' cottage on such an errand.

∞

"What about Mr. Hamilton?" William asked.

"He didn't mention anything," McKendry said. The smoke from his cigar curled upward into the air of the parlor, a fragrant cloud whose swirls looked almost like oracular patterns. "But you can have a word with him on the subject yourself—just now, at that."

The door was opening as he spoke, and Hamilton stepped in. He didn't look like a man who'd been up all night robbing graves. His eyes were bright and unshadowed, his smile was easy, and he walked with no visible sign of sore muscles. Comparative youth might have done as much, though—that and callousness.

"Good morning, Mr. Arundell. You wanted to ask me something?"

"Whether you'd seen or heard anything last night, around nine or so."

"It's to do with the matter in the churchyard," said McKendry, sighing. "Ghastly business, aye?"

"Aye," said Hamilton. "And I'd be glad to tell you anything I knew about it, only there isn't anything, as I wasn't here. I'd gone down to the pub for a pint or two at half past eight, and I stayed until past eleven. It wasn't a vast throng, but three or four men there could say I'm telling the truth."

His smile never flickered as he talked. If anything, it deepened.

McKendry, on the other hand, looked back and forth between Hamilton and William, and bristled once he realized what was happening, half rising from his chair. "Now see here—"

"It's all right, George," said Hamilton, making settling motions with one hand. "Hazard of the profession, and has been ever since Burke and Hare made a name for themselves. But that was well in the past, Mr. Arundell," he added. "It's been more than half a century since the dissection rooms have run short. Even the oldest of my professors couldn't call those days well to mind."

"Oh no," said McKendry, managing a genial little chuckle now that he didn't have to take umbrage on his friend's behalf. "The Anatomy Act was in…thirty-three? Thirty-two? Before I was even born, lad, and that's saying a good bit. And it may have its critics, but there's nobody with a need to go digging up graveyards. Besides, Hamilton's not been a student for years."

"Ah," said William, and he offered a sheepish smile. "Dreadfully sorry. Out of my area of expertise, I'm afraid."

"And why wouldn't it be?" Hamilton took a cigar from his friend's case, struck a match on the bottom of his boot, and leaned back, all learned man of the world. "I was in school when the Ripper was working, and didn't we get a lot of funny looks when one of us was about after dark? Ach, we've come a good long way from Galen and Hunter"—William only dimly recognized the first name as an ancient Greek surgeon and didn't know the second at all—"but a man who works with a knife is always bound to get as much fear as glory."

That last word poked like a pin into his mind. He'd read it in the endless notes he'd gone through at the central office—a spell from one French grimoire or other, newly come to light now that the Frenchies were inclined to be cooperative. Glorious Hand, Hand of Glory…it had been along those lines.

One took a criminal's hand and pickled it, making it into a candle or a candleholder. Then what?

"Yes," he said, so suddenly that both of his hosts started. "Pardon me." William got to his feet. "How does one reach the Gordons'?"

"Down the road westward," said McKendry. He was frowning, puzzled, but the directions came off his tongue almost automatically. "Left at the fork. It'll be the last house, set back near the woods."

"Thank you. I'm afraid I must be going. Sorry to have disturbed you."

"Don't give it another thought," said Hamilton. "Best of luck."

"Are you quite well?" McKendry asked, peering up at him.

"I hope to be better soon. Thank you."

William left McKendry's yard still not remembering what the Hand of Glory did. He knew that it was nothing good, though—and if Hamilton's alibi held, which he was sure it would, then Ross was quite probably making one.

And Judith was going to his house.

He reached the road and started to run.

❧

"He's gotten himself into trouble, I'm sure of it," said Mrs. MacDougal. Her face was hollow-cheeked, her lips so thin as to be nearly nonexistent. Age looked like worry, and worry like age, and in her countenance they'd merged. "He'd not tell me what sort. Said it was all for our sake—as if we'd ever asked it of him. As though his sister or I hadna' done well enough for ourselves."

"It's no crime to want better for your family, Mum," said Gillian mildly, after a concerned look at Judith. "And we'd not said no to any of the money he sent us, nor any of the fine things he brought back."

"Why do you think he's in trouble?" Judith asked, letting Gillian and her mother worry over morality. "Gillian said he was high-strung—"

"Jumpy as a colt, more like," said Mrs. MacDougal. "He couldna' hear a noise, the last few days, without flinching. 'Tis the letters that did it. He's had three of them since he came, all from London. Devil a one would he let me read, and each of them put him in a worse temper than the last. Debts, I shouldn't wonder. Or worse."

"Could be, I'm afraid," Judith said and meant it. Using magic to get money had never struck *her* as worth the time, but she'd never lacked for funds. A man with a little occult knowledge and a legion of creditors breathing down his neck might well try to turn lead to gold— and a man who knew of a wealthy and mysterious family might well try to discover the source of that wealth and see whether he could siphon off a bit. "I hate to ask, but do you know where he was last night?"

"No," said Mrs. MacDougal. "He went out after dinner, and he wasna' back when I fell asleep."

"We'd gone to bed too," said Gillian. "It's not as if we had to stay up to let him in—the door hardly locks. I didn't think much of it." She looked at Judith and her expression was her mother's in every particular. "He's in trouble here, if he isn't in London. Isn't that so, your ladyship?"

The door opened.

Judith started to turn and see who'd entered. Halfway through the motion, her neck froze in place, leaving her staring at the corner of the cottage. Every muscle in her body went rigid. She wasn't sure how she still lived, for the air was frozen in her lungs, but she had no sense of suffocation, only of complete and total paralysis.

At first she thought one of the other women would notice and raise an alarm, but at the sides of her vision, she saw that neither of them was moving. Flickering light danced across all three of their stiff forms—light from a source that Judith at first couldn't see.

It moved closer, in time with a man's steady footsteps. Ross MacDougal stepped into Judith's vision, tense and sorrowful as he looked back and forth between the three women in the room. In one hand was…another hand, this one long dead. Each of its desiccated fingers sprouted a wick, and a flame danced at all five: fingers of fire on fingers of flesh.

In his other hand, he held a long knife.

Thirty-two

THE TIME FOR SECRECY WAS OVER.

Anyone on the road, or on the farms to either side of it, could see William running. He didn't care. He registered a few people as he passed them, knew that they might have tried to speak, but didn't pause to respond or even to acknowledge them. Later, they'd understand. Or they wouldn't. The question had no weight to it.

As he ran, he silently cursed—cursed the rough ground underfoot, all rocks and loose dirt; cursed his body for the basic humanity that meant he couldn't move with the speed he wished; and cursed his mind for its failures of memory and connection. It had taken him too long to think of the Hand of Glory. He still wasn't sure he'd remembered all of the details right.

A candle made of, or resting in, a criminal's pickled hand: that was the basic gist. It should take a while to make…but it might not, for a man who'd already enlisted demons to his cause. That kind of power might let its adherents take shortcuts.

Make the candle. Light the candle.

There was the fork McKendry had mentioned. William veered left, almost ran into a man with a horse and cart, saw that it wasn't Ross—the bastard—and kept going with a breathless, muttered apology.

Light the candle. He wished the man *had* been Ross. He would have been off his guard, then, harmless and away from Judith. Damn him. Judith could probably take care of herself. But there were ways of killing even dragons. Hadn't William bluffed her with just that?

What did you do with the damned thing once you got it lit? It was a thief's trick. The grimoire had mentioned burglars. Doors wouldn't stay locked. He thought that was part of it. How many bloody farms were on this path? Why had he thought Loch Arach small? The place was vast. The road went on forever.

Unlocking doors wasn't dangerous. There had been more. A picture appeared in his head, one from a real nursery tale, though not one that featured dragons: a golden-haired girl lying on a bed, roses growing all around her. Sleeping Beauty. Sleep. Or stillness. Helplessness, either way. There'd been a verse in his notes, a possible correspondence from a folktale: *Be as the dead for the dead man's sake,* one of the lines had gone.

Sympathetic magic. Fairly simple. The dead were without motion or volition. A dead man's hand conferred the same qualities. Basic theory. Even he knew it.

Be as the dead.

Running should have been painful by then. Breathing should have been painful by then. William knew the depth of his fear by the fact that he could have kept going for hours. A house was coming up in the distance, small and set back, as McKendry had said, near the woods.

He drew his gun. He chose the one with silver bullets this time, though Ross was probably still human. William was taking no chances.

Be as the dead.

Four syllables. An easy rhythm for his feet to echo. Like a heartbeat, really. And did the heart keep moving when the rest of the body couldn't? Did the lungs? Was it only helplessness that the Hand brought to its victims, or the slow horror of suffocation? Was Judith—

There was the door. William stopped. He made himself stand still—*be as the dead*—and listen. He heard a voice from the other side: Ross. Nobody else was talking.

Careful now, said the voice of his reason.

None of his notes had told him the Hand's limits. It might be like Medusa and turn any onlooker to stone. Rushing in unprepared was never a good idea when there was time to do otherwise, and if Ross was talking, there was still time.

There was also a window.

❧

"I'm sorry, Mother. Gillian," Ross said. "And you too, Lady MacAlasdair. I hadn't intended any violence. No more than I could help," he added and swallowed.

Judith thought he was remembering the young man in Belholm, the one William had mentioned to her. She hoped so. She wanted the memory to rise up and reproach Ross, as she lacked the power to do. In that much he looked like he was gratifying her. He swallowed again, hard, and for a second she thought he might be ill.

She strained to move any part of her body, throwing her whole will toward motion, and nothing happened. In final desperation, Judith reached into herself and began the process of transformation—and nothing happened.

Her body was no longer her own.

Inside her head, she screamed for what felt like an age.

Ross was speaking again. "I heard you talking. From outside, I heard you. And I knew she'd not let the matter rest." He wasn't even looking at Judith now. "And I knew neither of you would defend me. Even though I've always had your interests at heart. And I—"

I panicked.

Ross didn't say that, but he might as well have. His eyes were wild, the whites and pupils both wide, with only a sliver of brown showing between. Sweat stood out on his forehead, despite the day's chill, and he kept licking his lips as he talked, his tongue darting out to the corners of his mouth at just about every third word. If he hadn't been holding the hand and the knife, Judith thought he'd have been wiping his palms on his trousers.

Dry mouth. Wet hands. Down through the centuries, she'd gotten to know the look of fear well, and the way it felt on the skin and in the throat. If she'd actually been breathing, she was sure she could have smelled it, acrid and metallic.

If Ross had let Judith go away, he might have had time to run. Before he went, he might even have had time to convince his mother or his sister, or both, that he was innocent, or at least justified.

Jumpy as a colt.

He *had* jumped, and come down running in the first direction he saw. Now he was reconsidering. Now he was thinking it was too late to reconsider. Ross was in very much over his head, and he knew it.

That made him more dangerous. You could reason with a calm man. You could play on his sympathy, talk him down, maybe buy him off if it came to that. Terrified men, like terrified stock, would kill at the sound of a stick breaking.

"I know I never explained myself. And I'd say that means some of the blame's mine—though if you'd only trusted me, as is proper... But you've been on your own up here a great deal, aye, and it's far from a natural place and never has been. I can't blame either of you. I'm so very sorry that things have come to such a pass."

Ross searched his mother's motionless face, then his sister's, hunting for a sign of understanding or forgiveness that he must have known wouldn't appear—*couldn't*, even if either of them had felt as he wanted. To Judith's eyes, he moved strangely, half a second too early or too late. When she thought about it, there'd been the same quality about his voice and the sound of his footsteps.

What any of that meant, she couldn't say. She suspected she might not have very much time to wonder.

G'bye, Stephen, Colin. Live well, and remember me to your bairns.

"The thing is," Ross said, because he was going to make her wait to die, like the black-hearted dog that he was, "it's not only the money, although there's certainly that, and I'd have supported you in grand style. It's about preserving the world as it should be. About preserving the *nation* as it should be. I'm doing a fine deed, truly, though I allow that it might not look that way. There's only one other man who has the courage to join me in it now, but once the others find out—we'll be heroes. To them and to everyone."

What?

Briefly, Judith was too puzzled to feel either fear or sorrow. She didn't have much choice about staring at Ross, but she would have even if she'd been able to move. Was he a would-be Saint George—or the mortals' version of that legend—who'd somehow gotten word of her family's secret? Or a modern version of the witch finders who'd held such dominion in her father's day?

He *would* have a time trying to hang her or burn her at the stake. A knife to the throat or the heart, on the other hand, would probably suffice. Those of her bloodline healed quickly and endured much, but vital organs were, well, vital, regardless of form, and it would be easy enough to hit the right spot when she couldn't move.

I'm sorry, William. I hope you don't take this too badly—and I hope you make an end of this bastard.

I'll miss you.

As if responding to her thoughts, Ross looked over his shoulder at her, then back to his mother. "I'll take Lady MacAlasdair out of here now. We'll go to

London. I'll not kill her if I can help it, and I don't think my brothers wish her a corpse. Perhaps knowing that will change your mind, and you'll not raise the alarm after I go. But just in case," he said and raised the knife, pommel pointing down.

If Judith had been able to breathe, she'd have stopped then. A blow to the skull would kill as often as it rendered the victim unconscious. If a young man knocked an old lady over the head, it was almost a sure thing. Silently, she cried out, but she still could make no sound.

◆

Although a farmer's cottage having glass windows was probably still a luxury in a village like Loch Arach, the window William peered through, once he'd raised his head to see above the sill, was no great specimen. Set in rows of small disks in lead frames—thus making the window impractical as an entrance—the glass was old and streaky. Every shape in the room blurred at the edges, and those farther away became merely suggestions of forms vaguely defined against the darker background of the cottage walls.

There was Mrs. MacDougal, sitting in a chair, and her daughter caught in the act of reaching for a dish. Judith stood by the older woman, half turned toward the door. All three of them were as motionless as wax figures. Light flickered over them. In the dim cottage, the additional source was quite apparent, even through the old glass.

That was the Hand of Glory. That was Ross MacDougal. And *that* was a knife.

Even as the threat registered in William's mind, tightening his hand around the grip of his gun, it lifted his spirits. A man wouldn't need a knife with a spell that killed instantly. Nor would he be standing there and talking. The actual words Ross used didn't come clearly through the window, but William heard the rise and fall of his voice, and in it he heard the whining of a frightened dog, one whose fear may drive it to spring at any moment.

Slowly, glad to find that he could still move, he brought the gun up to the window. As far as he could tell, Ross had a good grip on the Hand, but a good grip wouldn't necessarily last very long. If the intent of the Hand's wielder mattered, a distraction would help too—but the man was also conventionally armed, and he had three hostages. The trick would be timing.

William didn't look at Judith. Throat like the Sahara, every muscle in his body tense, he found a stable stance beneath the window and pressed the muzzle of the gun to the glass. Inside, Ross stood in front of his mother, looking sorrowful. Questions rose in William's mind, but none changed what he had to do now. He took aim.

Ross raised the knife.

The first shot broke the glass. The second bullet, a blink behind it, hit Ross in the hip as he spun around. William heard his cry and saw him sag at the middle, but didn't have time to observe more. He was up and running, throwing himself through the door and into the room, where the Hand had fallen to the floor and under the table, each of its fingers still burning.

He ignored blood, ignored screams. He was still

moving. The women weren't. There was some factor at work other than being able to see the Hand—some trick of time or intent. Good. How did he end it?

Put the Hand out.

How did that work?

Legends and notes crowded his memory. Thieves. Servant girls. Milk.

He seized one of the pails by the door and hurled the contents at the still-burning Hand. The pail hit the floor with a crash. The drenched flames sputtered and died, and milk flowed across the cottage floor and around the prone body of Ross MacDougal. By his side, it mingled with his rapidly flowing blood, forming red and white patterns like fluid roses.

Thirty-three

THERE WAS NO GRADUAL RETURN TO MOTION, NO
chance to stretch and feel sensation returning.
Paralysis left Judith as suddenly as it had struck her,
sending the jolting pain of a stubbed toe over her
whole body. She snarled one of the riper oaths she'd
learned during her years away before she remembered
her company.

Well, they were doubtless feeling the same. And
there were more surprising things in this house just
now than the local lady's profanity ever could be.

Judith spun to look where Ross had fallen. Her
weight went back as she moved, and her fists clenched,
but clearly none of that was necessary. Ross lay on his
back in a pool of mingled blood and milk. His chest
moved steadily, though shallowly, and his eyelids
twitched. Still alive. Damn. Well, it would be easy
enough to fix that.

But William was kneeling by Ross's side, his coat
and waistcoat in a carelessly discarded pile on the
floor, and pressing the crumpled remains of his shirt
against the wound on Ross's leg. The muscles on his

bare chest and back flexed with the effort, and Judith's body tightened, responding to her own survival instinct as much as to the view.

As always, there was neither time nor privacy. Gillian was rushing to her brother's side, and William's actions weren't just a source of arousal; they were a reminder. Judith was supposed to behave that way. She should be civilized. Merciful.

Human.

"I'll go and get the doctor," she said, but she took a quick look at Mrs. MacDougal and Gillian before she moved toward the door. She'd put on civilization for their sakes, but everyone in the room knew that her real concern lay with worthier recipients than the blackguard necromancer on the floor. "Are you both all right? Mr. Arundell?"

Gillian didn't even look up, but there was no blood on her, and she'd moved quickly enough. It took a moment for Mrs. MacDougal to focus her eyes on Judith's face. When she did, to Judith's relief, she nodded. If she'd looked grim before, she was a granite figure now, a remonstrating angel from the head of some tomb.

She asked no questions. But then, she wouldn't. She'd served Judith for forty years, and she was still under the *geas* that had held her then. Elspeth MacDougal might have learned very well not to ask about certain things.

The realization was another blow.

William's voice steadied Judith, even preoccupied as it was. "I'm fine. He'll live, I should think. The wound's in the fleshy part of his leg, and it's missed any vessels, as far as I can tell. Do get the doctor, though. I've been known to be wrong."

Judith went. Part of her wondered why she was bothering, and why she kept running once she was out of the MacDougals' sight. She could always just say she'd run, and save the nation the price of a rope—but she was at least half human, and this was here and now.

Acts were stones. Pile enough of them together, and you might have the shape you wanted, or one that was close enough to serve.

She gave Dr. McKendry the sanitized version of the story. Ross had attacked the three women with a knife, and William had shot him in the leg.

"My God," said the doctor. They were already on their way back to the Gordons' house, now in Dr. McKendry's carriage. He was driving—the horses, though bred from MacAlasdair stock, didn't have quite enough training not to find Judith intimidating—and so spared her the full force of the look she knew was on his face. "Why in heaven's name would a man act so?"

"I don't know," said Judith, not lying. She really didn't know why Ross had gone down his path—particularly not after his obscure attempts to justify himself.

She could think of any number of possibilities, though. She didn't know which of them—or what entirely different motive—would be the explanation. All of them still came to mind far too readily for her own comfort.

❧

To the best of Judith's knowledge, Dr. McKendry took his oaths very seriously. Certainly when he knelt by Ross MacDougal's bed, seemingly disregarding the hard floor and aging knees alike, he worked as hard and as carefully as she'd ever seen him with a patient. His face was grave—as it would have been with any other serious injury—and if he made less effort to avoid causing pain than usual, that might just have been because Ross never came back to full consciousness.

Eventually the doctor sat back, bloody handed and weary. "He'll do. I'll come tomorrow to make sure 'tis not festered." He washed his hands on the wet scrap of towel Gillian offered, then let William help him to his feet. "I'll have a look at the two of you lasses before I go, though."

"We're fine," said Mrs. MacDougal.

"I'm glad you think so," said the doctor. "However, your daughter's well along with child. Not a good time for a shock. And you're no' as young as you were, Lizzie, any more than I am."

Gillian let out a long sigh, like the hiss of a bellows, and leaned into the sheltering arm of her husband, now returned from his errand. "Might as well be safe, Mum." She looked back to Judith, hesitated, and then asked, "What about"—brown eyes flicked toward Ross—"him?"

"I'd best keep him at the castle," Judith said. "The rooms up there lock, and I've enough men to watch him. We'll figure out more later."

Loch Arach took care of minor crimes itself—sometimes diplomatically, often roughly. Judith rarely had to intervene much. The unfortunate Ryan, whose hand still lay under the table looking like a giant withered spider on its back, had been the last man to try outright murder. They'd hanged him. They'd had to ask the Queen, and the law hadn't been nearly as touchy then as it was now about a provincial lady serving as justice.

Thirty years later, Judith would have to contact her brothers again. She'd also have to decide what Ross's actual crime was. He'd said he wouldn't kill her if he could help it. What a gentleman he'd been.

"Lady?"

McKendry's voice was polite and concerned. William was looking at her too, brow furrowed. She'd been staring into space longer than she'd thought. Not really a surprise: that was the closest to death, or whatever, that she'd been in a very long time. Even battle hadn't been so bad. She'd been able to fight.

"The castle, for now," she repeated.

"I'll take him," said Ronald, slipping his arm from around his wife.

"The two of us," William said. "Eventually. Meanwhile—" Judith saw him looking at Gillian and her mother, balancing the doctor's concern with what he knew of them and what his mission required. She, who had herself judged the breaking strain of men and women more than once, thought it was an expert look. "I'm afraid I need to ask a few questions."

"Oh?" Gillian frowned. "I'm not ungrateful for your help, sir, but..." She trailed off, presumably because it was hard to put *What business is it of yours?* into diplomatic terms.

"Mr. Arundell does detective work back in London,"

said Judith. "If Ross was led into this—threatened, mayhap, or blackmailed—then I'll be finding the people who did it. Ross talked of improving the world, or at least the country, and of how the village wasn't natural. I'm not sure what he meant by that, or what he wanted with me."

"With you," William repeated. It might have been a question, but there was no inflection in it—no tone at all, only stillness.

Judith nodded. "Talked about his 'brothers' in London not wanting a corpse." She looked back over to Gillian. "And there were letters?"

"Aye," said Gillian. "Three. All with English post-marks, though I didn't note from where."

"Do you know where they are now?" William asked. He was very calm, almost casual. Only his mouth moved.

Gillian shook her head.

"He threw the last one on the fire," said Mrs. MacDougal. "I saw it burning. I had words with him about it this morning. Asked was it a girl he'd gotten in trouble, or was he on the wrong side of the law? He said I couldna' understand." She took a slow, rasping breath. "I shouldna' wonder if the others ended up as kindling too."

"I see."

"They weren't large, the letters," said Gillian, closing her eyes to aid her memory. "And they didn't seem like the sort a lass might write to her sweetheart—or to a man who had been. Plain paper. No perfume, nothing of that sort. And the hand looked like a man's, from what little I saw of it."

Judith, glancing involuntarily at the other hand that looked like a man's, had to stifle an inappropriate laugh. Hands and hands, she thought. *Never play poker with a surgeon, MacAlasdair—bastard always comes up with a good hand.* That had been King, in the War Between the States. Private at the beginning, corporal by the end. He'd taken a shot to the face, lost most of his jaw, and still lived for a day and a half.

She inched closer to the fire.

"If you recall anything else, do let me know," William said with a warm and sympathetic smile. "You know where I'm staying, of course."

"I'll give you more of the details of this"—Judith gestured around the room, vaguely—"up at the castle later. We'd best let the doctor make his examination."

"Of course," said William. "Mr. Gordon, perhaps we should start for the castle now. I'd imagine it'll take us longer to get there with him than it will for the lady."

He passed by Judith as he spoke, brushing her shoulder with his fingers: a quick touch, necessarily subtle because of their audience, but no accident.

It was a good reminder. She didn't necessarily *want* to remember—it would have been easier to sink back into plans and thoughts, into the inside of her head— but she was physical, human, and the lady of Loch Arach. Certain responsibilities attended on all three.

"Thank you," she said and then crossed the room to kneel in front of Mrs. MacDougal. "I'm sorry," she said. "I'm so very sorry."

"You didna' make him do it," said the old woman. Her eyes shone with tears, but none of them fell.

"You didna' make him do anything. You never asked him, nor I, nor Gillie. He went to the city and he came back wrong, that's all."

Plenty of men came back fine—or better. Judith knew that. So did everyone in the room, probably including Mrs. MacDougal herself. None of them said it, just as nobody mentioned all of what Ross had said or the hand that still lay beneath the table. If Ronald or Dr. McKendry saw it, they *didn't* see it.

The world turned on silences as much as on words. She'd had that thought before, but never so strongly.

"I'll come back tomorrow," Judith said, as she would to any of her people in crisis, and then her brain caught up with her mouth. This was no ordinary misfortune. "If you'd like."

"Of course," said Mrs. MacDougal, as she would have at any other time. "Very generous of you."

With that, Judith left. There was nothing else she could do.

❧

She wished she'd ridden. Walking home gave her too much time to think. Riding would have been quicker and would have occupied her mind more. The road held little to distract her—no bird sang in the sere brown-and-gray wilderness, no small animals fled her presence—and so she heard every crunch of shoe leather against dirt, felt every beat of her heart and each breath that filled her lungs, and still couldn't concentrate hard enough on them to get away from her thoughts.

Flight would help. Hunting would help. She hoped

so—and for the first time since she'd come back to
Loch Arach, she felt the village and her duties there as
a weight on her shoulders, or shackles on her wrists.
The village had bound her, and maybe that was right.
After all, she'd bound *it*, or her family had. Through
interest—through mystery—the MacAlasdairs had
linked an otherwise obscure village to the worst of
what lay in the outside world: greed, prying, and
whatever strange fanaticism had moved Ross.

The *geasa* that William had asked about were minor
in comparison.

Discipline kept Judith from swearing aloud. She
knew her own strength and the limits of her control
too well to risk kicking a fence post or punching a tree
on the way. But inside her mind, as the road widened
and wound and led her back to her own front gate, she
cursed steadily—and wearily.

The look on Janssen's face when she arrived could
have meant that Judith's own expression reflected her
mood, or just that the events of the day had shaken
the man. "Mr. Arundell and Mr. Gordon are in the
small downstairs drawing room, my lady. With Mr.
MacDougal. I didn't know where else to direct them."

"The green one, or the one with the mirrors?"

"The mirrors, my lady."

"It'll do," said Judith. "Better than the wine cellar."

When she'd been a child, MacAlasdair Keep had
possessed, if not proper dungeons in the Gothic
tradition, at least two cells near the wine cellar itself.
Floods and disuse had done good work there since
Ryan's day, and Judith had taken to storing the more
dilapidated bits of castle furniture there until she could

dispose of them. Currently a set of moth-eaten chairs and a writing desk missing half a leg were the prisoners in custody. She neither wanted to move them for Ross's sake nor to go down to the cells and check on him with any regularity.

No. She'd keep him upstairs. They'd do…whatever they ended up doing…quickly, and then he'd be gone and it would be done. Then she could think about the future, if she had to.

"Are they still there?" Judith asked.

Janssen shook his head. "Campbell's watching Ro—the prisoner," he said and dropped his eyes. He and Ross would have been children together, Judith realized. Friends? She didn't know—though in a small village, good friends or bitter rivals were the most likely options—and couldn't ask. "Mr. Arundell took the black mare down to Belholm. He said you'd understand. And that he'd come back soon."

"Thank you," said Judith.

She went inside. She'd check on Ross, then talk with her brothers. She didn't have time to think about how relieved Janssen's last statement had made her feel—nor how disappointed she'd felt a moment before.

Thirty-four

NECESSARY FACTS: THE HAND. THE KNIFE (AND WILLIAM did not want to think about that more than he had to, nor about how close his timing had been, nor about the myriad things "didn't want a corpse" might cover). Ross's apparent fit of idealism. The letters. Brothers in London.

Riding, William made the list over and over, devoting to it all of the consciousness he could spare. Placid as the mare was, that wasn't very much—even the best parts of the road were narrow and uneven—and William was almost thankful for the distraction. The border between analysis and overthinking was very fine at times. This was likely one of them.

By the time he reached the post office in Belholm, he and the horse were both dripping sweat despite the cold day. William patted her side on the way in, a manner of vague apology, and then rushed to the telegraph counter, where the young man in attendance looked up and stared. "Sir?" he managed.

"Telegram," said William. "I'll give you the addresses at the end."

Inwardly he felt for the boy. He hadn't stopped to tidy up before he'd flung himself on horseback, and now he stood hatless, shirtless beneath his coat, and disheveled, not to mention flushed and perspiring. He *had* made sure there was no blood left on him, though. The local constables wouldn't be bursting in to interrupt him.

"Begin," he said. "Initial quarry located and subdued. Stop. Resourceful man. Stop." The official euphemisms filled his head, all fairly and thankfully straightforward compared to the letter codes. "Doing favors for friends. Stop. Interested in local nobility. Stop."

Then *he* stopped, with the telegraph boy watching him in a blend of excitement and wariness, and tried to recall how to go on. The phrase for "necromancy" was more obscure than the ones for "sorcerer" and "suspected cult affiliation." Meanwhile, the two other customers were staring at him too.

One day, Clarke would be clever enough to invent a private bloody system of sending urgent messages. Meanwhile, if one of the cults was active in England—and lively enough to have its minions try to kidnap a MacAlasdair—D. Branch needed to know as immediately as he could manage.

"Used help from underground. Stop." There it was. "Exact membership unknown. Stop."

Ross hadn't woken up enough to talk, although neither William nor Ronald had been particularly gentle about carrying him. Once in the drawing room, William had stripped the unconscious man to the waist, to the puzzlement and scandal of Mr. Gordon.

"Looking for marks," William had explained, and a knowing look had entered the other man's eyes.

"Tattoos, aye? I've heard of that wi' criminals."

William had nodded and let Ronald have the half-truth. None of the cults would tattoo its members *just* for affiliation, but the Grey Duke's servants used certain designs as a conduit for dark power, and other forms of initiation left telltale scars. The old witch finders had been, mostly, as vile fanatics as anyone William had hunted, but their beliefs had somehow enveloped a shred of truth: certain beings left signs on their followers' bodies.

Aside from William's bullet wound, the only mark on Ross had been a scar along his right bicep: old enough for the wound itself to have healed, fresh enough still to be pink. It didn't look like a demon's mark or a god's. It looked like the sort of thing a man might pick up in a knife fight. Ross hadn't seemed like the knife-fighting type.

And yet—there'd been that moment of recognition when they'd met, that itch at the back of William's mind, and then Ross's hostility. William had a good memory, but even he might be hazy about a face he'd seen once before, and that during the chaos of a raid.

"Possible adviser," he added. "End message."

He gave the lad Baxter's address and the address of the central office in London, and handed a note across the counter. From the young man's expression, William thought he'd overpaid, but he didn't care, nor did he stay around to collect the change. Let the operator have the joy of it. He needed to get home.

From the wide-eyed way the stable boy looked

at him when he arrived at the castle, word of both Ross's trespasses and William's "real profession" must have spread rapidly. Fascination didn't keep the older groom from looking disapprovingly back and forth between the exhausted mare and William, nor from clicking his tongue in sympathetic reproach as he led the horse away. Stopping the Apocalypse itself might not have been a good enough reason, in the groom's eyes, for taxing a good beast in that manner.

When William reached the kitchen door, feeling far too disheveled for the front entrance, Janssen was sitting at the table, talking with the cook over bread and jam. Both rose when William entered.

"Lady MacAlasdair's out, sir," said Janssen. "She said, if you want to stay here, we're to give you tea in the kitchen until she returns. But if you want to find her, sir," he added, clearing his throat and continuing with the air of a man who didn't quite believe what he was saying, "she's in the forest. She said you'll know where."

"Then I will."

~❧~

When he wasn't running in the dark, the trip through the forest was actually rather pleasant, particularly after he'd borrowed a shirt and a hat from Janssen. Thus sheltered from the chilly air, he made his way along the paths he'd taken before, with the world quiet around him and the smell of pine in the air. Red light from the sky filtered down through the shadows of the trees, which made the forest look a trifle more infernal than William would have preferred, but it was calm and peaceful. He hadn't had much calm or peace in the last few hours.

He'd always had a good memory for directions—it was one of the reasons he'd done so well in D Branch—but the ease with which he found these particular paths surprised him. Perhaps it shouldn't have. Meeting a dragon was the sort of experience that branded itself on a man's mind. That would probably have been true even if the dragon hadn't been Judith.

As William walked, he kept looking up at the sky, or what parts of it he could see through breaks in the trees. He spotted two or three flying shapes. A moment's observation and a distinct *whooooo* in one case revealed them to be birds, but he stood still in each case until he was sure.

She said she'd meet you, he told himself sternly after the third time. *Why does it matter if you see her beforehand or not?*

He had no real answer for that—nothing save that he'd see her sooner, that he'd know she was unhurt when he had time and concentration to fix the fact of it in his mind. Before, in the Gordons' house, he'd had duty to think of. They both had.

Ahead was the point where William remembered leaving the path, or thereabouts. He took a step or two forward, looked off into the woods—and blinked in surprise.

Before, he'd pushed his way through a small wilderness of rocks and branches, hedges and briars. He'd thought he would have an easier time when he could go more slowly and carefully, and when the light was better, but he'd still anticipated the same obstacles.

Instead, a wide trail led off into the woods. A little wider than a man's body, it wound over crushed plants and beside uprooted brambles. In one place, a log that William had needed to climb over was gone, tossed into the forest beside the trail.

She hadn't known he'd be coming. She'd offered him another option. But she'd prepared just in case. That might have been hospitality—it was a strong tradition in older parts of the world and among the older races, and Judith was at least partly a daughter of both—but it made William smile, and the evening air was considerably less cold.

The way to the clearing felt short once he'd started down the new path, much shorter than it had on his previous trip. Despite the sorcery around Loch Arach, William knew *that* was subjective.

As the wind shifted, he could smell smoke, and before long, he saw the glow of flames through the trees ahead of him. William hesitated—uncontrolled, a fire out here would be a serious matter—but the flames stayed where they were, low to the ground and not apparently growing.

Besides, he thought then, Judith would probably have to be in some trouble if the forest itself was on fire.

Hoping for the best, but with a hand on his gun, William stepped quickly out into the clearing.

The fire was as he'd been wishing: a large, well-built pile of wood surrounded by a wide ring of bare earth and stones. The flames burned merrily, reaching up into the night sky like friendly hands.

At one side of the bonfire, Judith perched on a

rock. She was in human form, but she managed to perch nonetheless: knees drawn up to her chest, elbows resting on knees, chin in her hands. The dress she wore was dark, and in it, sitting quite still and watching the flames, she blended almost completely into the shadows.

Hearing him—probably, although given her other form, William thought that smell might be as reasonable a clue—she turned her head, a swift flick of her neck that would have been quite painful for a normal human. Her eyes glowed when they met his, all the more visibly so in the shifting shadows that passed over her face.

Her lips parted, full and dark.

"Hello," said William, all other speech driven momentarily from his head. He felt that his body went forward of its own will, knowing what he didn't and certain where he wasn't. There were instincts stronger than bodily survival.

"I didn't know whether to expect you or not," said Judith, the wood crackling in counterpoint to her voice. "I thought I'd wait until after twilight."

She was standing as she spoke, unfolding herself into her full height as a human, into the full force of her body's curves and its strength, and William watched like a lad at his first magic lantern show. Judith was here. She was alive and whole, and every move she made was as wondrous as the first transformation he'd seen.

"I'm glad you did," he managed.

They had business to talk about, he and Judith—questions of Ross's disposal and of the next steps between D Branch and the MacAlasdairs, even questions about the MacDougals and Dr. McKendry, the plundered graves and the snuffed hand. William knew that. He knew that his duty lay in discussing such things, and soon he would remember it enough to speak properly.

Before he could reach that moment, Judith was in his arms.

Thirty-five

WILLIAM REACTED FAST. NO SOONER HAD JUDITH come within his reach than he'd pulled her to him, one arm snug around her waist and the other hand twined in her hair. He kissed her roughly, desperately, his lips hard and demanding. In no mood to be passive, Judith dug her fingernails into his shoulders and wrapped her body around his, battling him for control and loving every second of the struggle. The speed with which he'd responded would by itself have taken her breath away.

Granted, she didn't think she'd exactly surprised him. She hadn't planned on congress. She'd built the fire thinking they would talk, and that anything more would come after. But his scent on the air and the sound of his footsteps had snapped her from unsettling thoughts to intense physical awareness, and she'd welcomed the change. From the moment she'd turned her head and seen William walk into the grove, she'd wanted him, been wet and tingling and open for him from the first word he'd said, and the sensation had filled all the space between them.

She could have held back, but why?

There would always be time to talk.

He palmed her breasts through her shirtwaist, rough caresses in which his talented hands squeezed and rubbed without any sign of his usual patience, and Judith groaned against his mouth. Her whole body hummed with lust—with *need*—strong enough to overwhelm all other awareness. This was like the hunt too: the cold air, the warmth of flame and flesh, the uncomplicated drive toward a single and increasingly urgent objective.

When she wrapped a leg around William's thigh, they both swayed, off balance, and William swore in an almost dragonish hiss. "Probably better places—" he muttered.

Before he could think too much about that, Judith dragged his mouth back down to hers again. As they kissed—he was easy to distract, thank God—she pulled both of them backward, stumbling blindly in her conflicting urges to find the right spot and to keep kissing William, keep feeling his hands on her breasts and the firm muscle of his arse beneath her palms.

At another time, the impact of the tree against her back might have hurt. Now it was cause for celebration. Judith grinned against William's neck. "Better place," she said and licked the hollow behind his ear. Pulling him against her, she slid her hands under his coat and raked her fingernails up his spine.

This time, William groaned, just before he pulled her head back and claimed her mouth again, his tongue as hot and insistent as the long, hard ridge of his cock was against Judith's aching sex. He thrust against her quickly, in a rhythm she welcomed and quickly echoed, one only disrupted by his hand as he tugged her skirts upward and out of the way. Even when it was accidental, the touch of his hand on her thigh made Judith shiver.

She reached for him, wrapping her hand around his rod for a teasing second to feel it pulse through the thin fabric of his trousers—but a second was all either of them could allow for teasing. Judith pulled her mouth away from William's and bit her lip as she flicked open the first button of his fly. The second got caught for a much-too-long second, and she was just on the verge of pulling it off, to hell with his trousers and either of their reputations, when it came free and the third followed. His cock sprang out, pushing against her hand, and he arched his hips to thrust into her grip.

"Do you need to—" she began, not wanting to stop and talk but wanting more to have him fully at his ease.

He shook his head. "I believe you."

"Good," Judith said and pulled his head down to kiss him again.

Then William pushed her back against the tree and wedged his body between her legs. With one hand, he spread her open, rubbing her sex in the process and making her cry out. She let out another cry when he thrust into her, mingling with his own growl, and let her head fall back against the supporting trunk. He was filling her, stretching her, as hot inside her body as the fire had been on her back. Cold behind her and to her sides; heat before her and inside her. The contrast left her gasping and frantic.

Now, with William's hands to aid her and the tree at her back, she could wrap her legs around his hips, holding him with all the muscles, inside and out, that she'd developed over an active life. She heard his appreciation in the half-choked curse that left his lips and felt it in the first of his thrusts, deep and hard, and in the heat of his mouth on her bare neck. She jerked her hips up to meet his, welcoming the contact and craving more.

He gave it to her: strong and smooth. Even on the edge of his self-control, he plunged deep into her again and again in a relentless series of thrusts that built and built until she was screaming, knowing that nothing in the forest could hear her and beyond caring even if that wasn't true. She called out his name, she urged him onward, and toward the end, she begged him with more desperation than she'd ever felt in her life, clawing at his back and shoulders, needing above everything to be fuller and closer and—there, *there*.

Climax was like a full-body blow. Blind and breathless, she could only lean against the tree, trusting in it and in William's arms as pleasure claimed her whole body. It went on for what seemed like hours, as William's steady pace quickened and became desperate itself, as he arched forward and spent himself inside her in a moment of warmth and sensation that blended with the last few seconds of her own peak. There was no thought in that moment, only instinct and sensation.

Judith wished it could have gone on forever.

❦

"I'll take Ross out to Aberdeen tomorrow," said William. "My contacts can see to transportation from there. And he should be able to stand the journey by morning."

It was the first either of them had spoken since finding the tree, and it was a firm tug back earthward. Judith went on picking pine needles out of her hair. "Well enough. It'll do the village good not to have him about," she said calmly.

She didn't ask if William would come back. She knew the answer.

"You should go with me," he said, which did make Judith look at him in surprise. "I wasn't there when he came in with the hand. I don't know all of what he said. Having a witness would help. Particularly one who knows the village."

"Particularly one who knows my family too, I'd think," said Judith. A piece of bark was stuck between her waistband and her shirt. She fished it out, knowing she'd find others, and that her shoulders and back would bear faint red marks. That was fine.

"Probably, yes."

She walked over to stand above the remains of the fire. Only a few flames licked at the air now, and they were small. The fire pit held mostly dark wood and glowing coals. The air had started to feel chilly again. Judith didn't mind; it felt good on her hot face and hands. "If we're to open relations"—oh, that was a nice double entendre now—"with your people, this might be a good chance to start, aye?"

"That too," said William.

He was careful, she thought, not to sound too

enthusiastic, not to try to persuade her that he had her own good at heart. If she hadn't had to keep her mind on business, she'd have kissed him for that.

Stephen might have been a better choice. He was more familiar with the city, and he'd had more to do with pure humans and modern humans and the world as a whole. If she put William in touch with him, Judith thought, she wouldn't have to leave Loch Arach.

She discarded that idea partly for the reason she'd told Stephen not to come up—he had a wife and a small child, and she was only willing to trust D Branch so far.

Partly she wanted to go. The thought squeezed her chest and throat, smoke from a much sloppier fire than she'd ever built. Loch Arach wasn't a refuge any longer.

"I'll come," she said and then cleared her throat and added, "I'll have to leave in a year or two anyhow."

She'd spoken half to herself, but when William asked, "Why?" the question was neither startling nor intrusive.

Judith shrugged, still not turning from the fire. She heard him walk forward, then felt his arms wrapping around her waist and pulling her back against his chest. Surrounded by warmth, breathing in William's scent, she leaned her head against his and felt her muscles unwind. "It's what we do," she said, and the words didn't hurt as much as she'd thought they would. "You can't have the same lord for two hundred years, can you? Not even for sixty, if he—or she—looks twenty the whole time. So I'll leave, and my 'nephew' will come and take over and inherit when I 'die overseas.'"

"You do that regularly?"

"Aye. I've stayed too long as it is." She sighed. "It's easy to do."

He nodded, his hair brushing lightly against her. "It's a peaceful place. And one gets tired of war—even the small ones I fight. I'd imagine it goes double for the larger sort."

"I'd really hoped to forget the way a bullet sounds going into flesh," Judith said, "or the smell of human blood. But that's not the way life happened, is it?" Regret was a waste of time. She'd learned that when she was still young, even by mortal standards. "Do you know who those 'brothers' Ross mentioned might be?"

"One of the cults I mentioned," he said after a second's hesitation. "The most likely call themselves the Consuasori—derived from a Latin word that means 'advisers.'"

"Seems like he had more than advice in mind. What do they want?"

"England the way it was in their day. Ruling the world—or at least the nation—to make sure it doesn't change very much."

Judith laughed, viciously satisfied. "They must be having a hell of a time lately, then."

"In more ways than one. We raided their main meeting place about half a year ago." William flexed the fingers of one hand absently against her stomach, a man recalling an old pain. "We were sure we'd gotten most of the cult—and I think we did capture or kill most of the major figures—but a few escaped. Apparently they're still better organized than we'd hoped."

"They always are," said Judith, "whoever they are. And if Ross was getting orders, then there's at least one or two more who I can hold to account for all this."

"You won't be the only one," William said, and his arms tightened about her, offering a promise that she didn't want to make him speak aloud. "We'll have to find them, of course."

"Or him," said Judith. "Ross said only one other man knew what he was doing up here."

"I'm not sure if that makes things easier or not."

"Well, I hear your people are good at finding things out." Judith looked up at William and smiled, then raised her head to brush a light kiss across his lips. "You managed better than any other mortal in my lifetime."

"Something to remember," he said lightly, "in my old age."

She expected that to sting, and it did, a little, but no matter. Pain passed like all other things. "I'd not tell your grandchildren much more about that, though," she replied, managing the same joking tone he had. "You'll quite scandalize them."

"Someone has to," said William, and he sighed. "Shall we?"

"The world waits," said Judith.

❧

They left early in the morning for Aberdeen. Trains didn't enter into it this time—Judith's carriage was waiting when William reached the castle, with a pair of sturdy horses in harness and one of the local young men at the reins, still blinking and surreptitiously rubbing his eyes. They were on their own schedule. Judith, William suspected, just wanted to get under way as soon as she could. He didn't blame her. Ross's final delivery into the hands of the men at the central office couldn't come soon enough for him either, though probably for different reasons.

The man himself was lying in the carriage when William boarded, taking up all of one side to keep the weight off his wounded leg. His wrists and ankles were manacled together. A faraway look in his eyes and a slackness about his mouth suggested that his bonds weren't the only things keeping Ross from being trouble.

"Been much of a conversationalist, has he?" William asked, sliding onto the bench next to Judith.

"Not to me," she said. Judith wore the same bottle-green hat and dark coat in which she'd come up to Aberdeen the time before, and from the green velvet at her hem and cuffs, the same dress as well. She sat tucked up against one wall of the coach, with her hands folded primly in her lap and her back so straight that William wondered if she could manage that posture all the way to Aberdeen. He longed to reach out to her, to touch her in reassurance, if only briefly, but witness and custom kept his hands at his sides.

He'd left the castle shortly after they'd gotten back the previous night. He and Judith had arrived walking a good distance from each other and speaking formally of plans for the journey. Judith had paused at the door, and William had waited himself, but they'd both known she couldn't invite him in. Whatever the rumors about them might be, it would do no good for her to have dinner, let alone spend the night, with the Englishman who'd be taking a local boy off to prison the next day.

That local boy couldn't do much in the village now, even if he was conscious of anything that happened, but he'd be answering questions at D Branch. It would be best for everything to appear impartial.

William met Judith's eyes and smiled, as sympathetically as he might have done to any comrade in arms. It was as far as he could go, and as far as she could accept. By her answering grin, faint and weary as it was, he knew she understood.

"Campbell said Ross talked in his sleep," Judith went on as the coachman snapped the reins and the carriage lurched forward onto the road.

"He's more than earned a few bad dreams," William said, glancing at the figure across from him, who looked back in sullen lethargy. "Anything specific?"

"Not that Campbell could make out. Of course, I doubt he was listening very closely."

Outside, Loch Arach dwindled behind them. William saw a flash of light as the rising sun glinted off the lake, and then the village was gone. Gray rock and dark trees shot up on either side of the carriage. The land had shut them in. It was an absurd thought, but William couldn't banish it as quickly as he would have liked. He rubbed at the back of his neck.

"Kenneth's a fair hand with the horses," Judith said, sounding like she spoke offhandedly. "I could swear he practices on the sly. I don't travel nearly often enough for his liking—though, of course, we all keep the road in good condition. There's none in this part of the country that'd take that charge less than seriously."

"Your faith in human nature is slightly reassuring."

Judith shrugged. "All parts of human nature. The railway didn't get here very long ago, and the roads were most people's way out. They'd do what was needful—and the man who didn't would hear of it."

On the other side of the carriage, Ross shifted and muttered. Like Campbell before him, William couldn't have said what the words were, if they were words at all.

"I had a driver once," William said, "who greatly resented me for wanting to keep all four carriage wheels on the road. Not a young man, oddly enough—I think he was in his eighties at the time."

"Less to lose?"

"That could be," William said and laughed, but his own words, even his feeling of amusement, took second place in his concentration.

He couldn't have said why. Instinct was an itch in the palms of his hands, the urge to shift forward in his seat, a restless twitch of one booted foot. He checked on Ross again. The man's eyes were closed now. He wasn't trying to sit up. His wrists and ankles were still bound.

William made himself count to ten.

The carriage went around a turn, sliding Judith toward him. Her weight against his side and the smell of her hair and skin were calming, no matter that the contact was brief. He fought back the urge to reach for her. After a second, she made herself move back to where she'd been, putting a few inches between them that seemed like a much longer distance.

He cleared his throat. He could have said a hundred things, asked her a thousand, if Ross hadn't been in the carriage. Now he couldn't think of anything. With that blank face in front of him, William's mind went just as blank, save only for the sense of unease that kept plaguing him.

Slowly, he slipped his pistol out of its holster and placed it on his knee. There he could hold it, keeping his finger well away from the trigger—wouldn't do for Ross to die before D Branch could ask their questions— and yet feeling better for the metal beneath his palm.

"The cuffs are good," said Judith mildly. "I checked myself."

"I don't doubt it," said William, and indeed it hadn't occurred to him to question the manacles. "What did you give him?"

"Morphine, I wouldn't doubt. It was McKendry who did that. I admit I didn't take much interest in his comfort."

"How long ago?"

Ross opened his eyes. They still didn't quite focus. His tongue slid out of his mouth, tapped at his upper lip, and then retreated. He kept watching the other side of the carriage.

"Midnight, roughly?" Judith hesitated and looked back and forth between Ross and William. "There are the two of us here. And we did make sure he'd nothing else on him."

"I know. I just—"

Ross smiled.

Stopping mid-sentence, William heard Judith's sudden, sharp inhalation and knew she was thinking along the same lines he was. Nobody in the carriage could have thought any differently.

That was *not* the smile of a drug-addled man. It was too deliberate and too knowing. There was still a haze about Ross, a sense that he wasn't quite himself, but his eyes weren't vacant anymore. They narrowed as he looked at William, and his smile widened.

Ross opened his mouth and said a word.

William didn't know it. He couldn't have spelled it. He wasn't even sure he could have pronounced it. Ross's mouth looked like it bent in the effort, all odd angles and distorted muscles. William only knew that the word began with *M* and that hearing it made the backs of his eyes hurt.

Beside him, Judith snarled like no human woman ever would have. William glimpsed her face and saw, in the seconds before she caught herself, her canines extend and her eyes start to glow.

No spell William had ever heard of took only a single word. He knew that, just as he'd known earlier that Ross was bound and drugged, and yet fear tightened his stomach and his chest.

"What was that?" Judith bit off each word, leaning toward Ross. "You *will* tell us—"

"You'll find out," he said quietly. "I expect it'll be harder on you this way. I wish you'd been sensible."

He smiled again.

And then he stopped. His mouth fell open like that of a man who'd been hit unexpectedly, and his eyes went huge with fear and more than fear—shock, William thought, and betrayal. "No," Ross mouthed. "But—no."

Judith cried out in pain and revulsion. When William turned to look, she had one hand pressed against her temple. She closed her eyes, then obviously forced them open. "What in God's name *are you*—"

Then Ross started screaming. As William hastily rapped on the ceiling of the carriage, hoping that stopping was the right idea and knowing only that he wanted Judith away from whatever was hurting her, Ross thrashed in his bonds like a fish on a hook. He had the same mindless look in his eyes as a wounded animal, and in that split second William pitied him. Whatever he'd done, whatever he'd given himself to, he'd gotten a reward that William wouldn't have wished on any man.

Pity didn't last very long—between one blink of the eye and another. After that, there was nothing *to* pity.

Ross unfolded in blood.

A sound from all around them took up his shrieking. It mingled with the screams of the panicking horses, the shouts of the driver, the rough sounds of dirt under speeding carriage wheels, and the wet noises of a human body...

William couldn't say what that body was doing, and he didn't want to. After a lifetime as investigator, soldier, and sometimes assassin for D Branch, he'd never seen anything like what happened to Ross MacDougal. He hoped he would die before he ever saw it again. He looked to Judith and saw the same horrified disbelief on her face. Two hundred years and this was foreign to her too.

His hands went cold. He grabbed his gun.

The shrieking sound was high-pitched now, a saw blade from the air around them. That air itself was deforming. The other side of the coach wasn't there; instead, there was a room, and in front of it, a human head pressing against some reddish barrier like cheesecloth that distorted and blurred all features. Other shapes lurked behind it. Most of them were much less human. Maybe they'd been human once.

The room expanded to either side, going beyond the blood-soaked carriage. The world twisted.

Outside, the coachman gave one cry of mortal terror, a panicked cry to God. Then the carriage was tilting, going over on its side—and space was twisting with it.

He was falling.

They were falling.

They were all falling: off the road, perhaps, or perhaps through a different place entirely. One thing stopped connecting to another.

The man behind the barrier was coming through, almost as entirely teeth and flaring mad eyes as the demons around him. He reached out one hand, and a knife was in it, black fire flaring along the blade.

Judith was snarling. He saw light—he didn't know from where—glint off green scales on a human-shaped arm.

How much time did it take to transform?

William aimed, as well as he could with the way that the world kept skipping around him, drew a breath, and fired as rapidly as he could: *one, two, three, four, five, six*. They punched little holes through the not-quite-air and made subdued popping sounds.

A drop of Ross's blood fell from the ceiling and hit William squarely in the middle of his hand, flowered red, and ran in all directions in rivulets.

One bullet grazed the intruder's cheek. Two hit the things directly behind him, which roared in pain and outrage. The other three bullets sprayed a route down the man's shoulder and along his chest. As the air became air again, William could still see the bullets' flight and the trails they left behind.

He could see the knife too, when it left the man's hand. He knew the man was aiming for his heart.

Space still warped between them. The knife didn't fly entirely true. William almost dodged completely. But not quite.

Damn, he thought as he felt the blade sink in just below his ribs, burrowing forward with a mind of its own. *This is going to be a problem.*

Then, darkness.

Thirty-six

JUDITH SCREAMED. IN DRAGON FORM, IT CAME OUT AS a roar, which scared Ross's ally and his pack of demons into brief stillness: a useful effect, but not her intention. She had no intention, hadn't since she'd lunged toward William and the stranger, too late and too slow to stop the knife. She just screamed.

The carriage smashed into the ground at the base of the hill. It landed in two halves, several feet apart from each other, all the edges severed with surgical neatness. The back, where Judith had burst the walls during her transformation, was a splintered contrast; so was the tangle of blood and leather and bone at the front, where the horses and Kenneth, poor lad, had been. Between the two were five demons—more-than-man-sized gray horrors with single eyes, four arms each, and too many teeth. William lay in front of them, almost at Judith's feet.

She thought she saw his chest move. She couldn't wait to find out.

The magician was slumping back toward his allies, blood pouring from his torso. His wounds might have been fatal. She didn't wait to find that out either.

Burn, God damn you all.

She didn't bother with control this time. Flame sprayed from her mouth in a swelling cloud, enveloping the demons and the coach behind them. The wood caught; so did the flesh of humans and horses, and Judith snarled at the scent of it. The magician didn't make a sound when he died, just charred and fell.

The demons stood unharmed in the middle of the flames and then rushed forward.

Judith sprang to meet them, landing at William's side. The first swipe of her clawed foreleg knocked two of them back against the smoldering wreckage of the coach, and one, as she'd hoped it might, landed with a spike of broken wood through the back of its head, struggling faintly and then moving no more. The other was getting to its feet, but it would take a few moments.

She whirled to meet the rest, just as one sank its claws into the side of her neck. The wound wasn't likely to be serious—she had *far* more between her veins and the air than a human or a beast would have—but Judith snarled at the pain and felt blood begin to flow. She shook herself, but the demon hung on, and then the other two were on her.

They weren't humans, she thought, in an insight as painful as the wound to her neck. They didn't fight the same way—and they didn't need weapons. Judith's experience wouldn't serve her as well in this battle. It might even be a drawback. Aside from the rat-things, much smaller than these and vulnerable to fire, she'd never been in a real fight as a dragon—and she knew she wouldn't survive for long in human form.

But she had fought while wounded before. That much was familiar. She knew how to ignore the pain, set aside the weakness, and push onward—and never before had she had quite so much reason.

Judith roared again and bent to face her enemies.

One was easy enough to dispose of. A quick dart of her head and its neck was between her jaws. The taste was foul, and its blood actually seemed to burn her tongue, but she had no time to care. Quickly, savagely, Judith bit down and snarled again, this time triumphantly, at the resulting crunch.

That left three alive.

At her neck, the demon ripped and tore, and Judith felt her skin and flesh giving way before its onslaught. She clawed it away with one leg, closing her talons around its body. The larger demons' flesh was as liquidly insubstantial as their smaller counterparts' had been. The demon squeezed through her grip, falling bruised but alive to the ground.

Blood was flowing down her neck now. That happened. She'd live.

At least she hoped so.

This was no quick battle like the one in Aberdeen had been. The demons were too large and too hard to kill—the one she'd thrown against the carriage was already rushing toward her again—and she had no ally with a gun. She didn't have any ally at all.

When her claws sheared off one of their arms and it started growing another, she knew she was in trouble. Another slash opened up its stomach—a fatal wound for a mortal—but nothing came out. The demon fell back a few steps but kept moving, and one of its friends took its chance to wrap around Judith's flank and fasten itself—claws *and* teeth, the bastard—on her side, right under her ribs. It didn't make its predecessor's mistake either, but raked through her scales and then leaped away as she struck.

She had to destroy the heads then. *Because this would have been too damn* easy *otherwise.*

But now she knew.

Judith threw herself into the fight once more, striking out with claws and teeth, tail and head and even wings, knocking the demons back with the force of her buffeting. It was messy and far harder than she was used to. Judith's muscles were burning, aching with long use and becoming more and more feeble as she bled from her neck and her side. The struggle was desperate. It was uncertain.

It was exhilarating.

Wounded, worried, tired, Judith was still a dragon, and in dragon shape. All of her old joy in the hunt and battle, her love for testing her strength and quickness against long odds, ran through her veins: rain on earth she'd kept parched for too long. When she threw one of the demons to the ground and crushed its head with her hind foot, she lashed her head back and roared once more, and this time there was laughter in it. The human part of her would have regretted that, but it wasn't in control.

She was a MacAlasdair, the daughter of Andrew and a thousand other ancestors more savage and less human, and this was still her land—her people—her lover. Any that tried to take them, mortal or otherwise, would answer to her.

The last demon fell before her, and she was, for an instinctual and completely inhuman moment, sad to see it go. Was that all? Would nothing else stand forth against her? She showed her teeth to the brightening sky: a challenge to the world.

She didn't even see the demon before it hit her. It must have been hiding, perhaps behind the body of one of its fellows, but Judith never knew. She saw the movement in time to jerk her head left, saving her eye by an inch or less. Pain and weight hit her face at the same moment. The demon ripped its way downward, shredding skin and flesh as it went, and Judith clawed at her own face in half-blind agony.

Her first swipe at the thing missed. So did her second, and she knew it was nearing the base of her neck, where the veins and arteries clustered thick and a deep enough wound might kill even her. The demon was on too firmly, too close. She snarled, futile, and lashed her neck from side to side, but it hung on and dug deeper.

All at once it fell away.

She felt its weight drop first, then saw the creature squirming on the ground. Judith pounced—but it was already going still. Its head was missing.

Judith swung her head to the side, peering at the spot where she knew William had fallen.

He lay on his stomach now. One hand grasped his pistol—he had a second—and he'd braced his arm on his other elbow. William's face was almost bloodless, his eyes huge and bright blue.

"Always one you don't see," he said hoarsely.

Almost before she had time to think about it, Judith

was human again and stumbling toward him on legs that barely worked. She knew so little about human physicking. She had to turn him over. She didn't want to move him. She had to.

She was as gentle as she could be, but her hands felt as unwieldy as if she'd still been trying to use claws.

The knife hilt stuck out of his torso, just below his ribs. A malign list immediately marched through Judith's head: liver, guts, stomach, spleen. Kidneys were toward the back. Blood vessels were everywhere. The blood oozing up around the knife hilt proved that. William's jacket was dark, so she couldn't see how much he'd bled already, but his face was white, with an almost bluish undertone. She'd seen that look before.

Ripping up her petticoats, Judith swore under her breath, long and low, in three different languages.

"An educated woman," said William.

She pressed the wadded cloth against the wound. Never pull the knife out. She'd learned that somewhere. It might have been a hundred years in the past or the day before. "Stop talking. Don't move."

William smiled. "Anything for you, love."

It was not a joke. Judith gasped as if for air, thinking at once that she'd gladly take another demon's claws to her face if it meant hearing those words again, or seeing that smile—and that no bargain she made would guarantee either. "Stay," she said, and she heard her voice crack. "Just stay."

But his eyes had closed.

In the stillness of the morning, her lone sob almost echoed.

With a shaking breath, she got herself back under control. There was still a chance.

William still breathed: shallowly, not healthily, but steadily. That was a start. It wasn't enough for Judith to thank Anyone or to feel any significant sense of relief, however. Breathing at the moment was no guarantee. Judith knew that too well to even try fooling herself.

The hilt of the knife was very small. Against William, a man with a powerful frame and a good bit of muscle on it, one might not have even seen the glint of metal.

She could cheerfully have rent Ross into his component parts once again, or done the same to the other sorcerer. She would have done so in an instant if it would have helped.

It never did.

Judith looked between the rocky valley where they had landed and William's body, still save for the faint movement of his chest. How long would it take her to get out? To get help?

Too long.

She knew that without any calculation at all.

At least, when she didn't have a plan, she didn't need much time to change it.

The transformation strained every atom of her body, every fiber of her will. Shape-changing had never been so hard before. When it was over, she was shaking with the effort, and she fought back her urgency to make herself sit for a moment, telling herself that haste wasn't the only thing that mattered.

As gently as she was able, wincing with every rough movement, Judith picked up William in her fore claws. It was not ideal. She kept his body as straight as she could, but she had claws, and even humans weren't supposed to move the wounded—not without stretchers. She didn't have a stretcher. She didn't have many things she would have wanted, and she was conscious of every single lack, just as she saw every rise and fall of William's chest.

Concentration was as good as prayer. A gunner's mate had told Judith that, with the sea wide around them and gunpowder gritty beneath her fingernails, and she hoped he'd been right. She didn't have time for both.

Judith closed her eyes, breathed in, and became aware of her body. She knew the ground where she stood and adjusted her balance; she tested her muscles, feeling the stiffness coming on and the weakness that she couldn't quite push aside as blood flowed from her own wounds; she felt William's not-inconsiderable weight and how it swung her center forward.

Her wings opened with a crack like a gunshot.

She waited. Tested the wind. Crouched. Then, with the smoothest and most conscious leap she'd ever taken, she sprang into the air and away from the ruin below.

Nobody was on the street when she landed, and the sky was still dark, with only a glimmer of sun showing at the horizon. Farmers would likely be up with cattle or sheep. One of them might have seen her. Judith didn't care.

Lights did go on in McKendry's windows. Setting William down on the lawn, Judith saw them at the edges of both her vision and her awareness. They were probably worried about earthquakes inside—or would be until one of them went to a window. Then they'd have other worries altogether.

She stepped away from William, closed her eyes, and shifted.

"Lady Mac*Alasdair*?" The voice was male and young. Sure enough, when Judith opened her eyes, she saw the door open and Hamilton staring at her with his mouth open.

He had seen *something*. Whether he'd looked out the window before coming down or had opened the door mid-transformation, he looked at Judith now with the knowledge that she wasn't quite human.

Of course, the blood running down from her face probably didn't help—not to mention the long gashes on her outer thigh, the general state of her clothes, or the fact that her arms were bloody to the elbows. Damn. She'd forgotten how she would look as a human.

"You—what—he—my God, what happened?" Hamilton finally managed a sentence.

"More than I wanted," she answered tersely. "Help me bring William inside. Then get the doctor. It's what *will* happen that matters now."

Thirty-seven

FOR THE FIRST TIME IN HER LIFE, JUDITH WISHED THAT Loch Arach was a city, or was much closer to one. A city would have hospitals—not the wretched places of her youth, where the poor and desperate went to die—but the modern sort, where a man with a gut wound would end up under the sharp eyes and quick hands of practiced surgeons in a clean, bright operating theater. McKendry was a very good doctor, but middle age was behind him, and Judith couldn't think where and when he would have seen an injury like William's before. His surgery was small, too, lit as best as he could manage by gas lamps, and Hamilton and his maid served as the only nurses.

Exiled from the surgery, pacing the parlor and deliberately not looking at the clock nor measuring the amount of sun coming in the window, Judith wished she at least didn't know how little they had to work with. Aware that she'd be no help, she hadn't protested when Hamilton had shut the door in her face, but complete ignorance might be better than the limbo where she now found herself, knowing too little to act usefully and too much for peace. She followed the paths of her thoughts, pulled together what plans she could, and then reached the end of useful forethought, where her mind circled like a hungry shark.

Eventually she ducked into the kitchen, stole a bowl of water, and returned to the parlor, where she used the cleaner remains of her petticoat to wash and bind her own wounds. They weren't so bad. She had to bite her lip when she washed out the deeper spots on her collarbone, and she shivered all over afterward like a frightened horse, but she'd had worse. Her hands worked from memory as much as conscious thought: too many battlefields in the past, too many hours of waiting to hear news of victory or defeat, life or death. Had she really thought she could escape that for good?

Best to be glad of the reprieve she'd won for herself, however long it had lasted. The world didn't have to give anyone one year of peace, much less thirty. William hadn't gotten that.

She heard the thought in her own head, heard the epitaph air of it, and almost slapped herself. She couldn't go outside, not and miss an announcement of any kind, but there wasn't nearly enough air in the parlor. The windows didn't open when she tried, and her hands were shaking too badly to try more than once.

She tried sitting down, but stood up again almost at once. She couldn't be still. And she didn't want to bleed on the furniture if the cuts on her thigh resisted the bandage. Walking was most likely bad for them too. If Judith had any sense, she'd stand still. The thought made her feel like the earth was going to shake and buck her off, throwing her to her knees—which actually did appeal as a posture, except that she was in McKendry's parlor and she was the Lady MacAlasdair and she would not curl up on the floor and scream, no matter how much she wanted to.

She would not.

She would hold out as long as she could.

The door opened. Judith spun immediately to face the new arrival—arrivals, as it turned out. McKendry and Hamilton were both at the door. By that, she knew the news would be bad. Their faces confirmed it.

And she couldn't even feel surprised. She'd seen too much to ever have really hoped. "Is he dead?" Judith asked before they could say anything. She discovered that she couldn't raise her voice above a whisper.

"Not yet," said McKendry. His face was haggard, as Judith had seen it before when he'd known he would lose a patient, but there was a sympathy in it that had never appeared when he'd talked to her: his talking-to-the-loved-ones expression. If he hadn't known earlier that her feelings for William went beyond a working partnership, she thought, her face now probably made it clear. God knew they were clear enough to her now.

Too late. Too late. Ah, God, *everything* was too late, and not even she was quick enough for this world at times. She longed for some dark place where she could go to ground.

But McKendry was still talking. "He's lost too much blood to live. Even if he hadn't, the injuries themselves might be fatal. Particularly here." He looked down at his hands with tight lips. "I'm sorry, Lady MacAlasdair."

"Is he conscious?" she asked, feeling every movement of her lips and tongue.

"No. Nor is he likely to be."

She'd expected no better. But William wasn't dead, not yet, and so Judith checked her desire to retreat, pulled herself back from the darkness, and faced the decision she'd thought about since she'd first seen Hamilton on the doorstep.

It wasn't a decision that anyone should make for another. Even less, perhaps, was it a decision that someone who'd never been entirely human should make for someone who'd never been anything else. The women who'd married into the bloodline had known the consequences and been conscious. They'd made their own choices.

William couldn't.

Nobody else would. Nobody else even knew.

"Mr. Hamilton," said Judith, "get your equipment and come back to the surgery. You'll give Mr. Arundell my blood."

"That—Lady MacAlasdair, there's only a chance that it'll help," Hamilton said. "And I can't say how great that chance is."

"I know," said Judith.

She did. Human wives among the MacAlasdairs died—not very often, but often enough—when their bodies couldn't handle the dragon blood they got from their unborn children. They were generally strong and healthy, and nobody had stuck a knife in them. Even if Judith's blood made things better for William, the healing might not take effect until too late—or it might not be enough.

"I'll be in the surgery," Judith said. "Waiting for you." She looked down at her body. "Might be a good idea to send in soap and water too."

⁓

And then she was lying on her back on a none-too-comfortable table, looking up at the ceiling of McKendry's surgery and listening to William's slow, shallow breathing. He wasn't even an arm's length away, but it was best not to touch him. She knew that and kept her arms firmly at her sides, resisting any stray impulses.

Waiting.

It didn't come easily.

Lying still, she itched. There'd not been much time for cleaning. The maid had cut off the remains of one of Judith's sleeves, and she'd scrubbed that arm until the skin was red and stinging. The rest of her remained a patchwork of grime, sweat, and at least two people's blood, not to mention whatever hard-to-see remnants the demons had left drying on her. She hadn't really thought about that until she'd lain down. Then she'd started feeling every molecule of filth.

She knew why. She didn't try too hard to ignore the sensation.

Out of the corner of her eye, she saw McKendry and Hamilton moving around the surgery. They'd reversed their usual roles. McKendry was the assistant now, taking down equipment and passing it to Hamilton, periodically stepping away to check William's pulse. Judith heard their footsteps, steady but irregular thumps on the floor, and the *thunk* and *click* of instruments on wood.

She swallowed.

"Just about ready, my lady," said Dr. McKendry, rounding the table. If she'd been one of the village lasses, he'd have patted her on the shoulder. Conscious of her rank, he halted his hand an inch or so short of contact and coughed. "We'd not think a bit worse of you if you'd changed your mind, ye ken. 'Tis a new procedure, and you've lost blood already."

"I'll be all right," Judith said and hoped it was true. She felt all right, in that she'd felt worse, at least physically. The cuts on her chest were shallow, those on her thigh a little deeper, but they'd stopped bleeding. "I'll tell you if I'm not. Word of honor."

McKendry made a small sound in his throat, one that didn't quite dare to be frank disbelief but nonetheless indicated that he'd be keeping an eye on her, whatever she said. He started to move off, then stopped and looked at Judith. "Funny thing," he said. "I've no recollection that I've ever had you in here before."

"I've always been healthy," said Judith, and she wondered if he'd have even made the remark a year ago. "And lucky."

He didn't regard her with the same knowledge Hamilton did—and she couldn't entirely curse that knowledge either, as she suspected it was the only thing that had finally persuaded Hamilton to try the experiment in the end—but McKendry's gaze wasn't credulous either. *There is more here than meets the eye,* it said. *I won't press you to tell me what, but don't get the notion that I'm blind.*

"We'll pray your luck holds, then," he said at last. "Hamilton?"

"I'm as ready as I'm likely to be, given the need for haste." Stepping over to Judith's side, Hamilton passed a porcelain basin—incongruously robin's-egg blue—and a complicated mechanism of tubes and syringes over to the doctor. He himself held a thick strip of white cloth. "Your arm, my lady?"

Holding up her arm for the tourniquet felt odd—not the constriction itself, though it was mildly uncomfortable, but the passive obedience of the gesture.

Hamilton didn't look at Judith's face as he readied the syringe. If she existed beyond her vein, he clearly didn't know it just then—or he didn't want to think about it. McKendry's face was worried and present; Hamilton had retreated into the abstract details of procedure. Judith was "patient A" in his mind, or perhaps "the donor," not the woman he'd chatted with at the harvest festival or the inexplicable creature who'd appeared on his doorstep. That was necessary.

Knowing a bit about doctors, Judith thought it might even have been necessary had she been just a mortal woman.

She felt a pinch as the syringe's needle went into her arm. The pain was almost nothing. But as the needle slipped farther past the skin and she felt the metal inside her body, Judith's stomach clenched. She looked away from her arm and the tube that was now attached to it, back up at the ceiling.

"Good," said Hamilton. "Now the recipient."

Before she'd looked away, she'd seen that the tube fed into a metal column, and that another tube ran out, with a needle on its end. When McKendry and

Hamilton walked around to the other side, she knew they were inserting the needle into William's arm. That was good; that was progress. The needle in *her* arm wiggled a little in the process. Her insides lurched.

She *had* been lucky. And healthy. The closest she'd come to surgery was having bullets dug out of her after battles. Usually she'd been drunk then. The last time had been by a stream in the colonies, Pennsylvania or Delaware or one of those states with hills, and if the man with the knife had been trained anywhere, it hadn't been in medical school. That should have been worse.

But there'd been the shock of battle to keep her numb then, not to mention rotgut. Besides, the damage there had already been done. Clawing foreign bodies away from her flesh was instinct. Lying quietly while someone inserted them, Judith found, went against every natural inclination. She wanted to snarl and fight. Failing that, she wanted to be sick.

She bit down hard on her lip and looked over at William.

His eyes were closed, dark auburn lashes vivid even against his tanned skin. Unconsciousness took all animation from his face, whether cheer or worry, and left Judith aware of just how much there normally was, how much of this man was dedicated to expression—or willful concealment.

She'd never seen him asleep. Of course she'd never seen him asleep. She'd never even considered it, but now the thought saddened her, made her think of trains she'd barely missed and mementoes she'd lost without knowing their absence. Judith closed her eyes.

"Check his pulse," said Hamilton.

Judith heard the faint sounds of cloth and flesh that went with motion. A minute passed. "Steady," said McKendry's voice. "Still too quick, but steady."

"Good."

Time crawled on. Judith didn't count the seconds, but kept her eyes closed and tried to think of anything but where she was or the sensation of the needle in her arm or William's condition. It didn't go very well. She'd once memorized a poem for such occasions, one by Dryden that began with "Fair Iris I love," but the years had taken it away.

Every so often, McKendry would take William's pulse. A little less frequently, he'd ask how Judith was feeling. She always said she was fine. It wasn't quite a lie; he was really asking if she could go on.

"Color's returning," McKendry said, after the fifth or sixth such time. "And his pulse is going back to normal." He cleared his throat. "I'll not say anything yet, but—"

"Not yet," said Judith, shaking her head. She clamped down hard on her own relief. "This has only been the first step."

Thirty-eight

THE FIRST THING WILLIAM KNEW WAS PAIN.

Centered in his stomach, where the Consuasori brother had stabbed him, it spread jellyfish tentacles through his whole frame. He was pain and the *world* was pain, as if some deity much less merciful than the god he'd been raised with had taken it upon itself to revise the first lines of Genesis. *Let there be agony. Let there be torment. And the Lord saw that it was not good—that it was very bad, in fact—but damned if he'd do anything about it.*

That went on for a long time. Gradually he found he had enough energy to scream. At least he thought he was screaming. He didn't hear himself. Screaming hurt his throat more, so he stopped, and was aware once more that he had a throat. Other bits of his body returned to his consciousness: stomach, head, arms and legs that he couldn't move, any more than he could lift his eyelids.

Was he paralyzed? No. He could feel every finger, every toe. They hurt. The nerves were still there.

Hands tilted his head up. Other hands set a spoon at his lips and tilted. Cool liquid flowed down his throat.

The pain receded—not gone, but fainter, behind a barrier.

William thought he slept.

There came a time when he could open his eyes, and when the sounds around him reached his ears. He knew that he was in a bed in a room, and not dead. A shape perched beside him, feeding him broth. He swallowed what was put into his mouth and tasted none of it. Another figure stood nearby, frowning at an object in its hand.

"One hundred and two," said the figure. The voice was male, with a Scottish accent. McKendry? Most likely. "No change there."

"His eyes are open," said the figure feeding him, also male and probably Hamilton. "It's a good sign. Mr. Arundell?"

William swallowed broth and tried to respond. He succeeded in making a noise in his throat, all nasal *n*'s and a *g* at the end that he barely got out. He tried again. "Present," he rasped.

"Don't exert yourself, lad," said McKendry. "But I'm glad you're with us."

Then it was later. William knew it was later because Hamilton was gone, and another figure sat by his bed. He knew this one even before she spoke, knew her by form and face and even smell: Judith. She bathed his face, her hands cool and strong and sure.

McKendry was talking. "…some awareness of his surroundings, aye. And there's no infection showing. The wound's healed quite cleanly, though it's likely done some permanent damage. But his fever's still very high."

"Yes," said Judith remotely. Her hands never stopped moving—dipping the rag into a bowl of cool water, wringing it out, and wiping William's brow again. "It will be."

The grave certainty in her voice was unmistakable. William looked up at her. Her green eyes were the only real color in her face. The rest was pallor and shadows.

"Lady MacAlasdair—" McKendry began.

"I tell you as much as I can," she said, "and if I knew anything that would help, I'd tell you that. I swear it."

"You dinna' need to," said the doctor. "I've only to look at you to know as much."

She laughed silently. "That's something. Can I ask you to leave us for a moment?"

"Aye, of course."

McKendry took his leave. William heard the footfalls and then the solid *thunk* of the closing door. "Judith," he said and touched her wrist with one hand.

"No moving around," she said, but she took his hand, lacing their fingers together. "I've a confession."

"Another one?" William would have raised his eyebrows, but it hurt too much.

"I never really confessed to the rest of it," she said and squeezed his hand. "I gave you my blood. It was—the only thing I could think of. You were in a bad way. You may still be."

"Figured that," said William, glancing down at his unresponsive body. "How bad?"

"You would have died," she said, so tonelessly that it had to be with deliberate control. "We heal from things mortals don't. But the transfer doesn't always work. Your body resists the change."

"Oh." He had no strength for emotion either, and the world was starting to slip away again. "What do I do?"

"Hold on." She leaned forward and brushed her lips against his. "I wish I could tell you more. I wish I knew. As far as I know, none of us has done this with a mortal before. Just—hold on. If you want to."

"Yes," he said, though the word was half exhale. Her kiss had sent warmth and strength through him for a second, but it was fading fast. Images and sounds broke into small bits. He focused on Judith's face. "Sleep. You should sleep."

"Don't tell me what to do," she said, pretending anger. Her voice thickened on the last word. Judith looked away again, then met his eyes, her own shining green in the rapidly closing darkness. "I love you," she said, each word as slow and serious as her oath had been, back when she'd sworn not to harm him. Her hand tightened on his, and when she drew in another breath, it shook. "I couldn't let you die. Not if I could do anything. Not if anything I know or am could help you. I don't know if it will, but—I love you. I want you to hold on. I don't know if that will help either."

"Love," he said, and wonder shone in the whirling void that was rapidly overtaking his mind. He said the word again, the feeling alien on his tongue.

It was the last time he spoke for a long while.

Hours or maybe days went by in broken moments, like moving landscapes seen from the window of a train. By turns William was cold and hot; by turns his senses receded, cut off from the world by a thick blanket of numbness and then sharpened to the point where he could smell steel across the room and hear birds on top of the house. The pain dwindled, but the disorientation grew as it did.

Someone was always in the room—at least, he never came back to awareness without seeing at least one person close at hand, and from that he inferred that they never left him completely alone. The constant presence of other people was reassuring; what it implied about his condition wasn't.

Most of the time his companion was Hamilton, McKendry, Judith, or some combination. Once in a while, particularly later, others were there. William opened his eyes once, when his senses were acute but not blindingly so, to see a strange couple standing in the room with Judith. The man was tall and dark, and the lines of his face were a masculine cast of Judith's, though his eyes were gold rather than green. The woman had dark blond hair and the forbiddingly businesslike air of a head nurse.

She was the one speaking. Judith and her brother, probably, were glaring at each other, Judith's hands on her hips and the man's arms folded across his chest. If Judith had slept in the time since their conversation, William noticed, her face didn't show it.

"It was different for me, naturally," the blond woman said, looking at William with a sigh. There was no trace of Scotland in her voice. He heard the East End there, with education buttoned tightly up over it so that only the edges showed. "More gradual, like. I wish I could be more helpful. I think he's worse than I ever got, but I never saw myself from the outside."

Her eyes were dark blue. William saw the rings of iris and pupil stand out sharply. When she blinked, he saw every eyelash. He looked away. The shadows in the corner of the room, dark in the sunlight, rippled like pools.

"Maybe a bit worse," said the man, his lips going thin. "Not very much, as I remember."

"You're biased. And this is exactly the sort of thing you'd have done, Stephen." The woman left William and put a hand on Stephen's arm. Their shadows were rippling too now, and their motions left small shining trails in the air. He thought of falling stars and then of traveling slugs.

"Exactly the sort of thing he *did*, I'd say—" Judith began.

The scene shattered. Voices became notes; people became blips of color and motion; everything was too close to make sense. When William pulled himself back from that edge again, it was night, or at least no sun came from outside. Judith's probable brother and his probable wife had gone. Judith sat in one chair in the corner, a cup of tea in one hand and a meat pie in front of her. At least she was eating.

Baxter sat in the other. His round face was somber, his clothing funereal—although William had never seen him in any other attire. He looked at the teapot as if it contained all the world's sorrows.

The look on Judith's face was familiar. She'd regarded William himself that way more than once, with that mixture of forced trust and profound suspicion. Her clothing was crisp and sober tweed, every hair had been pinned up under a dark hat, and her back was ramrod-straight. The emerald ring on her finger shone green, even in the dim light.

"...chose to come here, I'll remind you," she was saying. "Or rather, you chose to send him. I'm grateful for his assistance and yours, but I'll not be rushed into anything. Nor will my brother, but I expect you already know that."

Baxter had the grace to look embarrassed. He was a good man for gathering information, but no great hand at diplomacy. He was also easily ten years older than William and naturally would have tried to talk first with a man and the head of the family. William would have done that himself, had the option been available. He was glad now that it hadn't. His vision kept doubling and he had the energy to lick his dry lips for the first time in God knows how long, but he was still glad.

"Lady MacAlasdair," Baxter said, calmly and probably gently, "I mean no offense, but you do know that you were likely the reason for Mr. MacDougal's activities here? And while it seems that he only had one confederate, the fact remains that there are matters you can't understand."

Judith froze in place. One hand still held the teacup, which might have been funny if not for her expression. William had seen that pain elsewhere before, generally just when a knife had entered some vital organ; the guilt was less usual. Baxter had said nothing she hadn't thought of before, clearly. Rather, he'd given voice to every silent reproach that had haunted her since they'd discovered Ross.

"Mr. Baxter," she said, maintaining a very arctic composure, "I am very well aware of that."

"Baxter." William moved his lips, but the sound that emerged was only a hard breath. He thought of solidity: the room's, Baxter's, and mostly his own, whatever that consisted of now. He had a throat. He cleared it, summoned air into his lungs—did they hold more than they had, or had it just been a long time since he'd had to breathe deeply?—and spoke the other man's name again, loudly enough that he and Judith both turned, shocked, toward the bed. "This is still my mission."

William felt the truth of that settle on him, into his very blood and bones. He welcomed it. It was a weight, but one that would keep him pinned to the world. Duty was a decent handhold.

He watched Judith hurry to his side, forgetting both tea and Baxter—who, to his credit, had left off speech himself and was following her. The pain was gone from her face; hope was all that remained.

Duty was a decent handhold. Love was an even better one.

Thirty-nine

TIME HAD A VILE SENSE OF HUMOR.

For the first six days after the transfusion, while William had drifted in and out of consciousness and nobody had been able to give odds on his survival, there had been almost nothing to occupy Judith's time. Without Ross's disruptive presence, Loch Arach was settling peacefully in for the winter; the Connohs' new store was going up smoothly; and Judith's own recovery would have kept her from hunting in either form, even if she had wanted to go that far from William. The days had ticked by while she sat at his bed or attended to the minor tasks that did wait for her in the castle.

Stephen and Mina's arrival, with little Anna, had been a relief. Even Baxter had been a welcome distraction in his own way—but the day after his arrival, when Judith had taken him to the sickroom, William had come back to himself enough to speak, and to speak lucidly. After that, his periods of consciousness came closer together, and a day later, McKendry said that his fever had subsided as well.

He would live.

Judith went home, slept for twelve hours, and then ate all of the huge breakfast that someone—probably Stephen, who'd always been a favorite with the kitchen staff—had sent up on a tray. She held back from too much joy—joy was a fragile thing and a temptation to old and malicious forces. When she opened the note from McKendry, she made herself expect the worst.

Mr. Arundell is awake and of sound mind.

The letters blurred and danced in front of Judith's eyes. She set the note down, blinked hard, and picked it up again.

I don't advise much conversation just yet, as he still seems easily tired, but I believe your company would be welcome.

She dressed quickly but carefully, glad that she had slept and more aware than ever before of the face looking back from the mirror. It was a much paler face than it had been nine days ago, and it had a hollow look as well. Judith wished she'd had time and strength to hunt, but thankful for small blessings, she was just glad she'd slept.

William was sitting up in bed when she entered the sickroom, wearing a dressing gown more ornate than anything a villager would have owned, and eating a meal nearly as large as her breakfast had been. For a second, Judith could neither speak nor move. She stood in the doorway and drank in the sight.

Looking up, William smiled. If Judith was pale, he was paler. If she was thin, he was damned near skeletal. But his eyes were clear and unclouded, and his smile was as warm as ever—if a little diffident just then. "This is the third breakfast I've had today," he said. "I assume one does stop gorging, eventually?"

"I—yes." Judith caught herself, midway through tumbling down toward some abyss of feeling, and pulled her mind back onto a rational and slightly businesslike ledge. "At least I think so. You've not eaten much in a while, aye? And we've always done ourselves proud at mealtimes."

She watched his face when she said *we* and *ourselves*, waiting for revulsion or resentment. It didn't come. She didn't think so, anyhow, and she realized that she couldn't trust her judgment. She wanted too much. She feared too much.

"Sit, please," William said and gestured to the chair by his bed. "You were there often enough, as I recall—when I recall anything. Thank you for that."

"'Twas the least I could do," Judith said and sat stiffly on the edge of the chair, hands folded in her lap. She had too many questions, and it wasn't fair to ask any of them, so she started with a statement. "You'll want more meat, generally. And rarer. Mina—my brother's wife—said to tell you that. Though she'd not eaten much before, so perhaps there'll be less difference for you."

William nodded slowly. "I'd imagine the process was more—complicated—for her."

"Yes and no." Judith pushed back her hat, which didn't need adjusting. "Different complications."

"Will I"—he made a few vague gestures, fork still in hand, before settling on speech—"transform?"

"I don't think so," said Judith. "None of the women have. I think you have to be born to that part of the blood." She didn't let her gaze leave his. "You'll live longer, though. At least that's generally how it works."

William's mouth turned up at the corners. "Better not let that get around, I'd say." Then, more soberly, "As long as you will?"

"More or less. As long as you don't get stabbed again."

His eyes revealed nothing. "Although I do hear that I can heal from a number of wounds now."

"A number," said Judith, and she felt her hands tighten on each other. "Not everything. Fire harms us less, and silver more. And we don't often get ill, so you'll not need to worry about spring colds. I hope—"

There she teetered on the edge of a question it wasn't fair to ask. If he *did* object to what she'd done, if he would have preferred to die as a mortal man, he was too much of a gentleman to tell her now, and she would not force him to lie. "I hope Stephen or Mina can answer any questions I can't. She's been through it, and he knows more of our history."

"You'll have to introduce me," he said.

And then McKendry's maid knocked at the door. "Lady MacAlasdair? I'm sorry to disturb you, but your brother says there's important business up at the castle."

Of course there was. And when that was done—a matter of flooding in the cellars, and Stephen panicking as if he were a Londoner born and bred—then

Baxter came calling to have a formal tea and talk carefully around the terms of alliance, with nobody involved willing to make any kind of direct commitment or even *statement* just yet. It would have been Stephen's forte, except that he was still uncertain about the entire situation and inclined to glare like a subdued volcano.

Judith did the best she could, avoided dumping the teapot over Baxter's head, and tried not to think about how else the conversation with William might have gone.

Time had a *vile* sense of humor.

Later she thought that maybe it was better this way. A man recovering might not welcome attention— God knew she was surly and inclined to crawl into holes when she was hurt—and the more she was around him, the more she would be tempted to open her mouth and let stupid things fall out.

Judith had told him she loved him. At the time, it had felt more than appropriate—it had been the only thing to do. Now, when she wasn't writing lists or showing Mina the storerooms, she remembered the expression on William's face, the way he'd repeated just the one word, and wondered whether it had been wonder, distress, or simple surprise—or delirium.

Confessions were much less risky when the listener was non compos mentis, easier still when she hadn't entirely expected him to survive. Of course she was glad, but—she felt exposed in remembering her declaration, far worse than she had been just shedding her clothes in front of him. She could fight naked, if she had to. It didn't make her weak, and it wasn't—these days—showing anything that could be used against her.

She couldn't wish she hadn't spoken, but she did wonder whether William remembered or not, and what answer he might give her.

And the next day he came to the castle.

The family was in the drawing room when he arrived, save for Anna, who was upstairs napping while the adults played an inattentive hand of commerce.

"She'll be spoiled before you've been here a month, you know," Judith said, rearranging her cards. The draw had not been good to her. She made a face, since Stephen would see through any attempt to hide her reaction. Brothers made the worst opponents at the table—or most other places.

"*I* wasn't."

"Hah," said Judith, and Mina grinned over her cards.

"We'll just need a good nurse," she said. "Or I'll get my mum to come up—I doubt anyone could grow up spoiled with her around." A memory made her grimace, but affectionately so.

"Mothers are far sterner than grandmothers, Cerberus," said Stephen, "even if they're the same woman. Like sisters and aunts—you'll see. Judith will be the worst of the lot, for all her talk."

"You know I can't be here very often," said Judith.

"I know no such thing."

"We've always—"

Stephen snorted, just as he did when transformed, and Janssen chose that moment to announce, "Mr. Arundell, my lady."

"See," Stephen said as William walked slowly in,

"you can't leave. They'll never recognize my authority. Mr. Arundell, come sit with us and tell my sister that she's being unreasonable. You're looking well," he added.

Relatively speaking, William was. He wasn't walking easily, but he *was* walking, and he'd already regained some of the color that had been so long absent from his face. As he entered the room, he looked first to Judith, and only as Stephen spoke did his eyes leave hers.

She shook her head. "Unfair. But it is good to see you up and about." It was the mildest thing she could manage, and the most revealing she could stand to say.

William sat, Janssen closed the door, and Stephen, never one to give up a fight easily, turned back to Judith. "If we'll be working with mortals—and the English government yet—then we can bloody well stand it if a few people in the village ask questions."

"They're recording births now," Mina put in, "and taking photographs. Moving around won't be much of a disguise for any of us much longer."

"They're trying to get me to stay," Judith explained to William, though she suspected she didn't need to. It was something she could say. She shrugged. "Two against one—but I'm not trying to recruit you."

"Good," said William. He stood up again. "May I speak with you alone for a minute? If you'll excuse us, of course," he added to Stephen and Mina.

"No," said Stephen, rising, "we'll go. Best to check that the wee lass isn't terrorizing the servants yet."

On his way past Judith, he grinned in an encouraging fashion that left her convinced he knew, if not everything that had passed between her and William, at least the better part of it. She hadn't discussed her feelings with Stephen—she'd barely admitted them to herself—but, well, *brothers*. She reminded herself to give him a thick ear when he returned.

"I think you should stay," William said, even before Stephen and Mina had entirely left the room. "Your brother and Lady Mina are right, and I've never gotten the impression that you wanted to leave. I'm prepared to admit I'm wrong, if I am. That's not important."

"No?" Judith asked with a faint smile. "Maybe not to you."

"No, it's very important to me. Or I'd like it to be. If you stay, I'd like to stay with you—and if you want to leave, I'd like to go at your side."

The world stopped.

As Judith looked up at him, trying to figure out whether he meant what she thought he did, William smiled wryly. "I'm afraid I really must ask to be let out of the down-on-one-knee aspect of the ritual. McKendry was very keen on that. But"—he reached into his pocket and removed a small package: a blue silk handkerchief, many times wrapped—"he did offer this."

Gold gleamed as William unwrapped it: gold, and then a small stone, dark blue with flashes of green and silver inside it. "It was his mother's, he said, and he's not likely to pass it on to anyone else. He was quite insistent when he, ah, figured out my plans. Which he did with embarrassing ease, I might add."

"You've been wounded," Judith said, laughing in wonder as much as humor. "Nobody can expect top form—but what about your superiors? And your work?"

"I'll not be much use as a field agent for a while," he said. "As a diplomatic liaison to a new ally, I expect I'll prove my worth, even if the arrangement is irregular. You have my word, though, that this will have no impact on the alliance. You can say no if you'd like. I won't make a scene, and I think McKendry will take the ring back without question."

A smile took over Judith's whole face; she had to talk around it. "I'm sure he would," she said and stood up so that her face and William's were only a few inches away. "But it won't be necessary. If *you're* certain, that is."

"I love you. I'd say I was as certain as I was of anything in the world, but I'm not nearly as sure of anything else. I never have been. Any other questions?"

"No," said Judith, and she stepped forward. Trapping the ring in its box between them, she slid her arms around William's neck and kissed him.

She had intended the embrace to be both light and brief, in consideration of his injuries, but William had other ideas. Even one-handed, he had no trouble pulling her against him, and while his fingers were light against the small of her back, their caress was insistent and thrilling. When he stepped reluctantly back, they were both flushed and breathing quickly.

Judith could have wished for more time before the door to the hallway opened again, but she didn't get it. "You could not," she said as her brother and Mina walked in, "have gone to the nursery and back by now."

"Just down the hall to talk to the maids," Stephen said and grinned again. "It seemed time enough. Congratulations—though properly, you know, you should've asked my permission beforehand."

"Like hell he should have," said Judith, and she held out her hand for the ring. It was warm when William slipped it onto her finger, and the dark stone shone out at her: mystery, with flashes of light. "Let's begin as we mean to go on. Together."

Acknowledgments

As usual, I'd like to thank the Sourcebooks editorial team, particularly my editor, Mary Altman.

A Sword for His Lady

by Mary Wine

A *Publishers Weekly* Top 10 Pick for Spring 2015

❧

He'd defend her keep...

After proving himself on the field of battle, Ramon de Segrave is appointed to the Council of Barons by Richard the Lionheart. But instead of taking his most formidable warrior on his latest Crusade, the king assigns Ramon an even more dangerous task—woo and win the Lady of Thistle Keep.

If only she'd yield her heart

Isabel of Camoys has fought long and hard for her independence, and if the price is loneliness, then so be it. She will not yield...even if she does find the powerful knight's heated embrace impossible to ignore. But when her land is threatened, Isabel reluctantly agrees to allow Ramon to defend the keep—knowing that the price may very well be her heart.

❧

Praise for Mary Wine:

"I always find the emotional and philosophical tugs of war interesting between Wine's characters. Her main characters are always admirable and there are always some true baddies to root against." —*For the Love of Books*

For more Mary Wine, visit:

www.sourcebooks.com

About the Author

Isabel Cooper lives in Boston in an apartment with two houseplants, an inordinate number of stairs, a silver sword, and a basket of sequined fruit. By day, she works as a theoretically mild-mannered legal editor; by night, she tries to sleep. She has a house in the country, but hopes she doesn't encounter mysterious and handsome strangers nearby, as vacation generally involves a lot of fuzzy bathrobes. You can find out more at www.isabelcooper.org.